ICARUS

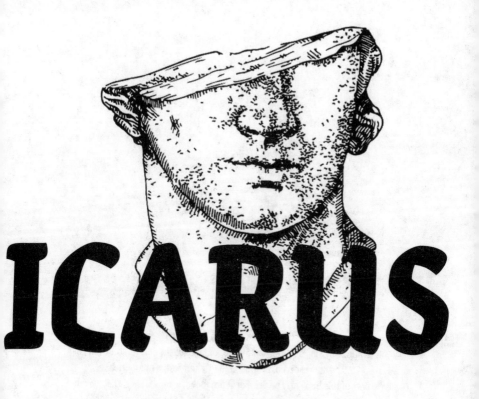

ICARUS

K. ANCRUM

HARPER TEEN
An Imprint of HarperCollinsPublishers

HarperTeen is an imprint of HarperCollins Publishers.

Icarus
Copyright © 2024 by K. Ancrum
Illustrations by aln_dek, Dedraw Studio, and Bibadash / Shutterstock Images
All rights reserved. Printed in the United States of America.
No part of this book may be used or reproduced in any manner whatsoever
without written permission except in the case of brief quotations
embodied in critical articles and reviews.
For information address HarperCollins Children's Books,
a division of HarperCollins Publishers, 195 Broadway, New York, NY 10007.
www.epicreads.com

Library of Congress Control Number: 2023937636
ISBN 978-0-06-328578-1

Typography by Jenna Stempel-Lobell
24 25 26 27 28 LBC 5 4 3 2 1
First Edition

Some of us lead lives that would require suspension of belief from others. The strange, the magical, the devastating, and the unbelievable. You deserve to have someone walk beside you. You deserve outstretched hands. You shouldn't have to live to house secrets. You should be allowed to just live.

Love,
Kayla

WEDNESDAY

It was dark in this house.

The air was still and warm.

Cat burglars rarely wear shoes. Instead, they wear socks. Icarus's were old and wool and his father had hand sewn fine black leather to the bottoms for traction.

Icarus crept across the edge of the main hall, then slipped into a drawing room.

Mr. Black's house had many useless spaces, many alcoves filled with junk. It was a monstrosity of metal and wood. Icarus had been here thousands of times over the years and he never felt comfortable. It was not a home; it was as empty and lifeless as a dollhouse.

Above a desk—protected from light and dust by a thin sheet—was Warhol's *Red Lenin*.

Icarus scanned the area around the painting, searching for the glint of a camera lens. He checked every time, like each visit was the first. It wasn't good to get too comfortable. Icarus crossed the room quickly and began dismantling the installation. He placed small tacks and screws on the floor, turned the protective glass pane onto its inside face to avoid disturbing the dust on the front. Then, Icarus pulled the black, flat case he carried off his back and unpacked his father's work: Warhol's *Red Lenin*.

It wasn't an expensive print, but Mr. Black was familiar with his belongings. He knew the works in this home. But Icarus's father knew Mr. Black and that made all the difference.

Icarus framed the forgery and hung it on the wall. He packaged the original painting and slid it into his carrying case. He backed out of the room, stepping into his own impressions, brushing back against the grain to erase his footprints. Then, he pulled the door softly closed.

Icarus left the house, scurried over the fence, shoved his feet into his Chelsea boots, and walked quickly home.

Icarus filiformis

Icarus was his father's son.

They were of a height, they had the same wiry frame, the same limp black hair, the same big ears, the same deep-set brown eyes, the same unhappy mouth. Icarus thought his father was ugly, so he knew he must be ugly too.

They were both artists, though Icarus was slightly worse.

Both thieves, but Icarus was faster.

Both quiet, but Icarus knew how to talk to other people.

Both friendless, but Icarus knew how to make people like him.

They walked at the same pace, moved with the same grace, had the same size hands and similar handwriting.

They both knelt in penance, chins to the sky, fisted rosary. His father liked to keep his eyes closed. Icarus needed to keep his eyes open to stay tethered to faith.

And wasn't that just the way?

Angus Gallagher shut tight like a sarcophagus. Icarus Gallagher, eyes open, mouth open, waiting.

BOUNTY

Icarus and his father lived in a small apartment in a part of town that had been nice maybe forty years ago.

The inside of their home smelled strongly of wood, linseed, minerals, herbs, and canvas, so that's what Icarus smelled like too.

The lights were all dim specialized bulbs designed to reduce light damage to paint. There were landscapes and portraits, repeated theme. A woman in green, brushed over and over, smiling, laughing, lying among them, her face an open secret. The only room where the walls weren't dotted with paint or paintings was the kitchen. In that room, where the sun was brightest, there were ferns in every corner that could house one.

In a few years, when Icarus and his father didn't live there anymore, a little girl from the new family who moved in would tell her parents there was gold dust in the cracks of the wood, gold left over from years of gilding.

They wouldn't believe her.

It was an artist's house. A studio with beds. Crammed full to bursting.

HIM

Icarus slipped in and closed the door.

He slid across his own floors and made his way to the cold storage room.

This room *should* have been Icarus's bedroom, but their art needed the space.

Icarus swung the case off his back and prepared *Red Lenin* for storage. Delicately smoothing the paper out onto a backing its size, slipping it into a protective sleeve, labeling it in fine print, and placing it in a storage locker with other originals of its size and environmental temperament.

"Is it un-damaged?"

Icarus whirled around.

His father, Angus Gallagher, never wore special socks but he was silent as death, always.

"It's fine, I think," Icarus replied. "I didn't inspect it. The air felt heavy . . . like I wasn't alone." Admitting his negligence made him nervous.

Angus grunted in disapproval and opened the storage unit.

Icarus stood there, cheeks blazing, as his father undid all of his work, pulling *Red Lenin* back out into the light.

He scrutinized the print. Sniffed it, peering closely at the detail with the small retractable microscope he kept on a loop at his waist as Icarus waited. When he was finally satisfied, he resealed the painting.

"This is one I've seen in person. It was one of the first Mr. Black purchased. He had it in his room when we were in school . . ." Angus trailed off without elaborating further. "I'll re-review security around the perimeter of the building. We'll break for two weeks, then start again if there aren't any discrepancies. Anything else out of the ordinary?"

"No, sir," Icarus said, eyes to the floor.

Angus Gallagher hummed low in his throat, then thrust an envelope under Icarus's chin.

"Your pay for the repair work you did on the frame of the Rothko. Spend what you need, save what you don't." Angus left as quietly as he arrived.

Icarus deflated with relief.

BREATH

Icarus's bedroom was a walk-in closet. He kept it very clean because he *had* to; there wasn't enough room for mess.

The small space was taken up by his twin-size bed and the shelves that lined it. At the foot of his bed the shelves were neatly packed with his books, trinkets, and work supplies. On the shelves at the head of his bed, his clothes were rolled tightly, military style, and organized by type and color. They were black or neutral so that it wasn't noticeable that he didn't have a wide selection. All pieces of impeccable quality.

When Icarus was fourteen, he had painted the ceiling of his closet-bedroom the colors of the sunrise. Now that he was planning to leave, he was considering a repaint.

Icarus tossed his backpack onto his bed and changed his clothes in the hallway. He crept into bed, closing the closet door behind him.

The envelope his father had given him was bulky and exciting. Icarus spread out the stack of fifty-dollar bills and counted them quickly, separating out $1,000 for savings, $500 for new supplies. Normally Angus didn't give him this much, but his work was getting really good. He had taken his time. His cheeks pinked with pride.

Icarus tucked most of the bills into his small safe and put the rest in his spending pile to be taken to the bank. He had just under $7,000 but he wouldn't feel comfortable until it was $10,000. Couldn't feel safe until it was $15,000. Couldn't feel free unless it was $20,000. Enough to start over anywhere in the world.

He curled up under his quilt and went to sleep.

TIME

Icarus and Angus Gallagher had been stealing from Stuart Black for years.

Icarus's father had started alone, of course, but when Icarus was old enough and well trained, Angus began bringing him along.

Then, after a time, Angus made Icarus do it alone.

It was such a normal part of Icarus's life that he didn't think about it much anymore.

When he was in elementary school, he used to whine about not being able to have friends over to their house. He resented the gymnastics lessons and having to outwit their home security system to go to the bathroom in the middle of the night.

By middle school, he was irritated because it was obvious that they didn't need the money. His father's real job was art restoration and he got paid a pretty penny for it. Most of which he spent on the stupid replications they shoved into Mr. Black's house.

By the time high school started, breaking into the Black house was so easy for Icarus that it was just like any other extracurricular activity. The last time he'd almost been caught was in freshman year and he was a senior now. His spirit had settled on the matter.

More, Icarus was now old enough to know why they were robbing him.

TENTH

The one other thing that was a constant negative was this: Icarus was only allowed to have friends that stayed at school.

Everyone understands how friendship circles work. You have your four tiers:

1. People you talk to in class, gym, maybe after-school sports.
2. People you'd hang out with if no one better was around. You might get stuck with them after school, then depending on how that goes they could move up or down a tier.
3. People in the same direct social group as you who aren't your absolute besties. You'd let them sleep over at your house as a group but you wouldn't go to a solo sleepover at theirs.
4. Friends that feel like siblings.

Icarus was only allowed acquaintances—people to talk with during class. Everyone else tended to start asking questions that Icarus was not allowed to answer.

This was a negative for obvious reasons. The worst of which was that Icarus *wasn't* unpopular.

He wasn't a wallflower, shy, or awkward. He didn't eat by himself at lunch and stare pensively out the window, or curl up in the library to read alone because he *had* to.

He was funny and outgoing, girls and guys liked him, he got invited to parties. He just wasn't allowed to *go*.

It was lonely. He hated it.

BOON

He made one acquaintance in every class.

First period was Julian. He sat directly in front of Icarus in history and had moved all the way from across the room to do it. He had bushy brown curls, a round freckly face, and braces. Sometimes, he brought Icarus coffee in the morning. He was rude but he'd been the one to start talking to Icarus first.

Aspen was second period, math. She was a horribly unpopular girl, with long red hair, who wore grungy military-inspired clothes and didn't like talking to anyone. Icarus regularly let Aspen cheat off of him by holding his tests up so that Aspen could see the answers over his shoulder. Aspen was a gamer geek and much better at science and English than math. Algebra was her Achilles' heel and Icarus felt a bit bad for her.

Third period and fifth period were both Luca: English and gym. Icarus had him in both classes and couldn't get away with talking to him in one and completely ignoring him in the other. Luca was tall, brawny, and a bit of a party boy. He always greeted Icarus by pushing him, punching him, or flicking him on the back of the head like the world's gentlest bully. He was easy to talk to and liked to complain about his girl problems.

Fourth-period history was Celestina, and Icarus was very glad she and Luca didn't know each other. She was Luca's type and that would mess up the entire system. Celestina was pretty, with long black box braids and brown skin, and she picked on Icarus in a flirty way. He always blushed when she bothered him and he valiantly tried to suppress it.

Sixth period, and last of the day, was Sorrel. A gentle, quiet boy with white-blond hair. Icarus could tell he overwhelmed Sorrel just as much as he delighted him.

It was a perfect roster for the year.

Everyone was in distant social groups and would never come together to ask him to hang out.

Julian was too geeky for Celestina and Luca, but too forward for Sorrel and Aspen. Aspen and Sorrel were so far outside of Luca's and Celestina's social circles that they probably didn't even know each other's names. It was stable. Efficient. Devastating.

JULIAN

"Today you get a chai latte," Julian announced, then turned back around in his chair. Julian brought Icarus stuff, but he never let him choose. It was always random and a lot of the time it was stuff he 100 percent didn't like.

Icarus drank it anyway.

"Did you finish the notes for last night? I was super busy and didn't get to them." Icarus leaned forward on his arms and tried to look apologetic.

Julian scowled; he wasn't impressed. "Perhaps if you spent less time doing whatever it is you do all night instead of homework, we wouldn't be in this situation."

"Come on, please," Icarus griped.

Julian thankfully didn't push him and just handed his notes backward. Icarus immediately began copying them.

"You can't keep copying off me, Icarus. Eventually someone is going to notice," Julian murmured.

"I know, I'll keep it to a minimum."

Icarus managed to finish before their work was collected and handed Julian back his notebook.

"You know they can cancel your acceptance to schools if you mess up senior year," Julian said. "I knew someone who got into Brown and got their offer rescinded. It does happen."

Icarus rolled his eyes. "Thanks for the warning."

Julian scowled ferociously and pulled Icarus's drink away.

"Dude, come on. I'm actually not doing bad in my other classes, I'm just not a morning person. I promise I won't ask again."

Julian pushed the drink back, narrowing his eyes. "I'm going to stop bringing coffee if you don't start doing your work. The Morning Person thing is obvious; that's why I'm bringing it in the first place."

Icarus nodded. "Okay. That's fair . . . A bit . . . authoritative but fair."

Julian smacked the top of Icarus's hand when he wrapped it back around the cup.

"You're too smart to become a fuck-up. Don't be pathetic."

Icarus was about to ask why Julian cared so much, but class was beginning to start.

BIDE

The sun lit up the small curls on the back of Julian's neck. His tag was stick-ing up out of his brown striped sweater.

Icarus leaned on his hand and stared.

Julian wouldn't be angry if Icarus tucked it back in. He would probably just bat at his hand and say something snappy.

But if he touched Julian's tag, he might accidentally touch Julian's neck.

If he touched Julian's neck, he would know what Julian felt like. If he knew what Julian felt like, Icarus was afraid he wouldn't forget it.

Icarus didn't get touched very often and the few times it happened by accident it felt . . . like so much. His face burned when someone handed him something and their fingers brushed. It made his chest feel tight and out of order, like the discord of strumming your fingers across all the strings of a guitar.

Julian scratched absentmindedly at the place where the thick fabric square irritated his skin but still didn't push the tag inside.

Julian wasn't mean but he wasn't exactly nice. Icarus couldn't just do things to him and assume he'd react normally. Julian was like . . . if someone had fused a bully and a nerd and a mom together into one. Unpredictable.

LUCA

There was a track that circled the hill. You could travel it in a loop for the full gym period if you didn't feel like playing. Icarus preferred this unless Mr. Collins specifically dragged him over to do team sports. Mostly because it was easier.

"Why do we always have to walk the mile?" Luca griped. "We could be playing kickball. You're so freakin' good at it."

"You're good at kickball too," Icarus reminded Luca. "You could totally opt to not walk with me. That's always an option on the table."

Luca sighed dramatically and pushed his fingers through his wavy brown hair. "Whatever man. I'm fine on the field, but not crazy like you. I'm sure if there was an Olympic track for kickball, you'd get a scholarship."

"This is better though. I like having at least one class where we don't have to try our hardest and we can just wander outside for a while." Icarus looked up at him, fondly.

Luca was quiet for a bit, gazing off at the other kids playing in the field. Then he pushed Icarus hard with one arm.

"Yeah yeah, whatever. Stop giving me doe-eyes or I'll ditch you and join them."

"I'll stop doing it when you stop liking it," Icarus shot back, with an eyebrow wiggle.

Luca huffed and pushed him again.

"You get on my nerves," he said, the tips of his ears pinking. "Anyway. Are you ready to listen to what happened with Amber last night or do we have to do more manly bonding before you give me advice?"

Icarus listened. He thought about what Luca looked like at night, pleasantly drunk and laughing with everyone else. How he saved his memories of it for Icarus in third-period gym.

CELESTINA

Celestina was one of those popular girls who just did whatever she wanted whenever she felt like it.

He had to admit that it thrilled him. As they passed each other in the hallway, she yanked Icarus by his backpack and pulled him outside, right toward the parking lot.

"I wasn't planning to ditch today," he said, struggling against her grip.

"You look exhausted this morning so we're taking a nap," she announced.

"What?"

"You look like a wet ghost—haven't you ever heard of self-care?" Celestina said, making a beeline for her pickup truck, which was parked all the way at the back corner.

Icarus stood there, overwhelmed, as Celestina tossed a blanket into the bed of the truck. Then she hopped in and turned to stare down at him expectantly.

"Get in, weirdo. I know you already have horrible attendance."

Icarus scrambled over the side. "You don't have to be like this."

Celestina scowled. "I *do* actually." She turned away from him to untie the sleeping bag she kept in her truck and unzip it into a fluffy comforter. "Lie down."

Icarus scrunched low. Celestina tossed the comforter over them both and the world plunged into darkness.

"Mom-friends are supposed to be nice," he muttered, shifting until he was comfortable.

"Niceness and kindness are two different things," Celestina said, suddenly much quieter now that they were under the cover.

The small pricks of sunlight that filtered through the cloth cast her in a gentle glow. Celestina looked back at him with her brown eyes and brown skin, and Icarus thought of a painting of a sable in winter. She reached over and touched the neck of his sweater.

"All of your clothes are so soft," Celestina remarked. "What fabric softener does your mom use?"

His sweater was cashmere, but Celestina's truck was rusted and she colored in spots of wear on her boots with Sharpie.

"Downy," Icarus lied. "And a cup of vinegar in with the wash. I do my own laundry."

Celestina hummed and closed her eyes.

"I'll have to try that someday."

Icarus wanted to take off his sweater right then and there and give it to her. He wanted to buy her an entire new truck. Instead, he scrunched a bit closer and closed his eyes too. Helplessly.

GRIT

The sound of wheels on pavement shook him from sleep and he struggled against the pull to consciousness.

Celestina's arm tightened around the back of his head and he nosed deeper into the curve of her neck, falling back asleep. He had never been this warm in his life, had never been held like this—held at all. It felt like his bones were wrapped in a quilt made of sunlight.

Suddenly Celestina gasped and sat up, wrenching the cover off them violently. Icarus groaned and covered his eyes. There were students pouring out of the building and getting in their cars to head home.

"Oh shit, it's after school?! I've gotta get to practice!" Celestina exclaimed. She frantically gathered the blanket and shoved it back into its pack. Icarus rubbed his face and curled up until he could rest his cheek on his knees as she scrambled.

"I'm sorry," Icarus said reflexively.

Celestina stopped. Without warning, she grabbed his chin and turned his face around to look at him closely.

"Much better," she declared. "Sleep some more later."

Icarus did all he could not to gasp and shiver. The press of her thumb and forefinger against his skin reverberated down his entire body like an electric shock. The lax, easy acceptance of touch he'd been granted in half sleep was gone entirely.

When Celestina let go and turned from him, it felt like being dropped into the middle of a snow storm without a jacket. He pressed his fingers hard into his thigh to ground himself, gritting his teeth.

"You can stay if you want. I can give you a ride home with the rest of the girls if you wait an hour," Celestina said, oblivious.

"N-no. I'm good. Thanks for the nap," Icarus stammered as he pulled himself up out of the truck. Celestina grinned, gave him a friendly slap on the back, and jogged off toward the school.

Icarus watched her go. Then, he stretched his aching back and started the long walk home.

TRICK

It was Icarus's job to do laundry for his whole house. It was also his job to make dinner, tidy the house, and maintain the many ferns. Move the ones in darker rooms into the sun on a schedule. Clean the ashes from their altar.

It didn't feel great that he had to do everything most kids would consider "mom stuff," but at the very least his father didn't march around the house creating extra messes for him to deal with. Angus contained most of his chaos in his workshop.

Icarus dropped his bag by the door, took a soda out of the fridge, and then started on the dishes. There was machinery whirring in the back of the house, and the air smelled sharp and chemical. His father was probably working on deglazing something wood.

Icarus turned on the radio by the sink to drown out the noise.

ROCK

They lived in a row house on the third of four floors, with one long main hallway and five rooms branching off on either side. The first was his father's vault, the second was the bathroom, the third was the storage room, the fourth was the supply library, and the last and largest room—the room that should have been a formal dining room—was the workshop.

It had large windows that Angus had painted over years ago. A door had been installed in what should have been an open welcoming space. There was a large expensive island in the middle of the room with a humidifier, dehumidifier, and air purifier. Several lamps lined the left wall, each with different types of bulbs and filters attached to them. There were shelves on the right, built painstakingly into the wall, to hold a selection of tools and chemicals.

Angus himself was standing at the table, wearing a heavy-duty mask, gloves, and a headlight.

Icarus grabbed a cheap disposable mask from the bin by the door and put on a pair of gloves. He wasn't allowed in this room without them.

Angus poured a bit of liquid onto the painting he was working on, then gently scraped away at the yellowing glaze crusting the surface.

"How was school?" Angus asked, without looking up.

Icarus shrugged. "It was okay."

The detail work on an ermine fur–trimmed purple dress revealed itself beneath his father's expert hand. It wasn't a painting Icarus recognized, but it was always fun to watch old lacquer get removed.

Angus painted only two things: commissions and portraits of Icarus's mother, Evangeline. He was grand in his variety of course, painting her in different styles and eras, historical and modern. In watercolors, oils, acrylics, every expression, every gesture. Her face peeking out of all corners of their apartment, but always wearing green. Icarus could always tell when Angus was working on something for sale or preservation. Because it wasn't *her*.

"I reviewed security footage from the cameras facing Black's property. There have been no updates to his security system unless he purchased and installed it himself, and only indoors," Angus said. "That's not to say your concerns are unfounded. We have senses for a reason . . . "

Angus paused and pulled up the mask he was wearing so he could look at Icarus face to face.

"However, this is not enough of a hindrance to delay your next visit. The opportunity is too good and you'll be making several trips," he said.

"What would you do," Icarus asked bravely, "if he caught me?"

Angus's eyes narrowed.

"I would pick up whatever pieces he left of you and take them home."

SPIN

Icarus was furious.

Angus's words circled in his head as he lay in bed. Over and over again.

Angus wasn't a real parent. It was like living with a college professor that Icarus didn't know or like. He was fair and could be gentle, but he was also cruel and thoughtless. He had no idea what to say to anyone he was supposed to love.

He wouldn't have to pick up "pieces" if he cared enough about taking these concerns seriously, Icarus thought bitterly.

The fact that his father had said it unflinchingly, without hesitation. Like Icarus being a sacrifice was an acceptable ending to any plan.

For a man who didn't have much, Angus wasn't being that careful with what he had left.

DRY

When the itch under Icarus's skin got bad, he climbed up to the roof to smoke.

The roof was flat, white, and industrial. The sides curled up in a way that caught rainwater and held it for days, and the edges were covered in pigeon poop, but it was as good a place as any. Since they weren't the apartment on the very top, he'd had to negotiate with their upstairs neighbor to let him install a ladder on the side of the building.

Celestina would like it up here.

Icarus used to spend his nights walking the streets trying to make himself tired enough for sleep.

But the harsh wind and wide sky were enough to cool his blood, now that he was older.

Icarus smoked sage and clove. Angus didn't like the smell of tobacco, and traditional cigarettes caused more noticeable damage on canvas than Icarus's herbs ever would.

The flame in the dark and the smoke curling into the night were both, also, enough.

Icarus closed his eyes and touched where Celestina's fingers had gripped his chin, but the magic was gone. His own hands didn't feel the same.

Icarus took another draw on his cigarette and blew the smoke up into the sky. Then he reached behind his neck and grazed his fingertips across his nape, tickling the short spiky hairs where Julian had curls, and finally, he shivered.

BONE

Icarus awoke to yelling. He gasped to full consciousness, alarmed to find himself still on the roof. He scrambled down the ladder and hoisted himself back into the house.

"You're going to be late." Angus seized him by the arm and frog-marched him to the kitchen, where a bowl of oatmeal was waiting for him.

His clothes for the day were neatly pressed and folded on the table and his backpack was set out on the chair.

Angus scowled, huffed air through his nose hard in irritation, and then disappeared into his workshop.

Icarus hadn't had oatmeal in ages.

Angus stopped making it when Icarus had gotten old enough to get himself ready. He'd also stopped ironing and folding Icarus's clothes and bringing his school things to the front of the house. Then, after a while, he stopped cooking at all.

This morning, as uncomfortable as it was, felt like stepping back in time. Maybe some parents are better suited to parenting children instead of teenagers, Icarus thought. Maybe all they know eventually just runs out.

Even though Icarus was late and clearly in a bit of trouble, he savored the taste of his oatmeal and let the steam warm his face.

STRICT

There was a test in first period, so Icarus and Julian didn't get to talk much. Julian did tell him that his hair was sticking straight up and handed him a double-cream hot chocolate, but that was about it.

Aspen was in class today. She slung her backpack on the floor by Icarus's and settled into the seat next to him instead of behind him like usual.

"Hey."

Aspen was wearing her usual camo jacket and cargo pants. She smelled a bit musty, but for once Icarus didn't mind. He was sure *he* still smelled like the outdoors himself.

"Where were you yesterday?" Icarus asked quietly.

Aspen shrugged and stared resolutely at her notebook. "Migraine."

"You didn't miss much. We're on linear momentum and collisions now, but we barely started the chapter before class ended," Icarus said.

Aspen nodded. She combed her fingers through her hair and began absent-mindedly twisting the ends. Icarus watched her. He wondered whether Celestina, Julian, and Luca felt about him the way *he* felt about Aspen: a mixture of curiosity and pity.

Icarus knew that if he didn't talk to Aspen, no one else would.

More than that, it wasn't a mystery as to why.

Aspen gave off very intense "stay away from me" vibes, in a way that Icarus sincerely hoped he didn't. But that was also a thing they had in common. Aspen didn't know why Icarus kept to himself outside of school, but she did understand both that it was important and that it wasn't exactly what Icarus really wanted. Part of the reason Icarus liked Aspen was because it felt good that someone noticed this part of him. It was as close to knowing his secret as someone could get.

When the bell rang, Aspen stood up and faced Icarus directly.

"Some people saw you get out of Celestina's truck with her," she said bluntly. "You should get a handle on that unless you want attention from people like her."

Icarus nodded and Aspen left.

HUMDRUM

He walked the mile with Luca and sat through the rest of the day without any issue, but still he felt anxiety creep under his skin.

Tonight was the first night of this multi-heist. He had two more before the week was done.

It went like this:

Mr. Black rarely moved his works unless he was selling them or he was adding something new to his collection.

So, Icarus would break in to take pictures. He would bring these images home and his father would study them. Angus would research their sale history and validate their origins. Mr. Black didn't have many fakes in his home aside from theirs, but he wasn't an infallible collector and a few slipped under even *his* watchful eye. Angus didn't make those kinds of mistakes. If it wasn't real, it remained untouched.

Then, his father would begin the reproduction. If it was a painting, there was print work involved and hideously expensive historical paints. If it was a sculpture, he would source marble, wood, plaster, gold, whatever was necessary. Depending on the piece, it could take months to complete a replica and cost thousands in supplies.

Finally, location of the work was vital to understanding how quickly Icarus could get in and out with a piece, and what tools he might need to remove it. The larger the piece, the more elaborate the break-in. Paintings were a swift in-and-out, one-and-done sort of job. Sculptures couldn't be heavier than Icarus or Angus could carry one-handed and could only be delivered when Mr. Black was confirmed to be out of town.

Angus had placed cameras all around the Black residence, far enough down the street to not be associated with the property, but close enough that all entrances and exits were under twenty-four-hour surveillance. No one watched them during the day, but they were intensely useful for studying later for schedule and interference.

So.

Three break-ins were scheduled before the week was over because, according to Angus, Mr. Black was headed to New York.

VESSEL

People rarely returned home within three hours of taking a flight. There was a danger zone within the first two hours: if they forgot something, they'd have enough time to turn back. Breaking in during the scheduled time of Mr. Black's flight seemed good enough, but it wasn't. On the off chance there was a cancellation, there was still enough time to return. Ten to twenty-four hours after a flight were also dangerous, because there was enough time to turn a three-day trip into a one-day trip and head back.

But three hours after take-off? If they were coming back home without leaving, they would already have arrived. If they'd actually left, they would still be in the sky.

It was a treat, and it happened maybe once or twice a year.

Which was why—three hours after Mr. Black's flight out—Icarus could use the back door.

He placed the large bone-china urn on the ground and unlocked Mr. Black's house with a key. The alarm began to beep, but the newest code had been in their possession for a year, easily taken from video through a window. He quickly turned it off.

The eerie feeling in the house still remained. A silence louder than noise.

Normally when Mr. Black was gone, when he knew the house was empty, Icarus could relax and make his way through the property with a regular amount of noise, but this time, in spite of his father's reassurance, he just couldn't.

He crept gently up the back stairs to the smaller library and did his job. One urn removed, one urn replaced, he fled back down and out the door, his heart racing like a coward.

STRIKE

The sculpture delivery went off without a hitch, but photography was a day-time activity. So, on Thursday, the second day of the heist, Icarus got called out of school.

He was supposed to take pictures of some of the empty bedrooms. But he followed the jangling of his nerves and went down into the dark storage instead to take pictures of the pieces that were too fragile or not grand enough to display.

Hopefully his father would be so excited to see this untouched work that he'd let the disobedience go.

The painting delivery haunted him though. It was *not* optional and definitely located in one of the most commonly used areas of the mansion. The delivery was on the worst day as well: the day of Mr. Black's return home.

Anything could happen. Mr. Black could come in eight hours early, he could arrive hours late, there could be delays, or he could arrive a whole day later. Then there was the whole thing about the house maybe not being empty. Icarus hadn't heard anything during his first visit but the air felt so heavy in there, there was a hum like more electricity was being used. Something. He couldn't just shrug it off, it itched at him.

Uncertainty felt like death at his back.

TITLE

Icarus clattered around the house like a grain of rice at the bottom of an empty tin, picking things up and putting them down. Tidying objects he would never normally tidy.

Angus sat at the kitchen table eating hard dark bread and sweet cream butter. He had a book in one hand. Every so often he would look up to watch Icarus.

"You have half an hour. Do you have everything you need?" he asked softly.

Icarus startled, then composed himself, putting down a small figurine he was dusting.

"Yeah. I think so. This one is in the second master bedroom. I haven't been in that room since the images were taken." It was the closest he could come to admitting that he was nervous.

Icarus's father chewed for a bit.

"If anything happens . . . I'll come for you. I won't . . . let you fall," he said, his gaze returning to his book.

Icarus stopped fidgeting. It was the first time his father had ever offered that to Icarus in his entire life.

"Dad . . . " Icarus said softly.

Angus nodded. "Don't forget to be careful," he said unnecessarily.

"I won't."

GONG

Icarus slid into the window on the second floor. The back door wasn't a viable option so close to Mr. Black's return.

This wing of the mansion was blue. Blue carpet, blue walls, silver sconces every ten feet or so, all unlit. There was a guest bathroom, big and white with gold fixtures, a small study packed tightly with old children's books, a playroom filled with unused junk toys, and finally: a large bedroom meant for a child.

Icarus and his father never spoke about Mr. Black's personal life. But it wasn't inconceivable to imagine that he'd had kids at some point. There had never been anyone else in this house the entire time Icarus had been coming here. He was twelve when he started; now he was almost eighteen.

Icarus pressed himself against the wall and paused, listening hard. He could hear the trees blowing in the wind outside, the ticking of a clock in one of the rooms, the light buzz of electricity in the walls, but nothing else.

Icarus darted across the mezzanine and into the hallway. He paused, holding his breath, to calm his heart.

HUFF

This room was ornate, designed by Mr. Black's ex-wife. On one side there was a large, four-poster bed with drapes all the way to the floor. Stacks of books spilled out onto the ground. There was a record player that looked dusty and unused, and a giant wardrobe with clothing sticking out every which way.

All of it dusty and untouched, like someone years ago had left in a very big hurry.

It was currently too dark to see the other half of the room, but the place where Icarus needed to be was easy to find.

Directly across from the bed there was a large landscape painting of haystacks at dusk. A Monet. It was one of the most beautiful paintings in the house.

Icarus rarely spent time watching his father reproduce pieces, but this one felt . . . crisp, like a winter morning before it truly got cold. When the dew gathers, wavering between frost and water, and the air smells like wood. Like metal.

Even the destruction of the forgery felt obscene: the layer of yellowed volatile lacquer to replicate the age, the dash of green crayon, the heat exposure, and resulting cracks. But, still, it was a masterpiece.

Icarus stood in front of the original, set into the wall in the center of a built-in bookcase, and took it in. The glare of his headlamp illuminated the real cracks, the real crayon, in a circle of yellow light.

Icarus pulled out a few volumes from the bookcase to stand on and delicately placed them on the floor. Then he climbed up to face the masterpiece.

IKE

He lowered the Monet to the ground and unfastened the backing from the frame. Now that he had them side by side, he could tell that the forgery was lighter in weight, the canvas it was painted on much softer and more delicate than the original cloth.

The painting his father had made was slightly too yellow, but without the other work next to it, it wouldn't be easy to tell. This clearly was not a room that Mr. Black went into particularly often.

Icarus pinned the replacement painting to the old frame and folded a protective sheath of silk around the original Monet before placing it in the carrier on his back.

Then he hung the forgery where it belonged in the center of the wall. When Icarus bent down to pick up the books and replace them, the light of his headlamp landed on two feet.

Icarus jerked up with a gasp and whirled around.

He stumbled backward over the books, catching himself against the bookcase. His headlight spun crazily around the room as he faltered, eventually landing steady on the person in front of him.

Dressed in a slightly too-small blue linen pajama set, another boy stared back, very calm. He had bright red hair—mussed, as he'd obviously been asleep—and soft brown eyes. He was taller than Icarus and broader in the shoulders. But he wasn't armed or standing like he was about to attack.

He looked resigned, but curious.

"How long have you been doing this?" he asked.

BRUSH

The sound of the boy's voice—rough and low—was enough to break the spell of shock that pinned Icarus to the wall.

He tried to dart to the side, but the boy caught his arm quick and pushed him bodily up against the bookshelf. Icarus's head banged against the middle of the fake Monet and he let out a terrible noise. So throaty and desperate he could hardly believe it came from him.

Icarus had *never* had someone this close, pressed along every inch of him, and it was more than he could take. His eyes rolled back as the heat of a palm squeezed his forearm. Strong thighs bracketed his, preventing his escape. Icarus's knees felt like they were about to fail him.

"Who are you?" the boy demanded, but Icarus couldn't answer even if he wanted to.

Up close, it was worse. There was breath on his face that he could feel even through the balaclava he wore, and the boy was so near that some of his hair was brushing the sliver of skin that showed around Icarus's eyes.

The boy grabbed the edge of Icarus's balaclava. With a thrum of fear, Icarus reached up to keep it down. But his assailant was quick and then Icarus was unmoored: naked and shaking in the circle of his own light.

The boy backed up, startled, but did not release Icarus's arm.

"Angus," he whispered, then shaking his head he tried again. "Too young. You must be the son."

Icarus pushed the boy hard, grabbed the real Monet, and dashed for the door.

"Helios!" he heard the boy call from behind him. Far enough that Icarus knew he wasn't being followed. But Icarus wasn't foolish enough to stop running.

It didn't keep him from hearing the rest.

"I'm Helios Black. You rude idiot."

BLUR

Icarus ran all the way home. His heart was pounding so fast that he couldn't feel his legs. He slammed inside the front door, stumbling up the stairs to their apartment, breathless and raw, then stopped.

Standing there—panting—all his thoughts coalesced to a final conclusion:

He couldn't tell his father.

First, Angus did *not* like being wrong. Enough that it was its own separate type of fear to consider informing him that Mr. Black had somehow gotten a whole person into his home without his father knowing. To tell him that the fail-safe surveillance that had kept them secure for over a decade of thievery had missed something so big.

Second, "Angus," Helios had said. It could mean many things, and nothing good. Icarus knew he looked a *lot* like his father, but the fact that this stranger was remotely expecting either of them was hideous to consider.

Third, Helios had seen his face. He had seen *him*. Had looked at him closely and touched him.

Icarus could still feel the ghost of Helios's hands, and it made him want to press his forehead against the wall and groan. The idea of trying to warn his father about this situation and having to explain his delayed reaction, to have his ears turn red without his permission while his father looked down on him in disappointment and disgust, was . . . violent.

Icarus took a moment to calm down. He wiped the sweat from his face with his shirt and pushed his hair back so his father wouldn't be able to tell he'd been running his fingers through it in anguish.

He breathed slowly. Willed his heart to stop racing. Then, he opened the door.

REAM

Icarus walked quickly to the storage room and began unpacking. The whir of machinery was a relief. At least if it stopped, he would know his father was coming.

He unwrapped the Monet, hands still shaking, and spread it out on the worktable. The crayon damage on the real painting would absolutely need to be handled by his father before sale. But right now it just needed to be cleaned and properly hung.

He hooked up the air brush and blew away the first layer of dust, then dry brushed it with soft fluffy bristles. The crayon could probably be removed. But if it had stained the oil paint beneath it, it might need more elaborate work that Icarus simply hadn't been trained for yet.

The crayon was bright green. A child's drawing of the sun and what looked like either a dog or maybe an attempt at a horse. The painting was already in terrible disrepair and extremely rare. It wouldn't sell at auction without press. But they might be able to offload it to a museum overseas that was willing to turn their head if Icarus could get it back to a reasonable condition.

Icarus eyed the bottle of diluted rubbing alcohol on the counter with the rest of the tools, then looked back at the painting.

The last Haystack Monet had sold for $110 million.

Instead, he opened their bottle of rarely used vinegar, set a few drops on the crayon to sit for a while. Then, he took a deep breath and on the furthest corner of the painting, swiped at the green.

To his immense relief it smeared, the younger oil liquifying immediately. Icarus alternated between the vinegar and the soft shop-paper towels, slowly removing Helios's clumsy drawing from this priceless—

"Trusting your instincts is the first sign you're ready for larger projects."

Icarus startled badly, nearly knocking the painting from the desk. The noise of the machine hadn't ceased, but Angus was leaning against the storage room doorway anyway.

"I'm sorry!" Icarus exclaimed, reflexively. But his father's eyes just crinkled with amusement.

"It's good work. Alcohol probably would have done a nice job on a newer oil painting, but would have been much too harsh on this one. It will have to be gone over again with spit and a shop cloth to remove the residue."

They stood together in silence.

"You can go, I'll finish this." It was the closest his father came to thanking him for any work he ever did.

Icarus took the out and scurried away gratefully.

STEAM

Icarus ran the hottest bath their house could manage. He boiled himself in it until he couldn't take it anymore and had to add some cold water.

He could still feel the ghost of Helios's hands on his arm, feel the tenderness where his knuckle had scraped his cheek when Helios had snatched off his mask.

The mask that was still in Mr. Black's house, Icarus realized.

He swore and let his head thunk back against the tile.

ANALYSIS

Helios looked a lot like Mr. Black. Icarus knew he hadn't been lying.

Mr. Black was extremely tall and athletic. He had a face like an old fox: sharp eyes and cheekbones, narrow and pinched. In the old pictures Icarus had seen of him, he had red hair like his son. Icarus had been told it was mostly gray now, even though he was probably only in his very late forties.

They had only been together for a moment, but it was vivid in his memory now that Icarus wasn't in a state of panic. He could analyze it.

Helios had a softer face than his father and brown eyes that were probably his mother's. Helios was wiry, but strong, and had big hands—larger than Icarus's. There were calluses on one, but the other was soft like Celestina's had been.

Nothing in the room had been disturbed very much, so he couldn't have been living in it for long. Helios's clothes fit like he had visited once, right before a growth spurt, gotten these pajamas, and never been back. They were too small to have been lent to him by Mr. Black—who still towered over all of them. But not small enough to be from the dusty dresser.

So, Helios's arrival to the Black mansion was recent and unexpected. He hadn't been allowed to bring most of his things, and he hadn't left the building since getting there. Even casually, to get something to eat.

Also, he was *alone*.

The first time Icarus's hackles were raised in the Black mansion was at least two weeks ago. Mr. Black had been inside the house the last time

Icarus had broken in, but the feeling of occupancy had stayed the same even when he'd gone to New York.

Helios was confident and unpredictable. He'd managed to take advantage of Icarus's focus on the theft to get out of bed and approach without Icarus hearing. Instead of screaming for help or calling the police, he was comfortable enough with his own strength and speed to force Icarus to stay in one place for his questions.

Worse, he'd asked, *"How long have you been doing this?"* before *"Who are you?"*

Icarus didn't know how to feel about that.

SHARK

Icarus was sure he would wake up to police banging on their door the next morning, but he didn't.

It was not enough to completely reassure him, whatever was going to happen to them wouldn't be a local law enforcement issue. If Helios had called the cops shortly after Icarus left, they would already be here. Mr. Black absolutely knew where they lived. Maybe it would be the FBI or Mr. Black would spring for an assassin.

Whatever happened, they deserved it.

Icarus turned over in his warm nest of blankets and closed his eyes.

Without knowing or being told about these circumstances, Angus was bound to send him back there. He wouldn't be able to get out of going without making this situation worse. But he just . . . couldn't. Not yet. He didn't know the parameters of what he'd stumbled upon; he needed more information or there was a chance he could unintentionally make things worse.

Saturday was the only day of the week that was Icarus's to do whatever he wished. The only thing he wanted was to sleep until this problem fixed itself.

SABBATH

There was no church in their town that mattered.

Icarus pressed his forehead to the ground and let the wood grain cut into his skin. Angus's voice chanting liturgy, solid and steady as water washing over stone, while Icarus both listened and didn't. The light from their foyer, golden and weak.

Icarus had been taken to big churches, gilded like palaces. Seen the bones of saints in small gold cages, caressed paint that hadn't been touched in decades with hot human fingertips. Knelt on marble, granite, limestone, cedar, pine, gravel, linoleum. Heard choirs that would make angels turn their faces in jealousy.

Seen all built in the name of God by men. Rosaries made of diamond, made of dental floss and paper.

He raised his face to the rafters, eyes open.

"Pater aeterne, offero tibi Corpus et Sanguinem, animam et divinitatem dilectissimi Filii Tui, Domini nostri, Iesu Christi, in propitiatione pro peccatis nostris et totius mundi."

He tasted bread from his father's hands, wine from his father's cups. They knelt, mirrored, grateful.

"Do you have any confessions?"

"No."

SMART

Icarus was good at secrets. He took this new frightening one and wrapped it up just like the others. He put it on a shelf in the back of his mind and labeled it firmly "to be addressed later."

Monday was wet with the rain from Sunday night. The gloom carried into the classroom, making lessons slow and irritable. Worse, gym class was held inside on rainy days, in the caustically bright gymnasium.

Their teacher didn't care what anyone did while gym was outside, so long as he had enough players for a game. But with less space indoors, anyone not playing was actively in the way. On rainy days, Icarus actually had to participate.

Floor hockey wasn't his favorite, but he got to be the goalie, which was nice. Normally people in other classes who walked the mile would fight over that position—seeing as it was the most sedentary. But Icarus's reflexes made him startlingly good. Team captains always picked him first and instantly assigned him that role.

Luca, who was on the other team, had made his way across the gym and parked himself near Icarus to chat. The center back defenders on Icarus's team watched him warily.

But Luca didn't care, he was blabbing about some video game that he thought Icarus might like.

"It's open world, I'm not sure if you're into that. You don't really seem like an FPS-type guy."

"I'm not." Icarus didn't play video games; he didn't have time for it.

"That's what I thought." Luca pushed his hair back and glanced up the court at their classmates loudly chasing the ball. Attentive, even still.

"But anyway, you can do whatever you want in it, which is pretty fun. You can do side quests, or mine or fish, you can be a hero or a villain or like . . . I don't know, a vagrant?"

Icarus snickered. "Middle Ages Fantasy Crust Punk Simulator?"

Luca laughed loudly. "Yeah man, if you want it to be."

The ball rolled quickly across the room, pursued by Janine Rodgers—one of the most athletic girls in their school. She scrunched her freckled nose in concentration and slapped it. Icarus tracked its trajectory. He easily parried it back into play right at the feet of one of the defenders on his team.

Luca whistled low. "Man, you should definitely try an FPS though. With that kind of reaction time . . . you'd be dangerous."

Icarus shrugged. "I like the sound of the other thing you were describing better. I . . . like the idea of getting to go wherever you want and do whatever you like."

Luca smiled, but it was an odd one. "Yeah . . . I thought you might."

The ball sailed in their direction again. This time Luca did his job and volleyed it sharply into Icarus's net. Reflexively, Icarus's body instantly fell to its knees and his arms jerked up to catch the ball with a painful smack.

"Fuck," one of his teammates gasped. "He's like a professional."

Icarus's ears burned at the attention. He climbed to his feet and gently tossed the ball back into action.

Luca was gazing at him, eyes dark with amusement. "You can't keep doing stuff like that and still turn me down when I try to recruit you for team sports."

"Yes, I can." Icarus smiled back shakily as he rubbed his smarting palms on his thighs.

"Come eat lunch with us next period. At least turn down Akeem in person so he gets off my back," Luca said, his eyes tracking the play toward his own team's net. "Literally no one else in school knows you well enough to ask. He's been bothering me about it every day."

It was rare that permanent solutions to social problems were dropped in his lap, so Icarus agreed.

BLUSH

Icarus usually ate in the photo room; it was dim, quiet, and almost always completely empty. On the rare occasion that someone was trying to work in there, he would switch to eating outside on the hill. If it was rainy, or winter, he would sneak to the back of the library and eat on the floor surrounded by books. The three or four times that the librarian caught him and firmly reminded him that there was no eating in the library, he waited twenty minutes until everyone had been served and went to eat in the kitchen with the lunch ladies.

He'd come up with this method after he accidentally fell in with a habitual group to sit with in freshman year and they started trying really hard to chill with him outside of school.

But even so—even when he was younger and less careful—Icarus would never have sat with Luca and his friends.

Luca led him through the loud, busy room to the back where the sporty popular kids sat. Akeem—tall, African American, and talented at baseball—sat at the center of the table leaning back against the window. To his left: Patrick—blond, big as a house, and better at football than most other things—was loudly talking about how he didn't want to read *Adventures of Huckleberry Finn* because it made him uncomfortable. To Akeem's right was his girlfriend, Trina, who was exceptionally nice, but so pretty she was completely unapproachable. There were two other guys at the same table, both on the basketball team. Each had two lunch trays with two portions of lunch each.

All of them perked up as Luca and Icarus approached.

"I see you brought something for show-and-tell," Patrick said, pausing in his tirade.

Luca grinned and put a firm hand on Icarus's shoulder. The other kids shifted to the side to make more room.

"So, which one of you is riding my boy Luca about making me join stuff?" Icarus said immediately, sitting down. He pulled out his sandwich and water bottle.

One of the basketball guys hooted. "Right to the point, huh. You're not playing any games!"

Akeem cocked his head to the side to appraise Icarus, shifting the vibe with weighted silence.

"Do you know how rare it is to get scouted?" Akeem said. "Especially right before we graduate. I'm not saying you gotta, I'm just saying that if there's anyone here who can start impressing recruiters immediately it's you." He ate a french fry and raised an eyebrow. "It would be rude of me not to try."

Luca stole a fry off Akeem's plate, even though somebody had clearly packed his unseasoned chicken, rice, and broccoli with care and consideration for his health.

"Bro, I told you. He doesn't like sports, he's just good at them," Luca griped.

"How could you not like something you're good at," Patrick complained. "I don't get it."

Icarus grinned. "Anyone can be good at anything. Doesn't mean I have to do it for my whole life. I start playing, recruiters start watching, and I'm stuck doing a thing I'm not into for what, five, ten years? Fifteen if it's baseball . . . statistically three if it's football."

"No way you're good at football too," Patrick groaned. "You're so small."

Luca nudged him hard. "Reflexes, man, you should see this kid dodge.

And he throws with precision. Not super far, but put him in the right place and he's golden."

Icarus scowled.

"Do you spend all of gym just watching me?" he snapped.

Luca looked at him, scandalized. "*Yes.*"

"I had gym with him sophomore year," said one of the basketball players that Icarus didn't recognize. "He did fifty pull-ups during the Presidential Fitness Test. The next closest guy was at like twenty-one."

Icarus rubbed his hands together under the table, feeling his calluses. Climbing the side of buildings meant that he *had* to know how to support his own weight enough to swing himself up quietly.

"Who even *are* you, dude?" Patrick said, clearly frustrated.

"My dad is ex-military," Icarus lied. "You should be glad you don't have to do the shit I do at home."

This got the whole table to laugh.

"Hmm." Akeem sat forward and steepled his hands. "I respect that, I respect that, I'll stop pushing. But let me know if you change your mind. We have about three weeks to get you on any team you want before time runs out and things get solid for the year."

Icarus nodded. "Thanks, man."

Akeem leaned back. "And let me know if your old man gets out of hand," he said casually.

Icarus's blood ran cold. He schooled his face to neutrality and met Akeem's eyes.

"Fifty pull-ups in two minutes is no joke," Akeem continued, around another french fry. "We don't gotta be friends, man, but my dad's a PD captain. You get tired of what you got going on at home, you come find me."

Icarus truly didn't know how to respond to that, so he chewed the last bite of his sandwich for longer than he usually would to think. The rest of the table watched him, including Luca, who seemed nervous for some reason.

"I feel like the belle of the ball," Icarus joked, finally. "You treat all guests to your table so sweet? Or am I just as pretty as Luca keeps telling me I am?"

Luca covered his face with his hands. "Oh my god, don't do this here."

The rest of the table laughed again. But Akeem stayed serious, waiting for a real reply.

Icarus nodded. "I got you, man. Thanks. I'll let you know."

SORREL

Icarus collapsed into the chair next to Sorrel. He had never been so relieved to be near someone low maintenance in his life. Luca's friends were nice, but meeting them on their level left Icarus exhausted. Sorrel glanced over at Icarus with his dishwater blue eyes and smiled shyly.

In art, they were working on still-life painting, which was honestly hilarious considering how much practice Icarus had. Each time they shifted mediums, they had a history lesson, wrote a paper, then submitted a subject request for approval. In the weeks after, they were left to do whatever they liked until the project was due—so long as they showed up to class to work on it.

Sorrel had chosen to paint a bowl of rapidly decaying flowers.

Icarus had chosen Sorrel's hands.

"It's coming out good," Icarus observed.

Sorrel's ears pinked. "Yeah. I think so."

Sorrel never spoke first; he always waited until he was spoken to.

"Mine's too simple." Icarus glanced over at his own work. "I can't believe she wouldn't just let me do your face."

Icarus didn't like drawing objects, just people. He liked to study people; they were much more interesting.

Sorrel raised one shoulder in disagreement as he looked at Icarus's canvas. "I think it looks really nice."

Icarus sighed and smiled back. The quiet of the room and the scratching of brushes and pencils pulled the tension from his shoulders and the tightness in his jaw.

He painted in silence next to Sorrel for the rest of the period, then packed his things and headed home.

FLEE

Icarus swung by the hardware store and picked up a small sampler of paint to color the ceiling of his closet. Gray blue, like the lake in winter. Like the walls of the rest of the house underneath their clutter.

There was plenty of paint in his house, of course, but he'd learned the hard way that wall paint and canvas paint weren't interchangeable.

He made a quick stew and tossed it in the pressure cooker so he'd have time to work on his room. He hoped it would be dry by the time he went to sleep.

It was halfway complete when his father knocked on his closet door and then opened it without waiting for Icarus to let him in.

"Do you have a lot of homework today?"

A thrum of dread settled in Icarus's stomach.

"No."

"I need you to make an exchange."

Icarus put his brush back in the can and faced his father. Angus sounded anxious, which was startling.

"What's . . . "

Angus pressed his lips together hard before continuing.

"I was sent a sculpture by the Musée d'Art Moderne for repair and it's a forgery. A good one, but a forgery nonetheless."

Icarus immediately closed the can and stood up, striding fast out of his room. This had happened to them three times before, and he knew what it meant. A museum owning a forgery is scandalous in most situations. But when a museum ships a work believed to be legitimate and upon its return it is recognized to be a reproduction, it is an emergency involving insurance, money, and law enforcement.

"Do I have to travel?" Icarus asked, already heading to where his coat was hung by the door.

"The photographs you sent of Black's storage," his father continued. "They contain an image of what I believe is the original. I need you to take the version sent to me by the museum and exchange it with Black's."

The thrum of dread became a roar.

"Tonight?" Icarus choked out.

"After dinner. It's still not dark yet. But yes, tonight."

CRIME

The stew settled in Icarus's stomach like it was ready to come right back out. It hadn't even been a full seventy-two hours since he'd left that place.

He felt cursed. Shaky.

Icarus had opened his mouth six or seven times to tell his father about what had happened the last time he was in that house, but the words never came out.

This was a bigger emergency than his fear. This could cost them their livelihood, bring an investigation to their home, and land them in prison far more quickly, efficiently, and permanently than even the situation with Mr. Black could.

With Mr. Black, they were just stealing from a guy. This, on the other hand, would be stealing from a private collection, a cultural artifact preservation site, and the country's government all in one, while also separately violating international law. Plus, if they somehow managed to wriggle out of those charges, Angus could never work as a restoration artist ever again. Icarus wasn't selfish enough to bring a second layer to his father's terror by adding his own, so he swallowed it.

He would have to be the quietest and quickest he'd ever been. Using the most dangerous door, at the most dangerous time.

Icarus looked across the table at his father and thought about Akeem's offer.

TOUGH

There was a diner across the street from the Black mansion. Their coffee was good. A little burned, but Icarus liked a lot of sugar in his coffee anyway.

He could almost see the back entrance of the Black house from the booth he was sitting in. The house was surrounded by thick trees blocking most of the neighborhood light and the noise from the highway. There were a few nice houses this far out—rich people definitely liked the acreage—but Mr. Black's was the biggest.

The street was quiet and clear. Icarus needed the extra time to gather his nerve.

The sculpture was small. Small enough to fit under his black jacket in an inside pocket. It was wood and not even particularly valuable compared to some of the rest of the pieces they'd worked on. A 1960's abstract piece, with a crack from heat damage.

Icarus ran his fingers over the shape of it from outside his coat. People had been banned from entering countries over a little thing like this.

"You need one last refill, dear?" the waitress asked. She looked tired; it was almost 2 a.m. "It's almost closing time."

Icarus shook his head and stood up to leave. "No, thank you." He put a few bills on the table and headed to work.

CRACK

The alarm was on. He could tell from the whine that had taken him years to notice. Icarus grit his teeth in irritation for a moment, then tilted his head back and took a calming breath. He could do this.

He took out his fabric-covered hammer and set about removing the back door from its hinges. Doing that was easier than most people with homes to protect would like to know. But it was loud, and that made it a liability. Icarus hated liabilities.

He pulled the door open a few inches and slithered through the crack, pressing it gently closed.

The house was quiet, but felt alive. Noticeably inhabited. He could hear the TV upstairs and laughter near it, hushed as mouse chatter.

Icarus flattened himself against the wall and slid along it toward the basement door. There was a thump a few floors above him, and his heart slammed in his chest.

He paused, waiting in the silence. After a minute of nothing, he flew across the rest of the hallway and quickly typed in the code for the storage room. The door opened with a soft hiss, and Icarus darted inside, closing it behind him. The room was about forty feet long and twenty feet wide with two aisles of shelves perpendicular to the door.

Unlike last time, when he could use his headlight camera to take pictures as slowly as he wanted, he was aiming for speed. So he turned the ceiling light on and sprinted down the first aisle.

Mr. Black's collection was organized like a library. The least valuable items were unwrapped and at the front of the storage unit. The most valuable were wrapped, in storage boxes or in the vault.

They were further organized by region, but in an unofficial way that made it hard to navigate. The sculpture was in the third row, on a shelf near the ground. It was next to a few other wood pieces Mr. Black clearly didn't value much. All of them unwrapped and covered in a fine layer of dust.

Icarus sighed. He pulled out a mask and tucked the straps over his ears. He picked up the original sculpture and placed it in his jacket pocket, making sure not to scrape any of the particulates off the surface of the shelf where it had rested. He took out the small container of fuller's earth that they used—rarely—to replicate dust. Placing the piece the museum had sent his father on the ground, Icarus crouched over it and gently tapped a kabuki makeup brush in the fuller's earth. He brushed his thumb over the bristles, sending a fine mist over the figurine from above. Glancing every so often at the remaining objects on the shelf, he matched the particle density as best he could.

Then he took two holding needles and pinned the figurine on either side. Using tension and steady strength, he lifted the statue off the ground, held fast between his two pins, to gingerly replace it on the shelf.

He could feel the sweat beading at his temples as he lowered the sculpture back into the circle of clean metal where the original piece had sat. Though he could feel his arms shaking, the base perfectly filled the circle without scraping or smudging the perimeter. Icarus pulled the needles slowly away from each side, leaving only pinprick-size dots where the sculpture had been handled. The adrenaline drained from Icarus in a dizzying wash and he let out a breath of relief.

He took a moment to study the figurine he was stealing. The forgery the museum had given them was worse work than Angus would have done himself. The real version was slightly lighter in color—they wouldn't have made this mistake and Icarus idly wished that they'd had time to make a better one. But that didn't matter nearly as much as making sure that it hadn't looked as though anything in this room had been touched.

Icarus stepped back. He closed his eyes and rubbed them, and had just turned to head out of the storage room when something caught his eye.

A gold that was too gold. Instead of leaving, like he knew he should, Icarus headed to the next aisle, to look closer.

It was a torque, about the size of his hands end to end, coated with dust. Icarus leaned in close, scrutinizing it. His heart started to race. To his delight, the metal bent at a hard press of his thumb.

Pre-Columbian gold was often solid. Closer to 24k than a significant number of ancient gold artifacts. This thing was so dusty it had to have been here for an extremely long time, and it wasn't in the safe like a pile of gold should be. If it was solid, it would be worth about $24–$50K. But that was small change to a man like Stuart Black. There were dozens of pieces in his home worth ten times more.

He'd probably gotten this early enough that he wouldn't have noticed if it was missing altogether. They never took without replacing as a rule. But if Icarus was never coming back after this, would that even matter?

Icarus bit his lip. He looked at the door nervously. They had never just taken something from here without replacing it.

But the opportunity was irresistible: $30K worth of gold that was easy to fence. More valuable to Icarus than all the Monets and Picassos in the world. Most of Mr. Black's art was valuable because of its provenance, its historical significance, or the fame of its artist. Its appearance on a traditional market would always raise red flags, and Icarus wasn't familiar enough with the black market for him to feel comfortable there. But gold . . . could be melted down into a block. It could be sold by the ounce regardless of its source. $30K was enough for a new start somewhere. With this torque,

Icarus would have his chance to start fresh. To start comfortably, far from his crimes and his father and this house.

Icarus opened his calipers and snatched a ceramic teacup from a nearby shelf. He scratched the raw bottom of the cup against the torque and turned it over—stomach in his chest—and the streak left behind was gold. *Yes!*

He gingerly placed the teacup back in its place and turned back to the torque. If he filled the gaps of dust left behind with fuller's earth, he'd be able to move it. This could be the last thing he ever stole—

The door to the storage room wasn't loud, but it wasn't silent. Icarus snatched his hand back from the torque. His head snapped up just in time to watch Helios enter the room.

Mr. Black's son closed the door behind him.

TINE

Helios turned the lock, tugged the handle, then gazed placidly down the aisle.

Icarus was ready this time. He squared his shoulders. Then he pulled his baton from inside his coat and shook the length out with a threatening snap.

"Let me out."

Helios tilted his head to the side, still assessing him, but said nothing.

Helios was wearing a soft black sweater and matching slacks, both of which fit him much better than the pajamas he was wearing when they met. They washed him out and made his red hair violently bright by comparison.

Icarus also noticed something else he'd missed: a thick silver cuff around Helios's ankle over his dark socks.

Then, strangely, Helios sat down cross-legged in front of the door.

"Please talk quieter, or he'll hear you," Helios said, low and soft. "What are you taking this time?"

Icarus looked at the figurine reflexively, and then back at Helios. He immediately felt stupid for giving himself away like an amateur.

"I . . ."

"Come here, sit down with me," Helios said. "I can't hear you from that far away."

Icarus's eyes darted around the storage room ceiling, checking for cameras and potential exits. He glanced back at the vault.

"Even I don't have the combination for that," Helios whispered. "Can you stop being so stubborn?"

Icarus grit his teeth and tightened his grip on the baton. He strode across the room, twisting his wrist so the rod swished through the air with the promise of violence. But Helios just watched calmly.

Icarus came to a stop two feet in front of the other boy and looked down at him. Helios's face was . . . like a statue come to life. Crests and shadows in alabaster and blue. Cow-eyed, dimple-chinned, long-lashed beauty. In spite of everything, for one horrible second, Icarus wished that he had time to paint him.

Icarus knew the figure he cut in black. He knew how he moved in uniform, but Helios stared up at him bravely, still. Without breaking eye contact, Icarus reached over Helios's head and unlocked the door. Helios's hand flew up to grab Icarus's wrist, but he jerked away.

"Stop touching me."

"Stop liking it," Helios shot back immediately and Icarus saw red.

He curled his fist into the front of Helios's sweater, lifting him up.

"Don't make me hurt you."

Helios grinned. "You think you'd be the first?"

Icarus shook him crisply. "What do you want?" he hissed.

"To have someone to talk to. I can't leave this house and I haven't spoken to anyone in weeks."

Icarus was so startled by that answer that he dropped Helios. Who miserably tried to pat down the wrinkle where Icarus had stretched out his sweater.

"Fine. But when we're done here, you turn me loose."

DROWN

They sat across from each other at the storeroom entrance. Icarus's back braced against the center shelf. His baton across his lap, knees bent to look relaxed but in optimal position to spring up and run.

"Take off your mask. I've already seen your face," Helios said.

"No," Icarus replied curtly.

Helios sighed. "Okay, whatever. So, is this like . . . your day job? Or, well, night job."

"It's a hobby."

"Cool hobby . . . genuinely. Do you make the fakes? How many of them are there?"

Icarus didn't answer. He just stared back at Helios.

Helios sighed and rubbed his temples. "Fuck me. Ugh. Okay. Let's start with introductions." He put his hand on his chest dramatically. "Hi, my name is Helios Black. Resident fuck-up and local prisoner of Stuart Black the second. Unable to talk to anyone, have access to a phone or computer, see any of my friends, and most importantly, leave—"

"Who is he to you, specifically?" Icarus demanded, cutting off Helios's stupid speech. He had an idea, but he wanted to know for sure.

Helios scrunched his nose up in disgust. "My dad. But I don't know him that well and he's . . . extremely mean. I haven't been back to this boring little town for over ten years. I left when I was like seven. Which is good because there is literally nothing to—"

"Why is he keeping you here?" Icarus interrupted, again.

Helios grinned but it didn't reach his eyes.

"Because, I'm trouble," he replied after a moment. "It's a punishment to keep me out of more of it." He flicked the silver cuff around his ankle and it made a sharp ping. "I like to have fun."

A delinquent, probably.

"What do I have to give you for you to let me out? I need to go home," Icarus said, shifting topics. "You didn't contact the authorities last time, so you probably want something from me instead. What is it?"

Helios crossed his arms and thought for a while.

"Will you come back?" he asked.

Icarus considered lying, but seeing as this was the second time this quiet fucker had managed to catch him it was probably useless to try.

"Yes," he admitted.

"For the art? Or is it money too?"

Icarus shook his head sharply and lied. "Just art."

"For how long?"

Icarus shrugged. Hopefully his part in this would be over soon, but this guy didn't need to know that.

Helios took a deep breath and let it out in a whoosh. Then he glanced up at the doorknob and back at Icarus.

"You're the only person I can see that's not . . . him. It's presumptuous to assume we'll like each other and kind of weird to demand that we be friends. If *you* have to be here and *I* have to be here, can you at least talk to me sometimes?"

"Are you blackmailing me?" Icarus asked softly.

Helios pressed his fingers into his eyes. "No, fuck. My dad is keeping me here alone for an entire year until I turn eighteen. Whatever your price

70

is, I'll do it. Not telling the cops, not telling him—I'll even help you out with security or something. But I *can't* just sit here in the *silence* like this. Not for a year."

He pulled his hands down from his face.

"I've waited every night to hear you come in," Helios admitted. "You're good at your job, you didn't fuck up or anything. I was just waiting. You're an opportunity that I couldn't miss."

Icarus climbed to his feet and reached for the door again.

"Do you want me to call the police?"

Helios laughed. "I'm his son. Where else would they put me but where I belong?"

Icarus took a breath and closed his eyes. Loneliness he could understand.

"I'll be back."

"When?" Helios asked.

"When I need to," Icarus replied. He was not going to give this complete stranger information about his schedule. He turned the knob and Helios stood, backing away so he could open the door.

Icarus looked up at him for a moment, then opened one side of his jacket so Helios could see the top of the sculpture poking out of the inside pocket.

"It belongs to a museum. It was probably smuggled here. I'm returning it."

Helios nodded silently and moved farther away from him.

"I'll see you later . . . ?"

Icarus bit his lip. His name caught behind his teeth.

"Nothing you need to know," he said instead.

Helios smirked. "I'll see you later, Nothing."

BURR

Icarus slid across the hallway to the back door of the house, then squeezed himself back through the crack.

When he glanced behind him, Helios was still there. Backlit by the storeroom fluorescent, watching him.

Domini nostri, Iesu Christi.

Icarus closed the door. Reinstalled the hinges and walked back home.

WRATH

The farther he got from the mansion, the more irritated he became. No offense to Helios and his situation, but Icarus really didn't need this sort of pressure right now. If his dad had listened to him in the first place, he wouldn't even be in this position.

Icarus had never done anything that would make it reasonable for Angus to mistrust his instincts. He didn't deserve being ignored. It would never feel good to leave Helios hanging knowing the parameters of his . . . imprisonment. They could figure out a way to get child services involved and then take a long break.

Icarus didn't creep into his house. He walked in and closed the door hard. He strode down the main hall past his bedroom and the storage room and headed straight for his father's workshop.

Angus was dust blowing a granite piece that looked freshly sanded. He looked up in surprise as Icarus yanked the plug out of the wall.

Icarus took the figurine out of his jacket and slammed it down next to his father's right hand.

Angus let him leave without a word. Rare as it appeared, Angus never seemed like he knew what to do with Icarus's rage. He cowered before it.

THREE

Bereft, Icarus curled into a tight ball, squeezing his eyes hard until sparks danced behind his eyelids.

His ceiling was a mess, half done, gray cutting roughly into the sunset oranges and pinks. He'd have to go back and get some primer to hide the mistakes and start all over again, and somehow that was upsetting him even more than tonight's chaotic events.

Usually after a large haul they stopped for a month or so before picking back up again. Angus's schedule varied and special opportunities were unpredictable but there were breaks. This would have been the beginning of one of those breaks, if they hadn't had to deal with this forgery.

Now, it was up to Icarus to show up there on his own. Helios probably wouldn't wait a month or two before assuming Icarus wasn't coming back. He would maybe wait a few days at most before freaking out and narcing on him. Icarus knew he would in that situation. This entire situation was so frustrating and frightening. He didn't like being so reckless.

"My Crucified Jesus, wash me with your most Precious Blood. Look upon me as the good thief, *qui iuxta te in Calvariae cruce pependit. Peccator, pro sceleribus suis reddens; sed cognoscit numen tuum et veniam petit et quaerit: Iesu, memento mei cum veneris in regnum tuum.*"

Icarus closed his eyes and rubbed his temples. Thief problems, Thief's prayer—but he hated to use it.

He shouldn't be having to do any of this at all.

BROWN

The statue was cleaned, wrapped, and shipped back with its authentication paperwork. It was accepted and placed back on display with the rest of the collection. Its minute differences in color, lacquer, and condition unchallenged and unaddressed.

Angus never accepted restoration jobs from that museum again, no matter the pay or significance of the piece.

When Icarus was older, he went to visit it as often as he was able. Until he couldn't visit anywhere anymore.

FLUSH

Icarus took a sip of the strawberry smoothie Julian had brought him and winced. It was sweeter than he'd expected, and not in a good way.

"If you don't want it, I can always take it back," Julian snapped.

Icarus pulled the drink toward himself, guarding it possessively. "I'll choke it down for you."

Julian smirked. "I'm only joking, loser. You don't have to if you really don't want to," he said, softer.

Icarus shrugged a shoulder and continued drinking it. It was Wednesday, two days after the most recent incident with Helios, and he had decided that today was the day that he would go back.

He had to assess what that would mean.

Everything about his approach to this break-in had to be different. He couldn't wear his gear: no silent socks, no jacket with hidden pockets, no tools, gadgets, or supplies, no mask—frightening as that might be.

His weapons . . . Icarus wanted to bring his baton very badly. But for all that it was just some stick, it was designed to break bones and legally classified as an assault weapon. He also had a knife that he mostly used for prying. But that would still be considered an armed break-in. Even rope to help with climbing might get sticky.

He had to consider worst-case scenarios, and the worst-case scenario for this would be Mr. Black catching him with Helios. It would be easier to be an apologetic friend of Helios's who'd managed to sneak in. A normal kid. Someone who might be more of a threat to whatever situation was making

Mr. Black trap Helios in the house than to Mr. Black's rapidly depreciating art collection.

Even if Mr. Black had him carted down to the police station: wearing normal clothes and having nothing of interest on him would hopefully get him driven back home with a stern warning, instead of a swift meeting with Interpol.

He didn't know what to do about the fact that he looked so much like his father, though. Mr. Black would instantly recognize him. Maybe he could—

"—carus? ICARUS."

Icarus looked up from his notebook. His classmates were giggling.

"Do you have an answer or are you just keeping us all waiting for your own entertainment?" Mr. Harrison said dryly.

"Sorry, I didn't hear the question. Rough night," Icarus replied, rubbing a hand down his face. "What was it again?"

Mr. Harrison, a sarcastic and short-tempered man, stared at Icarus for a few seconds.

"Mr. Gallagher, can you step into the hallway for a minute?" he said.

A wave of exhaustion and irritation swept over Icarus as he stood. Worse, Mr. Harrison followed it up with a curt, "Bring your things."

Julian watched him, worried, but Icarus just grimaced and cleared his desk into his backpack.

He took one last sip of the smoothie, handed it back to Julian, and followed Mr. Harrison into the hallway.

GREAT

Mr. Harrison had a hammy red face and brown hair that was starting to salt and pepper. Icarus rarely spent much time talking privately with teachers, because he was simply too boring and average to catch their notice. He was a straight B student. He never caused the sort of problems that would warrant negative attention or made the kinds of achievements that would earn positive attention. His freedom depended on it.

It was uncomfortable to be in a mostly abandoned hallway alone with this man.

"Are you doing okay?"

That was *not* what Icarus thought he would hear.

"Uh, I'm fine, I just . . ." Icarus thought quickly. "My upstairs neighbors just had a new baby and the walls are thin."

Mr. Harrison nodded and crossed his arms with a short chuckle. "That would explain it. All that wailing and you don't even get to have a cute baby in the house. My wife and I didn't sleep for four months after our first. I was a mess, even walked right into a stop sign."

Icarus smiled and rubbed his eyes. "Yeah, it's . . . all night long and first thing in the morning. I'm sorry about earlier."

Mr. Harrison shook his head, "No problem, kid. I get it, but I'm still going to have to send you to the guidance counselor for the rest of the period. Talk to her, take a nap, whatever." He handed Icarus a bright pink hall pass, then put his hand on the doorknob to return to class.

Thinking again, Mr. Harrison turned back to him. "The key is to stop sleeping when you're supposed to and start sleeping whenever you can," he said. "See if the guidance counselor can work through your schedule to come up with one that works better for you. Good luck. And try not to let this happen again."

Icarus nodded and shoved the pass in his pocket.

DRAKE

The guidance counselor's office was small, cramped, and hot.

Her desk was at the back of the room in front of a window, which was wide open to let in the fall chill. There was a slender blue cot surrounded by a privacy curtain, where they sent kids who were sick if the nurse's office overflowed. There were two bean bag chairs and a small bookshelf filled with volumes with titles such as *Divorce and Me* and *Discovering My Sexuality* and *Children of Addicts*.

The guidance counselor herself, Mrs. Drake, seemed nice in a "lady you hope you never have to talk to" sort of way.

She looked up when Icarus opened the door, mid-bite of a sandwich.

"Oh! Sorry, excuse me. Come in," she said, waving him over and rewrapping her lunch. "What can I help you with?"

Icarus gave her the pink slip and settled into the chair across from her desk. "Mr. Harrison sent me here."

"So, what's going on?" She brushed crumbs off her pink sweater.

"I've been distracted because I'm tired," Icarus said bluntly. "He said I could sleep here?"

Mrs. Drake tilted her head to the side. "What has you so tired these days?" she asked, in a Therapy Voice.

Great.

Icarus closed his eyes and then opened them. "My neighbor just had a kid and it's loud in the middle of the night," he lied.

Mrs. Drake smiled. "So is this more of a recent thing?"

Icarus shrugged. "Yeah, it's only been a few days. I'm sure I'll get used to it and it won't be a problem in class anymore."

Mrs. Drake turned to her computer to figure him out. "Well, I haven't gotten anything from the other teachers about you, so you can feel free to use the cot. But while you're here, is there anything else you might need to talk about?"

There absolutely was, but Icarus instantly regretted his hesitation. He knew he had to say *something*, and something truthful or she would start digging.

"I'm . . . uh . . . anxious about what I'm going to be doing after graduation." That sounded safe. "I'm not sure what kind of jobs I'd be good at and it's . . . stressing me out."

"Oh! That's not a problem. I can set you up with a meeting with the post-secondary coach and he can advise you on college programs and trade schools. We can talk about it if you want. But discussion needs action like a cake needs salt," she said chipperly. "Want me to set an alarm for you?"

"Yes, please." Icarus got up and slung his backpack next to the cot. He took off his sweater and rolled it up into a pillow, then pulled the curtain shut around him.

He could hear Mrs. Drake take her sandwich back out, and let the crinkling and the hum of the boiler put him to sleep.

When the alarm rang, Icarus had a new hall pass and a meeting with the college coach that he had no intention of attending.

He didn't need it. He already had his occupation.

RISE

When Icarus got home, he threw together a lasagna and went to pick out his outfit.

Normally, Icarus wore Chelsea boots to school, but he did have tennis shoes. His gray corduroys had the most stretch for climbing, but they were too bright. He settled on navy blue chinos and just decided to be thankful they weren't jeans.

Icarus had a wool beanie that he had cut eye holes into years ago when he had to do a job and his balaclava was in the wash. He could probably roll it down in an emergency to shield his face, though it wouldn't be much use if Mr. Black grabbed him.

Icarus wore climbing gloves when he had to scale exteriors, but they just looked too professional, so instead he decided to tape his fingers with foam flex tape.

It wasn't the most . . . fashionable . . . outfit. Helios had only ever seen him in his insulated tights, tactical jacket, mask, and socks. So, he'd probably assume that however Icarus was dressed tonight was how he dressed all the time. This bothered Icarus more than he'd like to admit.

Angus scanned him from head to toe when Icarus settled down at the dinner table.

"You're going out tonight?"

Icarus nodded, but kept quiet.

Angus made a gruff noise in the back of his throat, but didn't ask any more questions.

LIGHT

Icarus rubbed his hands together and looked at the side of the Black mansion. This was going to hurt.

Helios's room was on the third floor, which meant three stories without gloves, rope, or protective padding. Icarus clenched his hands into fists and let them go, spreading his fingers out wide, then took a deep breath and jumped. His fingertips caught the familiar jut of the first-floor window and he swung the bottom of his body up to brace himself on the wall.

There were large trees on this side of the building, so he always entered from here and made his way wherever he needed in the house. The second floor had the easiest entrance, and the first was the hardest. The third was somewhere in the middle.

The wind rustled the leaves around him, loud enough to cover the scrape of his shoes against the brick. His fingers were already smarting from the uneven pressure of holding himself up. Icarus turned and reached out for the thick tree branch that you could only reach from fifteen feet up and with a sigh of relief, slithered onto it. He glanced down at the freefall beneath him, and then back up to the dark closed window.

Climbing the tree was much easier. Bark was worse on his hands than brick or siding, but at least if he fell, he would probably hit a branch and have a chance to catch himself, as opposed to just clean sailing right to the ground.

He slid up a weaker branch and edged toward the end of it, just managing to grip the bottom of Helios's windowsill. With a strength he was sure

Luca would be jealous of, Icarus dug his elbows into the brick to brace his feet on the vertical surface once more. Then he hoisted himself up until the tips of his toes were on the sill. The curtain was half drawn and the room was completely dark.

Normally, with his gloves, rope, and gear, he'd be able to hook himself to the outside so that he could use both hands to pry the window lock open and let himself in. But now if he leaned back at all, he would go hurtling twenty-five feet down. He pulled his pointer finger away from the window frame and tapped quietly on the glass.

The wind blew hard and he closed his eyes, hair whipping around his face, as he tightened his grip and tried not to fall.

RUSH

The window creaked quietly as Helios opened it with a dour expression. It shifted quickly to alarm as Icarus reached out and grabbed his forearm tight.

"Pull me in," he demanded. "I don't have ropes."

Helios hoisted him in. Icarus dropped to the floor on his toes, silent as a cat.

Helios rubbed at his arm, which was no doubt bruising rapidly.

"Why are you . . . where's your stuff?" Helios whispered, taking in Icarus's disheveled casual appearance.

Icarus shrugged.

"I'm here. What now," he said bluntly.

Helios moved back from Icarus and the window, slipping into the darkness behind him. Moonlight blue flowing down his form like the tide.

"Here," he said and slipped back onto his bed, pulling the curtain to the side for Icarus to follow him.

The drapery around the bed was thick enough to block most of the light and a good deal of noise. It was warmer behind these cloth walls and smelled curious. Like animal, like dust: this combination of young and old Helios.

Helios stuck his arm outside the curtain and rummaged around on his nightstand to pull in a flashlight as Icarus toed off his shoes.

Then, they were face to face, legs crisscrossed. The light between them casting their features in pink, red, and shadow.

"How have you been?" Helios asked. "Were you able to return the statue?"

Icarus hesitated for a moment, then nodded. "It's back where it belongs."

The silence between them was heavy. Icarus could feel the warm puff of Helios's breath in the small space. His knee was close enough to touch, but Icarus made sure they didn't.

Helios followed Icarus's gaze.

"It feels weird to be able to talk to you, but now you won't say anything," Helios admitted.

Icarus cleared his throat and tried.

"Do you still have my mask?"

Helios rolled his eyes and reached beyond the curtain again. Icarus heard a drawer opening and closing, then Helios shoved a familiar piece of cloth at him.

Icarus snatched it gratefully and without thinking, held it close to smell it.

"It reeks of chemicals. You do too," Helios commented, leaning back. "Like a Home Depot."

"That's probably what my house smells like," Icarus admitted, pulling the mask over his head.

"Wait—no. Don't put it back on!" Helios exclaimed.

Icarus paused. "What? Why?"

"I want to see your face."

Icarus grimaced. "It's not special." He tugged the rest of the mask on anyway.

Helios's frown was exaggerated by the flashlight underneath his chin.

"You seemed really upset when I took it off the first time. Worse than just the shock of getting caught," Helios said, clearly to himself. "I don't know why I expected any different now."

"I wasn't—it wasn't. I don't know you, and you were *touching* me," Icarus hissed.

"Oh. I was planning to ask about that. You're really weird about that. You don't seem to have any difficulty manhandling me, but god forbid we do the reverse."

"I don't want to talk about it," Icarus huffed; his face was starting to get hot.

"I'm not the kind of person who violates boundaries, dude, don't worry. I'm not going to touch you if you don't want." Helios threw both hands up defensively, accidentally dropping the flashlight in the process.

The beam wheeled crazily around the canopy, then before either of them could grab it, it fell onto the floor with a loud thunk.

"Shit," Helios hissed, snatching it off the ground.

He held up a hand in a quick gesture for silence and they both paused to listen. With a thrum of dread, Icarus heard footsteps advancing quickly toward the room.

Helios's clear eyes snapped to Icarus's in terror.

Icarus tugged back the bed's drapery and snatched his shoes from the ground. He hid in the corner of the bed, lying flat across the mattress, shoes tucked under his chest.

As Helios threw the thick comforter over Icarus's head, the door swung open.

CRY

"What are you doing in here?"

Mr. Black's voice . . . Icarus had never heard it so loud or so close.

Helios scooted up the bed, pulling Mr. Black's attention farther away from where Icarus was hiding.

"I'm sorry, I was reading. I dropped my flashlight, I'm sorry."

The footsteps came deeper into the room until Icarus could hear Mr. Black's breathing. He clutched the edge of the comforter tighter.

"When I say go to bed, I mean go to bed."

"Please, I'm sorry. I'm sorry," Helios stuttered apologies like punctuation.

There was a sound like nails scraping cardboard and a gasp as the bed jolted. Silence, then the unmistakable sound of a book slamming into a wall.

Then it was very quiet.

"Why is your window open?" Mr. Black demanded.

Icarus held his breath as Helios's father looked around the room.

"I . . . I . . ." Helios sounded truly shaken.

Mr. Black wrenched the window open farther to look outside it, then slammed it closed.

"I'm going to sleep, I'm sorry. It won't happen again! I'm sorry!" Helios begged shrilly as Mr. Black did something Icarus couldn't hear, but could feel as the bed trembled.

Icarus reached out a hand under the comforter and clasped Helios's ankle, firm. It wasn't much, it wasn't. But he hoped it helped.

Whatever Mr. Black was doing, he stopped, and Helios gave a soft gasp of relief.

"Go to sleep. Now," Mr. Black snapped.

The door slammed and his footsteps echoed down the hallway.

They took a solid two minutes to make sure he wouldn't return before Helios reached down and covered Icarus's hand with his.

MOVE

Helios wouldn't meet his eyes.

"Is he always like that?" Icarus asked quietly.

Helios just huffed, an angry frustrated sound. His hand was clasped firmly over his ear. His face was red, with embarrassment or anger or pain. Something.

Icarus reached out, then faltered.

"You don't have to stay," Helios said, sharply.

"It's . . . it's not—" Icarus pressed his lips together in frustration, trying to find the right words. "You didn't even do anything."

"You don't know that; you don't even know me," Helios snapped.

"I don't have to know you to know that was unwarranted," Icarus said firmly. "Don't be embarrassed about this. So what if you were scared in front of me? He's frightening. You're the one acting normal, he's not. That's all there is."

Helios shut his eyes very very tight and turned even further away.

Icarus pulled the curtains open and got up from the bed. He heel-toe soft-walked silently across the room and picked up the book that Mr. Black had thrown, bringing it back to Helios's nightstand.

"I won't leave you here alone in this situation," he promised.

Helios stayed facing the dark.

Icarus grit his teeth. He didn't know what else to say, so he slipped his shoes on and fled.

REAM

The next day felt like a thick soup.

He walked through the halls and sat in class, ate lunch, and went back to class in a haze dense enough to catch Celestina's notice.

She dragged him out behind the school and into the woods.

Icarus walked beside her in comfortable silence, thinking. He could still feel the bones shifting beneath Helios's skin. His skin had been so soft; softer than anyone's he'd ever felt. Hairy too. He thought about the scrape of Helios's ankle monitor against his forearm; the wire brushed metal was a tad too sharp. It should have been rounded and smoothed down for comfort, but it hadn't.

And in a house as grand as that, it had to be intentional. A part of his punishment.

The bed had shaken beneath him like nothing else Icarus had ever felt before. He'd only ever been in a bed alone. Sitting on someone's bed politely is one thing, but lying flat, his cheek crushed into the sheets, warm beneath the covers, and touching—regardless of the circumstances—was new.

New enough that, once the fear passed, his heart raced at the thought of it. Playing like a skipping track.

Celestina waved a hand in front of his face.

"You're really out of it today, huh?" she said sprightly.

Icarus forced a smile. If the look on Celestina's face was any indication, it didn't land.

"Are you okay?" she asked, her pretty eyebrows pinching together.

Icarus closed his eyes and tilted his head back. He opened them to the green canopy above them and stared up to the sun filtering through.

"I'll be okay," he said. "I just had a rough night. One of my . . . friends is having a hard time."

"Do you want to talk about it?"

Icarus shrugged one shoulder uncomfortably.

"Not really? It's nothing anyone can really do anything about."

Celestina looked very very sad for a moment.

"Come with me. I want to show you something."

ROTH

Celestina grabbed his hand and the feeling slammed him from the haze of memory and back to the now.

The vivid green of the woods around them, the rustle of the wind through leaves, and her hot grip. He was pulled forward and over a pile of rocks to a glittering expanse, brown as a pebble and lightly burbling.

She let go of his hand and threw her arms out wide.

"What do you think?!"

The pond was enclosed on most sides by piled up rocks, and it was about as big as a tennis court. The water splashed up against the side, reversing like waves in the ocean. This pond must be fed by an underground spring.

Celestina peeled off her sweatshirt and started unclasping the buttons on the side of her skirt.

"What are you doing?" Icarus exclaimed, alarmed.

"It's still super warm from summer. I'm going in," Celestina replied, lightly. "I have my volleyball stuff under, so don't get your panties twisted."

She threw her sweatshirt and skirt onto the rocks and splashed loudly into the water in her sports bra and shorts.

Icarus huffed a sigh of disbelief, took off his backpack, and tossed it by Celestina's clothes.

He rolled up his jeans and tentatively dipped his toes in. The water was shockingly warm, almost hot.

He looked up at Celestina, scandalized, but she just threw her head back and laughed.

"Come on, don't be a chicken. I'll even close my eyes and turn around so you can preserve your precious modesty," she teased.

Icarus blushed. "Fine, *fine*."

He peeled off his sweater and jeans and made his way into the water slowly. Arms wrapped around his own compact shoulders until the water lapped at his chest.

Celestina flopped onto her back and kicked her feet until they were near each other.

"It's not so bad, is it?" she said.

Icarus laughed and shook his head.

The prettiest girl in school ducked under the water and popped back up, droplets clinging to her eyelashes, and Icarus wondered—not for the first time—what he was doing here. What he'd done to deserve to see all this.

The pond. Celestina's toasty skin. The snot leaking imperfectly out of her nose as she sneezed water out and coughed.

Icarus floated quietly next to her and focused on being thankful.

LIM

Celestina splashed him until she got tired, then they floated alongside each other.

Her acrylic nails stretched out, just barely touching his ribs to make sure he stayed close. Icarus stared up at the sky and watched it change colors until it turned the indigo that meant it was time to go home.

They sloshed, waterlogged, onto the shore and pulled their dry clothes onto their bodies.

Celestina punched him in the arm hard enough to hurt, and smiled bright as daytime before they parted ways.

Icarus breathed in and out and in again. He didn't feel hollow anymore.

BRUSH

Luca walked beside him, uncharacteristically quiet. Icarus gazed out at the other kids, playing softball on the diamond while Mr. Collins yelled.

They weren't the only ones walking the mile. A few goth kids were about 500 feet in front of them, talking and smoking.

Icarus glanced at Luca again, but said nothing. It didn't feel right to break a silence that he didn't start.

After a while Luca sighed.

"Do you mind if I ask you a question?"

"No, go for it," Icarus replied.

"Are . . . you and Celestina dating?"

Icarus stopped walking entirely to gape at him.

"What? Why do you think that?" Icarus demanded.

Luca stopped as well. He rubbed his temples, then pushed his hair back in what Icarus was starting to believe might be anguish.

"You guys are just . . . hanging around all the time," Luca said. "You go places with her that you wouldn't go with me . . ." He trailed off.

"Dude, what?! She *makes* me. She's always grabbing me and dragging me here and there when she thinks I look tired or sad or whatever and I'm not just going to push her away or anything. She's nice. She's just really nice," Icarus tried to explain. "And it's not like I didn't 'go somewhere I didn't really want to go' when *you* asked me to come with you to lunch."

Luca looked flustered and embarrassed.

"Who even told you we were hanging out?"

Luca shrugged and turned to gaze into the wind.

Oh. *Oh.*

"Hey, Luca," Icarus said, softer, even as his heart picked up speed. "I'm not dating Celestina. We're friends. Just . . . just like you and me?"

Luca turned back quick; dark eyes bright. "I didn't know we were actually friends either. I thought you were just . . . tolerating me."

Icarus's heart was doing somersaults in his chest. He wanted this, he wanted this so bad. But he couldn't have it.

"Look, man—"

"Hey you two! Start walking or pick up a bat!"

It broke the spell. Luca waved to Mr. Collins and they both picked up a quick pace.

"You should have said you had a crush on me," Icarus joked tentatively. "You want to go steady? You wanna take me to the dance?"

Luca knocked into him. "No, dude. You're just playing with my bro-emotions. My bromotions. Sometimes I think we're tight and other times you make me feel like you secretly hate me or something. You never hang out with anyone, but then suddenly you're hanging out with Celestina—who is the weirdest person you could ever be hanging out with anyway. I don't even get how you guys met."

Icarus smiled at Luca fondly. "People think that about *us,* you know."

Luca began to laugh. He laughed so hard it turned to a wheeze and he had to slow down and put his hands on his knees.

"Do you do this on purpose?" Luca asked once they started walking again. "Manipulate supply and demand to make being with you feel like a luxury good?"

"You think I'm a luxury good?" Icarus replied in the most saccharine drippy voice he could. "Oh Mr. Luca, I do declare . . ."

"Nooo, you dick," Luca guffawed, pushing Icarus again. "Don't start with that."

Luca's cheeks burned pink as sunset at the teasing.

Icarus looked up, and his mind took a snapshot of Luca's face.

SPECK

Luca slapped him on the shoulder, then squeezed it firmly before they headed off to their classes. Icarus shivered and gripped the spot with his own hand.

He stumbled through the day, landing in art class before he finally got his footing. Beside him, Sorrel was nearly finished with his vase of flowers.

"You're going to have to really do crunch time to get that done," Sorrel commented, dryly, looking over at Icarus's work.

Icarus sighed. The drawing was complete and he had primed the canvas with a soft orange. Maybe he could get away with declaring it an homage to da Vinci's sketches and just filling in the highlighted areas.

"I'm sure Mrs. Sims won't be mad," Sorrel said, glancing over his shoulder at their art teacher. "Yours is already much better than everyone else's."

Icarus shrugged self-consciously. He didn't like anyone comparing themselves to him. Especially not over something like this; something he had trained in his entire life. "It's okay. I'm not really trying to do anything crazy here. I just want a grade that's not going to get me yelled at."

Sorrel reached over and dusted his fingertips along the edge of Icarus's canvas.

"Could you do a portrait for me one day?"

Icarus glanced at him sharply. He was already on edge from his earlier conversation with Luca and it was alarming to hear this tone in Sorrel's voice too. "What of?"

"My grandma? I can pay you and everything," Sorrel said quickly. "She's turning eighty-five and I think she'd really like it. You're the best artist I know."

Icarus took a deep breath and let it out with a stressed whoosh.

"Are you *sure* she wouldn't prefer a picture of her made by her own grandkid?"

Sorrel nodded and looked a bit pained by that admission. *God.*

"Yeah, okay, fine. See if she'll settle for a pencil and charcoal piece. Where would she want to sit for it?"

"In her garden probably. She doesn't live far from here, so we could do it after school sometime. . . . Her birthday is in a month, so we don't have to rush or anything. How much would you want to be paid?"

Icarus rolled his eyes. "You don't need to pay me, Sorrel. As long as this is a one-time thing, we're good to go."

He didn't want to do commissions for high-schooler wages.

Sorrel nodded, ears red, and turned back to his canvas.

TRIP

Every so often, Angus Gallagher traveled to give lectures. It was good for marketing his services and strengthened his relationship with larger institutions. When the opportunity came up, he always seized it.

Icarus was forced to attend when these appearances landed during their "off season" or at a particularly high-profile location. Angus was insistent upon Icarus's being recognizable to the people who might hire him someday, and there was nothing Icarus could do to wriggle out of it.

At least this one wasn't overseas. Angus only gave him eight hours' notice to pack before they flew to O'Hare. He reserved separate hotel rooms at the Palmer House so Icarus didn't have to deal with listening to him rehearse and snore. When they arrived, he squeezed the back of Icarus's neck in a silent good night, before warning him to be in the lobby, fed and ready to leave, by 9:30 a.m.

Icarus walked alone down the hallway to his room.

He opened the door with his keycard and stood there in the darkness for a while.

Chicago was orange at night.

The blackout curtains were pulled back, and the hazy drapes underneath blurred the cityscape to a glow. The streetlights spilled into the room, painting the furniture in strokes of burnt sienna.

Icarus left the lights off and unpacked. He brushed his teeth and washed his face in silhouette, then filled up the bathtub to soak.

He'd never lived in a city, but he liked them. There were more people, more noises, more lights. They hummed in a way that small towns did not, had movement in a way small towns did not. People who lived in cities probably didn't feel the energy of other people around them anymore. But, when you're from a quiet place, you can tell there are bodies stacked above you and feet moving below you. Like living in a burrow close to topsoil. Some people thought it felt like suffocation to be around so many things that are alive. But to Icarus it just felt warm.

He liked it warm. He liked orange.

The hotel shampoo made for slicker bubbles than the stuff Icarus had at home. He dunked his hair under the water and scrubbed his fingers into his scalp. Then he rinsed off, cold and crisp, and tucked himself between the sheets to dry off in the gloom.

THRUM

Angus walked past him in the hotel café at 9:30 a.m. on the dot. He tossed a firm "Let's go," over his shoulder as he headed toward the door.

Icarus scrambled up, threw his continental breakfast coffee cup in the trash, and followed.

The skyscrapers here seemed to never cast a shadow; there was just sun and lesser-sun on the streets downtown. Big families with wandering children sluggishly made their way down Michigan Avenue, popping in and out of shops, gaggling in front of store windows, lining up next to men selling ice cream and cotton candy on a stick.

Angus wove in between them with ease, leaving Icarus to bump into people, stuttering out *excuse me* and *pardon me*, jogging every so often to keep up. As they got closer to the Art Institute, the sound of street drummers got louder.

It was a pretty common sight on many street corners: Black men and boys with paint buckets upturned in their laps, giving symphony orchestra–level performances in percussion.

Tourists gaped or sneered as they walked past, while the native Chicagoans bobbed their heads, danced, and threw a few bucks in their pails on the ground. Academics sat on the stairs of the museum, eating their lunches and watching behind their glasses.

Angus took out his wallet, without breaking stride or slowing his pace, and tossed $50 in. *Ticket prices*, he used to say when Icarus first asked him about it. "I won't pay more to sit in an amphitheater and I won't pay less just because they're outside."

Icarus followed him up the limestone steps, past the grand bronze lions, and into the museum lobby.

BROW

Icarus's eyes darted to the ceiling, then scanned the lobby. Visitors entered through four doors made of glass. Each was twice as heavy as a normal door, but half as wide unless you pulled them both open at the same time. Security was planted by the entrance, next to each ticket counter, inside the info desk, next to the bag check, and in front of the gift shop, making for a grand total of seven officers with eyes on all entrances and exits.

The security at the ticket counter was plainclothes. None of the security officers in this section was over forty years old. There were cameras, of course, and the obvious ones were easy to spot with a quick eye flicker. The halls were wide, but the floors were a bit slippery and not conducive to running. The floorplan guided people to move throughout the space in a way that created obstacles. There were always two streams of traffic on both sides of any room, one going forward and one going backward. Any deviation from—

A hand clamped down hard on Icarus's shoulder.

"Stop casing the museum," his father hissed, tightening his grip painfully for a second before letting go.

Icarus tore his eyes away from the walls and pinned them to the ground. He followed his father's feet through the main entrance, past the Asian sculpture wing, and toward the members-only area.

He had been here only once before, when he was much younger, and it was tempting to continue looking around. The museum had very high ceilings with clean lines of steel and caramel-colored wood. There were multiple skylights and large windows to fill the rooms with natural light, and enough space between the pieces to see from all sides without congestion.

It was a large museum, and difficult to visit all the different sections in one day. Icarus knew there was a good photography section here, and an interesting architecture wing in the contemporary art section, but he'd never been here long enough to get to them.

Icarus followed Angus quickly away from the art and down to a plain white greenroom. Icarus's father immediately started unpacking his things.

"Mr. Gallagher!" They both looked up in unison to see an older woman with bright red hair, chunky glasses, and a big smile rushing toward them. "It's good to see you! Do you need anything? Coffee, water, a back rub?" she joked.

She pulled Icarus's father into a hug, which he barely returned, patting her crisply on the back.

"Good to see you, Wanda," Angus said, clearing his throat sharply. "Which hall am I in?"

The woman leaned back and pulled her glasses down a bit. "This must be Icarus, then," she said, ignoring Angus's question. Icarus grimaced and rubbed at his bruising shoulder.

"You're almost as tall as your father, and the spitting image of him," she said, looking him up and down. "What a thing, genetics."

"Thank you," Icarus said, glancing anxiously at his father, who just seemed angrier.

"Well, I'm sure you don't want to sit and listen to this old windbag talk for a few hours. Do you think you could spare him, Angus?"

"Which hall, Wanda? Concentrate," Angus snapped.

Wanda rolled her eyes at him and waved a hand. "Fullerton Hall. They have a podium set up and everything."

"Thank you," he replied curtly. "Go with her," he told Icarus, "and be on your best behavior. Don't touch anything."

"'Don't touch anything,' he says." Wanda shrugged dramatically. "Like a young man would confuse this place for a petting zoo. Come on, son, let's get you some breakfast."

Wanda guided Icarus from the greenroom with a brittle arm and a strong wave of perfume. He looked over his shoulder at his father, but Angus had turned around and was already walking away.

INSTITUTE

Wanda got him a muffin from the café, then set him free, pinching his cheek with a painful little shake.

This was a place with so much light.

Icarus walked slowly, watching the people instead of the art. He had seen so much of it already that it was a bit more interesting watching people's reactions. He watched a family with triplets in the Asian art section, a gaggle of students in the tapestries, a couple on a date in South Asian sculpture, and an old woman alone in Greek antiquities.

He was working his way through mid-century furniture and up toward their featured artist—when he saw it.

His father's work.

Icarus froze mid-step. He pushed through the wandering crowd until he was standing before it. Until he was sure. Icarus knew his father's hand no matter where it was, could almost smell him radiating off the paint.

This felt like blasphemy.

Their art shouldn't be here. It should never be in a museum like this.

It wasn't a restoration; it was an entire forgery. Icarus had carried the back end of this portrait up the Black mansion's main staircase when he was thirteen. Had ground charcoal for its darkest hues with a mortar and pestle. Mr. Black must have sold or loaned it to the museum.

He wanted to snatch it off the wall, but he couldn't. An old man was listening to an audio tour next to him with the volume all the way up. He was smiling and nodding, appreciating the narrator's remarks about the color and the history. Icarus felt sick and angry. This painting was not even five years old.

He pressed his palms into his eyes and forcibly calmed himself down. Then, disgusted with this entire experience, he went to find a place to sit outside the hall where Angus was speaking.

Icarus would never let his own work find itself here. This shame was enough.

FEED

Icarus kept his revelation to himself. When they were on their way out, he picked up an art book from the gift shop. He flipped through a few until he found one that had enough work he'd seen in person.

His father raised an eyebrow at it, but didn't say anything. Angus hated prints.

Icarus was left on his own to figure out dinner. He was expected to go and find some fun. But Icarus ordered in and sat down by the window so the orange light was bright enough to see.

He annotated the pieces he'd seen in person. Which ones he'd touched and what they felt like. Whether they were the same size they seemed in print or much bigger or smaller. How they smelled, if he'd gotten to touch them. And, if it felt necessary, how much they'd sold for.

Icarus worked through the night and slept on the plane ride home.

MONDAY

"Here."

Helios took the art book from Icarus's hands.

"I didn't wrap it because of the noise. I hope you understand," Icarus said.

He leaned back against the bedpost to watch Helios flip through it.

"I don't know much about art . . ." Helios murmured. "But I have been to the Art Institute with school. Do you take things from there too?"

"What? No?!" Icarus scowled. "That stuff belongs to the public."

Helios gazed at him over the top of the art book then tilted his head. "Interesting distinction . . . anyway, thank you for this. I'll read your notes."

"How is your ear?" Icarus asked.

"Better. He just twisted it, and you've been gone for a week."

Helios pushed the art book under his second pillow at the head of the bed, then sat up straighter to gaze at Icarus across the dark space.

"How often do you go out there? To Chicago," he asked.

Icarus shrugged. "I've only been there twice. But I've been to Denmark, France, Italy, London, LA, Detroit, Sweden—places with museums to visit. We only travel for lectures now, but a while back my dad would take commissions that had to be completed in person."

Helios looked interested.

"I've only been to New York, Chicago, and here. What are those other places like?"

Icarus looked through the gap in the draperies and out the window. He could see the light from the diner peeking over the trees.

"Cities are all the same. They have this sound, like a hum, that's the noise of people talking and cars and construction, birds and dogs and children playing, and electricity that kind of . . . bursts on your palate the moment you step off the plane. During the day it's louder; at night it's quieter. The streetlamps are different colors and it gives the whole place an aura. Chicago is orange, Paris is yellow, all the cities in Sweden are a greenish white."

Icarus paused, but Helios didn't say anything, so he continued.

"Everyone in each city has different personalities, of course. But there is also a haze for that as well. People go on and on about whether a place has nice people, but I think it's more noticeable whether there is a strong community. In the nicer places of London everyone is so much more isolated than in the nicer places of New York. I'm talking about . . . well . . . that feeling where you know you can go to your neighbor and ask for a cup of sugar or stop someone on the street to ask them for directions. In London, they won't stop at all. In New York, as you know, you'll get a bunch of street names and lefts and rights. In Chicago, they'll say, 'I'm headed that way too. Walk with me and I'll show you the way.'"

Helios pulled his legs up and wrapped his arms around them. He lay his head down on his own shoulder.

"What else?"

"Each place has a different smell, but the base notes are the same," Icarus went on. "Steel, piss, hot concrete, sweat, and skin. If you're near a body of water you can mix that scent in too. And women. The smell of women and the perfumes they prefer layered over it all. In Paris the women like to smell powdery, like old people. In New York their perfumes smell like colognes, there's a lot of spice and complexity. Nordic women like to smell green, more like gardens than like flower blossoms."

"Green streetlights, green women," Helios snickered.

Icarus shrugged. "Yeah. And eventually, the entire city begins to make an impression, like a Rothko. Just a haze of layers and sensations in color."

He crawled forward and pulled the art book from under Helios's pillow and flipped to a Rothko to show him. He pointed at the painting titled *Orange, Red, Yellow.*

"If someone mentions a city I've been to, it feels kind of like this. And the memory of all the sensory impressions sort of settles in your chest, as an ache with a name."

"An ache with a name . . ." Helios repeated, closing his eyes. Then he laughed dryly. "When I asked, I thought you would tell me about whether they had good restaurants or cool stuff to do. Not all of . . . that."

Icarus drew back, embarrassed. "I'm sorry. I—"

Helios shook his head sharply. "Don't be sorry. This was better, anyway."

Icarus frowned. Shrugged.

"What is the impression of here?"

"What?"

"This town. Where you're from," Helios asked seriously. "Describe it the way you did the others."

Icarus frowned and tried. "I don't think home has the same impact unless you're returning to it after a long time away."

Helios didn't say anything; he just waited.

"Small places are . . . lost in time," Icarus said. "Things move slower. The women still smell like the perfume my mom used to wear twenty years ago. There's a bottle on the mantle I used to . . . never mind. The haze here is like black smoke and gray fog. It's a rainy place and even when the sun is out you can tell. The air is prickly with possibility, but the ground is magnetic and heavy. Going anywhere or doing anything feels like running in a dream. It's an open-air prison."

"I see." Helios brushed his fingertips across the surface of his quilt.

"What is it for you?" Icarus asked boldly.

Helios shrugged. "The green of the wood, the blue of the sky, quiet, violence, and you. Perched in my window frame."

"Oh."

"Yeah, *oh*."

BLOWING

"What do you do when I'm not here?"

Helios stretched out his legs. His feet mercifully a full six inches away. Icarus eyed them dubiously and considered scooting even farther back.

"What do you think?" Helios replied. "I read, write sometimes . . . work out. Like I said, I'm not allowed to use computers or have a phone, but I also have chores. I'm not even allowed to have coffee or sleeping pills. Its excruciating."

"What do you write about?"

Helios smirked. "Nothing creative. Just journaling. I have a supervised phone call with a counselor every week and she's making me write down my life experiences so I can reflect on them. I'm not sharing my diary with you, so don't even ask."

Icarus grimaced. "I would never ask you that."

Helios tapped his fingers on the pillow next to him and chewed his lip.

"I think about it sometimes . . . what my friends back home would think of you."

"I'm sure they wouldn't think of me at all. I'm not entirely unlikable, but if they were anything like you I would probably avoid them."

"What do you mean, are you telling me you're popular or something?" Helios said, clearly joking. "You're always giving dark and broody; I didn't expect that."

"Well, expect it or not, I am," Icarus replied bluntly. "In a way. This whole . . . 'thing' consumes most of my time, but I'm not an outcast if that's what you were imagining. My friend Luca won prom prince last year."

He hadn't been friends with Luca then, but it was still true at the end of the day.

Helios laughed and shook his head. "Okay, whatever you say, buddy. Anyway, I think they would like you. There's this girl named Starr who is super into EDM. Boomerang and Snakebite both go to the High School of Art and Design, and they'd lose their minds over you. My best friend Ghost would be really into you for like . . . slutty reasons . . . but he's mostly into everyone for that."

Icarus rolled his eyes. "Does anyone you know have a real name?"

"Yeah, but nicknames are more fun. More personal."

"What was your nickname?"

Helios grinned. "Helios is strange enough. I didn't have one. Do your friends call you Nothing?"

Icarus rolled his eyes.

"No."

"What should I call you, then?"

Icarus didn't answer.

"Can I call you 'my friend?'" Helios pushed. He dragged the tips of his fingers across his own arm. Over the new bandages that Icarus didn't want to ask about. "That would preserve the allure of anonymity that you seem to enjoy."

"That's . . . that's fine."

"Well, my friend. I think you would have fit in with the people I knew before this. Would you like to meet them? When I get out of here, of course." Helios curled so much pleasure into the words "my friend" that Icarus could hear them dripping in the night air.

He shivered. "Maybe. I have to go."

Icarus got up and slipped his soft shoes back on. Helios watched in silence.

Icarus paused in the window.

"I'll bring you coffee, next time I come."

SWEET

Icarus picked a brand with a price that made his eyes water. Then, he ordered a pour-over brewing system and an insulated glass water bottle to transport it.

Coffee from the diner across the street was fine. This would be better.

TUESDAY

Julian gave him a curious pale orange drink with ice in it.

"What is this?"

"Orange Julius with a bit of caffeine. They don't make them at Starbucks so I had to give instructions," he said, plonking down in his seat.

Icarus took a sip and grimaced. "I won't say it's good, but it could be nastier."

Julian winked and clicked his tongue twice, cheekily. "Noted."

His frizzy curls were kind of flat on the left, like that was the side he slept on, and he was wearing a brown corduroy jacket. The way the sun was shining through the window lit up all the fuzzies on his clothes, the translucent hairs on his skin, the ends of his ringlets in gold.

The pencil in Icarus's hand started scratching his silhouette on the paper in front of him aimlessly. He smudged the graphite across the page until it caught the light, pressed until the shadows were dark as ink.

The hollow behind Julian's ear was sweet and soft, the stitching on his jacket was a lighter brown than the fabric. When he turned just right, Icarus could get the tip of an eyelash peeking out from behind his cheek.

"Do you want to be my partner?" Julian whirled around. "I've got some free library time today."

Julian paused and looked down at Icarus's work. Icarus startled and felt his cheeks begin to color, but Julian didn't comment on the drawing.

"We just got an assignment. It's due Friday and it's like fifteen percent of our grade. I figured you probably weren't paying attention and it looks like I was right." Julian scowled. "Don't you have an entire class to do this art shit?"

"You don't have to babysit me, Julian, I'm not going to forget to do my work." Icarus covered the drawing with his hand. He didn't like the way Julian was looking at it.

Julian flicked the top of Icarus's hand hard.

"Ow! What the fuck," Icarus hissed.

"You can do art whenever. Are you going to be my partner or not?"

"Why do you even want to be my partner?" Icarus rubbed at his new welt. "Why can't anyone else work with you?"

Julian rolled his eyes. "None of my other friends are in this class. I'll meet you in the library at fifth period." He stood up and slung his backpack on his shoulder.

"You better show up, idiot."

"You can't tell me what to do," Icarus called after him, but Julian was already halfway out the door.

"Fifth period, Gallagher!"

COST

Julian was waiting for him at the front door, practically pushed him through it.

"Glad you showed up."

Icarus slung his messenger bag over one of the chairs and settled down across from Julian. Julian took out a notebook and a permanent marker. He liked writing big and bold even when it bled through the page.

"I think we should split this project up into pieces we can do on our own and then come together in the library to arrange the presentation together before it's due," Julian said. "That way we don't have to keep meeting up outside of school hours for the rest of the semester."

"Sounds good. What are we supposed to be doing it about?"

Julian made a face. "We can choose, but since you *obviously* don't know or care about what we've been studying, I'm going to pick *for* us. I want to do a presentation on labor strikes. I'm liking the Bread and Roses Strike or the Memphis sanitation workers strike from 1968. One is about textile mill workers—mostly women—and the other is about Black sanitation workers."

Icarus thought for a moment.

"We could do both, and then contrast and compare public reaction to each and give an analysis of social dynamic within protest?" He leaned his head on his arms. "That way we could each handle it as a separate research project, and then have our conclusion be more like a discussion."

Julian bit his lip and scribbled something down. "Hmm. That's . . . efficient. This took a lot less time than I thought it would. Do you want to do a slideshow?"

Icarus shook his head. That would require more collaboration.

"Let's do a photobook. We could probably get away with printing twenty-three copies, handing them out, and then leading a class discussion a few days afterward. Then we won't even have to do a real presentation. We'll just make everyone else talk and then say a few closing sentences and be good to go."

Julian hmmed low in his throat, then closed the notebook completely.

"Great. Now all we have to do is make sure you actually do the work and I don't wind up doing everything for us."

That was irritating.

"I have a question."

"What?"

"What's wrong with you?"

Julian frowned. "What's that supposed to mean?"

Icarus folded his arms. "I said I was going to do it and I will. The only class I'm doing C work in is this one, because it just starts too early for me. But that's because it doesn't affect anyone but me. Working on something with someone else changes that."

"And how was I supposed to know that, dingus?" Julian said. He leaned back in his chair, clearly nonplussed by Icarus's attitude. "I'm not hinging my grade on hopes and dreams. Just cause I think you're decent doesn't mean I'm ready to gamble on it."

That was it. He'd had enough of this.

"Why do you even care?" Icarus exploded, standing up. His chair scooted back with a loud screech.

Some other students were starting to watch them, curiously, but Icarus was too worked up to focus on being quiet.

Julian side-eyed the tables next to them, but said nothing.

"Why do you do this . . . this thing where you're nice and mean and nice again? I don't get it," Icarus said bluntly.

Julian sighed. "Can you be quieter? It's the library," he said. "And you shouldn't yell at people for caring about you—it's weird. Can you just like . . . sit down or whatever?"

"No." Icarus picked up his bag.

Julian flung his arms out, annoyed. "Dude, do you even remember the first week of class?"

Icarus didn't, but he also didn't walk away like he'd been planning to. Instead he waited. Julian sighed loudly, then leaned forward so the people next to them wouldn't hear.

"You nodded through every single day," he hissed. "Mr. Harrison was making fun of you. On Thursday you asked to borrow a pencil from me, then fell asleep before you could use it. On Friday, I accidentally got double my drink order on the way to school and gave the other one to you just so I wouldn't have to carry it around. You haven't slept in class much since."

Julian scowled at a girl who had stopped on her way to the shelves near them to listen. She walked quickly away.

"Dude, sit the fuck down, this is embarrassing."

Icarus could feel his ears getting hot. He pulled the chair back out and settled into it.

"I'm not your responsibility," he mumbled.

Julian leaned forward. "Obviously, you dipshit."

"Then—"

"There's a lot of bad things in life you can't control," Julian said. "That's why it's good to control the ones you can."

"What does that mean?" Icarus asked, when it was clear Julian wasn't about to elaborate.

Julian tapped his fingertips against the wood of the table.

"It means that if all it costs me is an extra two dollars a day to keep someone smart from fucking up their life over something stupid like being tired . . . it's worth paying."

"I don't need your money—" Icarus started.

"Don't fucking insult me, bro. Just accept the kindness and do your fucking work. Only a few of us are going to make it out of this town."

Icarus didn't know what to say. It wasn't . . . embarrassing, it was just . . . He usually had answers for things people said to him already pre-written in his head. He didn't have anything on deck for this.

Julian rubbed his nose straight up, pressing a little red line into the bridge of it, and sniffed.

"What do you do every night that makes you so tired? You working a job or something?"

Icarus rubbed his eyes until sparks flashed behind his lids. "Kind of. I guess I didn't think anyone would notice."

Julian tilted his head to the side, the way he had earlier this morning. Curious, gentle.

"People notice everything," he said. "I don't know why you thought you'd get away with it. Everyone else probably just decided it wasn't worth it to push."

"People *push*," he admitted.

"And I assume you punish them in some way for it? It's very unsatisfying, if you've ever wondered how you make people feel," Julian snapped.

"I know. I'm sorry."

Julian bit his lip and looked out the window over Icarus's shoulder.

"Yeah whatever," he huffed. "Sorry for assuming you'd fuck up our group project, for whatever it's worth."

Icarus shook his head. "No, it's fine, it . . . makes sense that you'd think that. Sorry for . . . not noticing you . . . caring."

Julian didn't smile, but his face softened a bit. The table got really interesting to him, suddenly.

"Just. Don't be weird about it. Try not to waste it."

Other people in the library were still staring. Icarus put his head in his hands and pressed his temples until they hurt.

DRY

He tore the drawing of Julian out of his notebook and trimmed the rough edges. He dated it and signed it.

Titled it *Art Shit*.

He folded it into quarters and slipped it into the vent of Julian McPherson's locker.

MEAT

He could feel his father watching him as he went straight from dinner to his room. He never asked if Icarus was okay. Ever.

But Icarus could always tell when Angus was concerned about him, because he would begin to stare and would only stop when he felt the issue had passed.

Icarus wanted to go to the roof to mope, but he needed to sleep a bit before he went to see Helios. Julian's words still burned. He thought about Julian's disappointed frown. He thought about Luca and Celestina and Sorrel too.

Their soft gestures, the hurt in Luca's eyes, Celestina reaching across the water. Sorrel's translucent lashes and pink cheeks, looking away to gather the bravery to ask him to come to his home.

And Icarus wanted. It boiled under his skin.

He had never felt so lonely in his life.

He curled his fingers into his sheets and gripped them hard, shut his eyes and squeezed them so tight that light burst behind them in red and orange. Tensed every muscle in his body until everything hurt.

When he let go, his breath wet and hot panting, it felt like being dropped from a great height. Or being dizzy with hunger.

SVELTE

The thermos was hot under his shirt as Icarus scaled the Black mansion, burning a scalding rectangle into his skin. He wondered if he could find some kind of silicone holder that would make this less excruciating.

Helios opened the window before Icarus even had to knock, reaching down to pull him up and into the blue-dark of his room.

"Hey."

"I have something for you," Icarus said immediately, ducking his head out of the lanyard and presenting the thermos to Helios. He bent down to take off his shoes as Helios shook it curiously.

"Soup?"

Icarus grinned sharply. "Mmm. No. Open it."

Helios grimaced at him in mock irritation and twisted the cap hard. He sniffed it, then groaned low in his throat, rolling his eyes back dramatically.

"Fuck. Coffee. You brought me coffee," he rasped. "I thought you were fucking *joking*, dude." He sniffed it again and let out another incredible noise. "Fuck, man. What the fuck."

Helios put the thermos down on the nightstand without trying it at all, and instead Icarus found himself being held very tight.

His cheek was touching Helios's neck, his face buried in the curve of Helios's shoulder. That blinding red hair was brushing his ear, warm and close, and Icarus felt weak and his heart was screaming and he could smell everything at once: cotton and Dove soap and something sharp and animal like the smell of Helios's bed. But fresh from the source.

When Helios pulled back, he clapped a hand on the back of Icarus's neck and squeezed.

For the first time ever it quelled that urge to reach out, like blowing the light off a candle. Icarus wanted to bite his lip and groan.

"Was that . . . okay?" Helios asked. He looked concerned.

"Yeah, yeah it was fine." Icarus knew his face was red. How could it be anything else?

"You look like I just punched you in the stomach." Helios laughed dryly. He glanced back at the thermos. "I can probably get some cream and a mug from downstairs. Do you mind waiting?"

"No . . . uh, no, that would be good."

Helios smiled, shy, and slipped out of the room.

WHEAT

Helios only brought one mug.

He shrugged at Icarus's curious gaze and didn't explain himself.

The room filled with the scent of French roast, woody and strong. Helios closed his eyes and let the steam caress his face, breathing in long and hard. His eyebrows pinched like he was about to cry.

It felt too intimate to watch.

Icarus got up and took off his sweatshirt. He slid across the floor and put it at the bottom of the door to cover the gap and block the scent from getting into the hallway.

When he turned to head back to the bed, Helios was taking a long drink.

"What do you think?" Icarus whispered.

"If you had brought me instant swill, worse than the kind they have at the airport, I'd still be fucking jazzed. But this tastes like . . . it reminds me of Intelligentsia but smoother. Sweeter," Helios said.

He pushed the mug into Icarus's hands. Icarus looked down at the rim, still wet from Helios's mouth. His eyes flickered up without his permission, and Helios was watching him. His gaze liquid in the dark.

Icarus took a sip and it was . . . coffee. Bitter, smoky, rich from what had to be full fat cream, but he wasn't a connoisseur of these things. He didn't swallow it slow, like liquor. Like Helios.

He handed the mug back.

Helios took another sip. They traded the mug back and forth until it was empty and Helios put it on the nightstand. Then he closed the thermos even though there was still some coffee left inside.

"Can I . . . keep it and give it back to you the next time you come?" Helios asked, hopefully.

"It's yours. It's . . . this is for you." Icarus cleared his throat. "I'll uh . . . I'll refill it when you're done."

Helios smiled.

"I . . . keep thinking about . . ." Icarus started then stopped. He twisted his fingers together in his lap.

"It's okay. What are you thinking about, my friend?" Helios whispered.

Icarus's heart kicked up and sweat broke out on the back of his neck. But the time seemed right and there was no going back from here. Not when he'd started so strong. Not when he was being looked at like this.

"I keep thinking about when we met. For the very first time."

Helios grinned, amused. "Oh? What about it?" He crossed his legs and put his chin in his hand.

"You said, 'How long have you been doing this?' and you weren't scared at all. Why?"

Helios watched him for a second before answering. "Because I recognized you. And I'm stronger than you."

A shiver of some feeling Icarus didn't have words for slammed into him so hard he had to hold back a gasp. Because I'm stronger than you. I'm *stronger* than you. I'm stronger than *you*. *He's* stronger than you? He *thinks* he's stronger.

"No you're not," Icarus said hotly.

Helios laughed quietly. "We could test it. Bet on it. Arm wrestle?"

Icarus could hold up his entire body with the strength of one hand.

"Fine. But if I win you can never say anything like that to me again," Icarus hissed.

Helios's amusement filled the room, like a cloud.

TORCH

Helios pulled the art book from under his pillow and placed it between them. There were new bookmarks sticking out.

They both sat in the middle of the bed, legs crossed, elbows on the edge of the book.

"You ready?" Helios asked.

"Shut the fuck up." Icarus clasped Helios's hand firmly, squeezing it in warning. To his surprise and delight, Helios squeezed back, possibly harder.

"Okay! One, two, three, go!" Helios said, then crushed Icarus's hand in a steel grip, pushing with surprising force.

Icarus was caught off guard. He fought the incredible pressure, pulling their combined hands further toward his side. Helios seemed pleased. He wasn't straining at all, which felt so strange. Helios wasn't stocky and athletic like Icarus was, he was willowy and graceful.

But Icarus remembered the way Helios's arm had felt across his throat, remembered his hands being wrenched behind his back, and . . . wondered. Helios's grin widened, and he brought their hands back from Icarus's winning side toward the middle and then a few centimeters in his direction.

"What the fuck," Icarus breathed, gripping the side of the bed hard for leverage.

Helios wasn't bracing against anything. His other hand lay inert on his thigh. There were bruises around his wrist.

"Oh, darling," Helios breathed. "You're very good."

"Don't call me that. I didn't say you could call me that," Icarus huffed, straining.

"Hmm," Helios said. Then he slammed Icarus's hand onto the bed in an easy win. Clearly, he had been holding back.

Icarus gasped, snatching his arm to his chest. He cradled it close. His fingers burned like Helios had ground the bones together. Careless, *careless* for someone who had to climb back down a wall.

"Oh, shit, are you okay? Here—let me . . ."

Helios tugged Icarus's arm to him very gently and stroked between Icarus's fingers. Too much feeling was bouncing around Icarus's chest, so he just let him. Icarus sighed, discordant and raw.

"I don't understand you," he whispered.

"Hmm?" Helios rubbed Icarus's joints like he knew what he was doing, and the pain was beginning to subside.

"I think about this . . . all the time," Icarus confessed. "I don't understand you. Everything about you throws me off guard and I feel like I don't know what I'm doing. I never feel like that."

"Never?" Helios seemed amused again. "Well. That sounds lucky."

"You *know* what I mean," Icarus said seriously.

Helios tucked his grin back into the corner of his mouth, like a secret, and looked up into Icarus's eyes.

"I'm a dancer. I lift a lot of people." Helios raised one shoulder, clearly trying to be casual. Clearly trying to brush it off. "Ballet, you know. People don't really think of us as strong, but we kind of have to be. Don't feel bad or anything. I'm sure if you spent the last couple years tossing around all your friends, you'd blow me out of the water."

He pressed into the webbing between Icarus's thumb and pointer finger and worried the skin until the throbbing faded to a warm glow.

"Thanks," Icarus said.

"Don't sweat it," Helios replied. He lay Icarus's hand down on Icarus's knee, and then folded his own in his lap.

"So. What do you want?" Icarus asked. "What did you win from me?"

Helios tilted his head back to gaze at the canopy above them.

"You bring me so much already," he sighed happily. "What more could I ask for?"

Icarus waited patiently in the silence. He wasn't a sore loser and he knew when it was important to be quiet.

"Can . . ." Helios started, then stopped, hesitant. "Can you hide with me under here?"

FLOW

It was even darker under the comforter.

Icarus could feel Helios's breath on his face, even though they were more than a foot away from each other. The proximity was dizzying. It was indescribable.

He was like a sunflower stretching toward the light.

"When I was a kid, I always used to imagine someone with me under here," Helios admitted. "When things got really bad."

Icarus stayed quiet.

"It would have been easier if I had siblings, I think. At least we could have talked to each other about it, or hid together," Helios whispered.

"If I had been there, I would have hid with you," Icarus moved closer.

Helios laughed softly. "Thanks. And thank you again for the coffee. It was a really nice gift."

"It's nothing," Icarus said, swallowing hard.

"It's *everything*," Helios insisted. "Some friend I am. You bring me coffee and I almost break your hand."

"I underestimated you. You just taught me never to do that again," Icarus said dryly. "But anyway, now I know you're a ballerina, you'll have to show me all of . . . that."

It was like he could feel Helios raising his eyebrows. "You'd watch me dance?"

"It'll either be very pretty or very funny, both of which appeal to me," Icarus said.

Helios laughed and the puff of air against his face made Icarus feel like he was drunk.

"Whatever, man, I'll knock your socks off."

"I don't even know if you could do it quiet enough for your dad to not burst in here like a maniac," Icarus said. "I'll probably never see it."

"He does leave sometimes. The hard part is letting you know when he'll be gone without a phone."

A fingertip grazed the side of Icarus's wrist. "He comes and goes randomly through the day." Helios stopped for a full minute, before saying, much quieter: "This Friday he has an overnight trip, though . . . you could come then?"

Icarus pulled back from the questioning touch. This coming Friday was homecoming. He had been trying to push it from his mind.

"I'll make some time."

DAWN

Icarus was terribly warm.

Someone was stroking a hand through his hair. He arched into the touch with a sigh, stretching his arms until his elbows cracked.

Gentle laughter puffed against the back of his neck.

"Oh, you're sweet like this."

Icarus's eyes snapped open. He was still at Helios's house.

He sat up sharply and hopped out of the bed.

"What time is it?" he said groggily.

"Four a.m. You have about a half hour until sunrise," Helios said. His hair was sticking up wildly, mussed from sleep. "You're lucky."

Icarus shoved his feet in his shoes.

"We can't do that again."

"Why not?" Helios asked.

Icarus decided not to answer him. He flexed his fingers to make sure they were still good for the climb down, then he wrenched open the window.

"Are you coming back?"

Icarus spared a precious second to really see him. Helios looked scared. Icarus didn't . . . He didn't like that look on Helios's face.

"Always," he promised. "I'll see you soon. Go back to sleep."

SPELL

Icarus wrapped his arms around himself in the early morning chill and jogged quickly across the street. Helios had been a bit off with his timing: the world was already light blue even though the sun hadn't come over the horizon yet. It was bright enough to see.

"Hey!"

"Hey kid!" Louder this time.

Icarus looked up.

A sweaty-looking man with a comb-over had his keys in the door of the diner. When Icarus made eye contact, he hooked his fingers to call him over.

Icarus gritted his teeth and changed direction.

"Do you need anything, sir?"

The man seemed to rethink what he was about to say, then shook his head resolutely.

"I know how it is. Young love and all that, probably sneaking into your girlfriend's house all hours of the night. Believe me, I've been a teenager, I get it," he said.

Icarus's heart raced in his chest but he forced his face into complete blankness.

The man, clearly the diner owner, rubbed a hammy palm across his forehead. "You should be careful with that one. I know she might seem worth it, buddy, I do. But the guy who lives in that house? He's not a gentleman, that's for sure."

"Okay," Icarus said, with a sharp nod. "Can I go, sir?"

"I mean it. Yous two can see each other at school or, hell, maybe even get a booth in the back here. It's not worth it." He shook his head and unlocked the door. "Fuckin' maniac," he muttered.

"Yes, sir . . . thanks for the warning." Icarus looked down the street, then reconsidered and asked, "Do . . . you see him often?"

The owner scoffed. "Oh no, him? He's banned. Ten years now. Broke a waitress's wrist, he grabbed her so hard. Just spilled a little coffee on him, once. I mean, it was her fault but y'don't have to get physical over all that. It's a matter of respect."

He pointed a finger at Icarus's chest. "I says to him, 'You can't treat the girls like that. Not in my house, not under my roof.' Then he broke a few glasses here and there, hollering. But he ain't been in since. We got a picture in the back so the new girls know not to let him in."

Icarus grimaced. "Okay. Thank you."

The owner sighed and reached out to pat Icarus hard on the shoulder. "You have a good day, kid. See you round."

LOST

Angus wasn't home when Icarus got in. It was more disconcerting than if he had been there and angry that Icarus was out all night.

Icarus headed straight to the bathroom and took a quick shower. He hoped that if his father had just stopped out for breakfast he'd be able to convince him he'd spent the night on the roof.

Icarus had nearly finished getting ready for school when he finally saw the note taped to the inside of the front door.

"Small emergency, be back on Friday. No visitors. Use the joint account if necessary. —Angus."

Well.

He let his bag slide off his shoulder, undressed, curled up in his closet, and went back to sleep.

BRIGHT

"Heads up!"

Icarus reached into the sky and plucked the football out of the air. He lobbed it back to the kids playing on the pitch nearby.

"I didn't say anything." Luca put his hands up, when Icarus glanced at him expectantly over his shoulder. "We're past that, man."

"Hmm." Icarus knocked into Luca's shoulder playfully. "Turning over a new leaf?"

Luca looked quietly thrilled at the contact, even glancing down at where they had touched. "Kind of. Anyway, I know you're all . . . you. But I wanted to invite you to a party at my house? Homecoming after-party. There'll be some people you know there . . ."

He trailed off, clearly expecting an immediate rejection.

"Who?" Icarus didn't know Luca even knew who Icarus had talked to. At the moment, that was more pressing than saying no.

"Julian, Celestina, James, Rita, Noelle . . . I think Brian said he might come." Luca scratched at his nose, then kicked a stick that was lying on the path.

Those were all previous acquaintances he'd had. Class friends, not real friends, all of whom he stopped talking to as soon as the class they shared was over. It was . . . uncomfortable that Luca was aware that they knew him.

"What is this, some kind of intervention? You cobble together everyone I've ever said hi to?" Icarus said in a voice he hoped sounded like he was joking.

"Not really? A lot of people are coming. And if it was an intervention I wouldn't even tell you, it would have to be a surprise. Obviously." He huffed. "I just asked Celestina and she rattled off some people who might make you feel comfortable enough to show up."

Icarus grimaced. That was less terrible. Celestina was a social butterfly and on student council. It was on-brand for her to be in the know about who talks to who.

"Okay . . . maybe. I'll think about it."

Luca shrugged and dragged a hand through his curls. "I should also mention I'm going to homecoming with her."

"Celestina?"

"You told me you weren't dating her, so I figured I'd take my shot," Luca said, a bit defensively.

Icarus stopped walking. "Dude, do what you want. Congratulations. I just didn't think you guys knew each other. Until now."

Luca shook his head. "Man, I forget sometimes," he mumbled, clearly to himself, then looked hard at Icarus. "Everybody knows *everybody* here, Icarus. Just because we don't hang out during the day doesn't mean we don't ever do stuff after hours."

Icarus rolled his eyes, his face getting hot. "You don't have to be a dick."

Luca crossed his arms. "Come to my party. We'll get drunk and get to talk to each other without having to be fucking walking the whole time."

Icarus rubbed his temples. His father was gone for the week. He could probably get away with it. This might be the only time he could *ever* get away with it.

"If you don't want to talk to Brian and Rita or whatever, we can just chill in my backyard and avoid them. Stick together the whole time like losers," Luca said, with a grin. "Come be a loser at my house."

Icarus took a deep breath.

PINK

Icarus's house felt warm and comfortable with Angus Gallagher missing from it.

The afternoon sun poured in through the kitchen window, golden and soft. No humming machinery or whining of a drill, no sharp scent of vinegar or varnish.

Just quiet. It felt like a different space entirely.

Icarus bought fresh vegetables, fruit, and flowers for the table. He set about making a cucumber salad and pan-fried pork chops. Even dinner would be better like this. Sitting alone at their small wood table, listening to the sound of their neighbors moving above and below him. Kids getting home from school and screaming with laughter as they walked up the path to the apartment.

Icarus glanced across the room at the note his father had left on the door.

When Icarus moved out, he would get to have this all the time. He would make sure of it.

The new place he'd live would have tall wide windows to let in so much light. The walls would be bare, not cluttered with frames, and it would be so clean inside. He would pick a place close to a grocery store so he could go shopping every day after classes. He would keep ferns of course, but would also have vases of flowers and bowls of fruit and the whole house would smell like their ripening. He would take one painting of his mom, just one so it had more meaning.

His bedroom would be the biggest room in the house. Even if he had to share it with the kitchen or put his bed in the living room. He'd have a mattress big enough to make snow angels.

Icarus finished his food and his daydream. Then he left the dishes in the sink, like he was never allowed to.

WORN

His father's office had been meticulously cleaned. It was eerie to see everything put away like this.

His angled desk was empty of work and had been rubbed down until it gleamed. All his paints, pigments, binders, and sealants, closed and arranged by name on the shelf. His stack of new canvases was gone, likely placed in the refrigeration room. All his reference books had been closed and shelved.

It was so immaculate, Icarus couldn't help but check for a trip wire. Or some other trap that would alert his father to the fact that he'd come in this room while he was away. But there was nothing.

The floor had even been cleaned as well as possible.

A chill passed over Icarus and he backed out of the room. He looked around the house at the portraits on the wall, running from one end of the apartment to the other, then burst into the cold room and yanked open the storage doors.

Relief.

It was all still here. The priceless work, the stolen pieces waiting for sale. Packaged away and organized, but still there.

"Fuck . . . fuck." Icarus slid down the wall of the cold room and put his head in his hands.

For a moment, he'd thought Angus had taken everything of value and left him. His father disappearing for a bit then coming back to announce where he'd been afterward wasn't exactly uncommon, but he rarely cleaned anything. That room had looked the same for the past three years. Untouched. In disarray.

It didn't take much to jump to the conclusion that the Feds were finally after them and Angus Gallagher had decided to flee with all the evidence and leave Icarus standing in their mess, bereft.

Icarus . . . couldn't do this anymore. He needed to have more insurance than this. His savings wouldn't keep him going if Angus never came home. He needed to stop being distracted with Helios and focus on getting the gold.

INHALE

There were only eight months left of school. Then Icarus would be the master of his own destiny.

He could leave this city, state, country. Hole himself up somewhere. Beg Helios to keep quiet . . . or maybe take Helios with him to start a new life. God knew that kid probably wanted one.

Helios was . . . something to him now. But he was still a stranger, a stranger who was backed against a wall and acting like it. Not someone Icarus could rely on in a federal investigation. It felt awful even imagining Helios being forced to speak on his behalf.

Icarus took a long drag on his clove cigarette, relishing the opportunity to smoke it in his own room. To fill his sheets with heavy spice.

Minors had been jailed over grand theft before, so even at seventeen he wasn't exactly home free. But he had always worn his mask, never faced the street cameras. He was the same height and build as his father and their faces looked so similar at a distance. He could wriggle out of it, if he was lucky. If his father didn't drag him down too.

And when he left, he could get work. Could do what Angus did. All he needed to do was show his face and prove he was almost as good as Angus, and he could be raking in $25k for a painting, $15k for a sculpture. Even if he did have to start small and work on-site, or for a restoration company, he'd have good references; he wouldn't have to beg.

Icarus put his cigarette out in the ashtray by his head, and stretched until his joints popped and a shiver of sweetness filled his bones. He lay his hands on his stomach, closed his eyes, and imagined a home with bright big windows, fresh fruit and flowers, with Helios in it this time.

Helios complaining that he smelled like vinegar and paint. Helios brushing flecks of it out of his hair, Helios peeling it off his skin. Helios sitting at golden hour, or by candlelight, letting himself be sketched over and over. Helios dancing in a living room without furniture, ankles free of cuffs and shackles. His vision filled with red, red, red hair, burnished and brilliant and bright.

Being as loud as they wanted.

They could have friends over and fill their house with noise.

And at night, they could lie next to each other with miles of sheets between them, together and alone.

PLUCKED

He woke up wanting terribly. He remained untouched, fingers shaking.

It didn't seem . . . appropriate. Respectful.

Icarus pressed his forehead against tile and breathed, letting cold water sluice down his back. Turn him holy again, *Ave Maria, gratia plena, Dominus tecum.*

He closed his eyes, shivering.

WEST

After four days of silence, on Friday a small cup was placed in front of him.

Espresso, bitter and dark.

Icarus drank it all.

He looked up into brown eyes and saw divinity in the quirk of a smile.

"That's all you get for now, until I'm happy with you again." Julian slid into his seat.

"Are you going to homecoming?" Icarus asked.

"Does it matter? You're not going to see us there. I might see you at Luca's party," Julian said without turning around. "If you'll *deign* to show your face there, at least."

"I'm showing up," Icarus admitted quietly.

"Which is weird to begin with, but I'm not going to bust your balls about it. It's not every day Queen Celestina walks up to you and begs you to do her the favor of showing your face at an event. My curiosity was piqued," Julian said, looking to the side, but still not facing him.

"Hmm." Icarus sat back.

"I'm not really mad at you," Julian mumbled. "If that means anything."

"I did miss it. The drinks. It really helps," Icarus replied. "I can pay you back for it."

"No, dude." Julian crossed his arms. "Stop making it weird, just like . . . get over yourself about it. Consider it my investment in not having to come back here after college and see you working at the factory with my dad."

Icarus frowned.

"Shit would be so depressing I'd set myself on fire," Julian mumbled.

"Uh . . . okay. Well. I'm half done on my outline for the project. What step are you on?"

Julian snorted. "Wouldn't you like to know."

He didn't turn around, but the side of his cheek rounded, and Icarus knew Julian was smiling.

RIPPED

Everyone was buzzing with energy, but Icarus was just nervous.

Luca gave him his address and warned him that the fun wouldn't start until 11 p.m. because the dance ended at 10, and if he got there early he would have to help set things up.

Apparently, Luca's parents were out for the evening to give everyone some space, which sounded as exciting as it did dangerous.

To Icarus's surprise, Aspen and Sorrel were both going to the dance but not Luca's party. Aspen was bringing a girl she'd met online who lived in a different town. She seemed wary and a bit disgusted that Icarus was going to a "popular kid's house" and warned him that it might be some kind of trap.

Sorrel told Icarus that he hadn't been invited to Luca's, and when Icarus insisted that it was open invitation, he still turned Icarus down.

"I wouldn't know what to do there. I'd feel out of my element," Sorrel had mumbled.

Celestina sat behind him and dragged her nails up and down his back until he bent like a willow and pressed his cheek to the desk. Tremors of pleasure turned his spine to liquid.

"It will be okay," she sighed. "I'll drive you back home in the end."

"Even if you can't come upstairs?" Icarus's eyes were hazy. He was falling apart in the middle of chemistry and he didn't care. He didn't care.

Celestina's laugh sounded like wind chimes. "Keep your secrets, love."

TIGHT

Getting ready in a silent house was . . . sublime. He could take as long as he wanted in the bathroom.

Icarus knew he could look passable in casual clothes, but he'd never be able to pull off the kind of cool things that everyone his age wore these days. He was sure he was ugly, but if he squinted, Icarus knew he could be 1950s handsome. He'd seen enough photography from that era to recognize it. Icarus liked older things, so he didn't mind.

He buzzed his nape down and smoothed his limp black hair back with brilliantine. His part was razor sharp, angled with the arch of his eyebrow.

He wore a black sweater with short sleeves that made his arms look strong and wool trousers borrowed from his father's closet.

He sprayed on a cologne that smelled like wood and fire. Tucked a pack of cigarettes into his back pocket.

Hand on the front doorknob, Icarus eyed the bouquet of flowers he'd gotten himself sitting in the middle of the breakfast table. He turned back, plucked a stem of lavender, and rubbed it behind his ears.

Then, Icarus Gallagher stepped into the night and headed for Helios Black's house.

THE FIRST NIGHT

Mr. Black shouldn't be home and the alarm wasn't on, but Icarus still came in through the back door.

He slipped off his shoes and socks, then paused, standing slowly. Right in the middle of this little foyer was a new acquisition. Icarus wondered how long it had been there. He hadn't come to this part of the house since the night he and Helios had officially met.

It was a bronze disc with three figures, a woman and two men looking at her in agony. It was weathered but clearly restored, and the room smelled . . . different with it so near. Icarus's clever eyes roved the space around it, looking for the telltale shine of a camera lens, but he saw none.

Still, the hair rose on the back of his neck. It was . . . improperly placed.

This piece was Italian, ancient and valuable. The sort of thing that should be in the vault, but it was here in the open, tantalizingly close to the door. There were rooms that would suit it better, rooms designed to make the viewing appealing, but it was here: downstairs in the modern common area surrounded by steel and linear shapes and dark colors. *All* of the rooms in this house had a theme and stuck with it, with no exception. This didn't belong here, but here it was, displayed.

It felt like bait. How long had this been here? He tried to remember if it had been in the shadows when he was rushing to replace the sculpture and he had just missed it. He couldn't be sure.

Icarus flattened himself against the wall as far from it as he could get and took a picture of it with his phone. Zoomed in on the plaque beneath boasting its name and provenance and took a picture of that too.

Orpheus Losing Eurydice, Veronese. He wanted to show his dad, but he couldn't. Not yet. Because of his decision to keep this situation to himself, he couldn't even text this picture to Angus. No matter how personally freaked out he was getting.

Icarus clenched his fists, took a few steadying breaths, and refocused. He couldn't make tonight about this.

He closed his eyes and listened.

Silence, until a toilet flushed upstairs. Icarus followed the sound to a wing of the mansion painted yellow. He knocked on the only closed door in the hallway and waited.

"What the f—" he heard Helios mutter.

The door swung open to reveal a small library. Helios looked down at him with an unreadable expression.

"Sorry for the unexpected entrance. I can't climb dressed like this so I had to use a door," Icarus explained. "Is your dad gone or am I about to be beaten to death?"

"Jesus Christ," Helios breathed. He swallowed hard. "Come in. He's— He's not home, he left at five."

Icarus strode into the library and looked around. Helios had strewn a few books across the ground in an arc, like he was researching something.

"Sorry about all this," Icarus said, crouching down to see what Helios was reading. "I'm going somewhere after this; I might not have time to change."

"Do you dress like this all the time?" Helios asked. He was still standing by the door, gawking.

Icarus laughed softly. "No. Just special occasions. Today is homecoming . . . is it really that much?"

Helios put a hand on his chest. "I don't even know how to answer that."

155

Icarus tilted his head. "If it looks bad maybe I'll *make* time to go home and change."

"NO! I mean *no*, it's good, it's really good." Helios still looked a bit spooked. "Do you by any chance want a tour of the house? Like with the lights on so it's more official? Then I could cook maybe? Are you hungry?"

"I could eat."

If you made something.

SWAN

Icarus had been here often of course. But it was either in pitch-black darkness, or he had to crawl in a very specific window, take pictures, and then crawl right back out.

He didn't have time to just wander around appreciating everything. It was interesting to see this through Helios's point of view.

"There are four wings. Each has its own bathroom and its own kitchen, even if they're hardly ever used," Helios said. "The wing painted blue—where we usually are—is where we lived when I was a kid. The rest was just guest bedrooms, but now I'm in my old room and my dad is in the white wing."

Icarus ran his fingertips across the banister as they headed down the stairs.

"There's the blue wing, the white wing, the red wing, and the yellow wing. Yellow has the library; blue has the biggest bathroom. White has the most storage, and red is mostly used for business."

Helios looked back at him with nervous brown eyes. He turned his head quickly when Icarus met his gaze.

So. Helios found him attractive.

Icarus hadn't been sure before, but he understood now. Icarus knew he wasn't handsome, but he had been eyed this way before and he knew what it meant.

He gazed at the nape of Helios's neck as he walked up the stairs in front of him.

Luca looked at him like that sometimes. He still didn't know what to make of it.

So he joked it away. Luca, in turn, had never asked. Never pushed. Touched him too rough for it to land.

He wondered what Helios would do.

CRUNCH

The blue wing was all memory. Pictures of Helios's mom, who looked so much like him. Dresses still hung up in an open closet. Floors caked with dust. Icarus didn't mention making this connection.

Yellow was warm, and seemed to be used half as much, if only for lack of occasion. There was a music room that Helios danced in sometimes, the library, a storage area with which Icarus was intimately familiar.

The red wing was also familiar. Impressive pieces in glass cases. Gaudy giant desks, books never meant to be removed from their shelves. There was a giant globe that Helios insisted they could sit inside sometime. Expensive telescopes and more.

The white wing was immaculate, but they didn't go inside many of the rooms. There were a few guest rooms and a storage closet that was large enough to echo when they spoke. It was messy and crowded with sheafs of paper and old art supplies.

"My dad spends almost all of his time in this wing. I'm pretty sure he'd notice anything we did in here, so let's just go back to the ground floor," Helios said.

He led Icarus to the main living room where the TV was, through a butler's pantry, and to the main kitchen.

"Do you have any dietary restrictions?" Helios asked.

Icarus shook his head. He sat down at the massive wood table and settled in to watch Helios cook.

Helios opened a large cabinet stocked full of pots and pans and turned on the stove.

"There are other things here, beyond the main house, that I would like to show you sometime," Helios said, as he filled a pot with water. "There's a really nice flower garden and a field. I can't leave the house but you can go out there if you want. People can't see you from the street because of the trees."

"Do you know how far you can go?"

Helios shrugged one shoulder without turning around. "I can't even get too far out the window. But I wouldn't be able to run away efficiently enough to not be caught. I don't know this town. I grew up in the city. My mom and I left this house when I was like seven. I spent one Christmas here when I was fourteen and then there's now. This isn't my home."

He started chopping while Icarus took some time to think about that.

"There's also a pool. If you weren't on your way somewhere we could have gone swimming," Helios said casually.

Icarus knew it wasn't casual for him. His ears were red and he said it too fast and had started cutting quieter to hear Icarus's answer.

"This is nice," Icarus said. "Being in here with you. It feels more normal than what we usually do."

RUB

Icarus made Helios take him up to the roof. There was a small ledge that stuck out under one of the windows in the yellow wing that was long enough to sit on with your legs outstretched.

He sat crisscross and pulled out his pack of cigarettes, offering one to Helios.

"I can't. He's coming home tomorrow; I feel like he would know somehow."

Icarus hmmed and lit his. He took a deep breath.

"We can share," Icarus said. "Come here. Open your mouth."

He took a drag. Then reached over and clasped Helios's chin, breathing into him. The smoke curled around their faces, making the edges of Icarus's eyes hurt.

"Fuck."

"Do you want more?" Icarus asked.

"Yes," Helios sighed and leaned in closer, their lips nearly brushing. But Icarus stopped him. Pressed his fingers to Helios's cheek, put his thumb on the swell of Helios's bottom lip, and caught him before their faces touched.

"Helios, no. I haven't done that before," he said, firmly. "I can't start with that."

Helios pulled back. His eyebrows knotted with the sting of rejection, but Icarus didn't let him go. Pain melted into confusion.

"It would be too much for me to handle," Icarus explained. "I don't get touched very often and it's overwhelming for me most of the time."

"Oh . . ." Helios said, curious. "That's . . . unique. Why?"

Icarus let his hand fall from Helios's cheek and took another drag.

"It's . . . it just wasn't as common for me growing up. Now I just feel things differently. More intense. And I know it's not in the same way other people do, because no one else reacts the way I do when it happens on accident," Icarus said.

Helios drummed his fingertips on the roof tile.

"And it's not when you touch other people, it's only when people touch you."

Icarus shrugged. "It's not fair. If I was in control of it, I would just stop it from happening. You want more?"

Helios leaned forward quickly and Icarus blew more smoke into his mouth. Helios made a soft noise, a wanting noise, as he pulled back.

"You're very beautiful," he said, eyes opening, hazy.

Icarus laughed at Helios, louder than was safe. "You don't have to flatter me. I'm already starting to want you."

Helios groaned and covered his face with his hands. "Why do you say everything so bluntly, god it's embarrassing."

Icarus shrugged and took another drag, blowing it out in rings. He just didn't care. When you don't have people to be responsible to, or relationships that you have to sustain, you don't get in the habit of saying things you don't mean. Icarus told the truth because if anyone didn't like it, he'd just never speak to them again.

"I'm really not beautiful, Helios, I'm just the only one who's around while you're in a tough spot," Icarus said. "But that's okay. When you're free you can go back and live your life."

Helios shook his head, then looked up at the sky.

"Let's change the subject," he said. "Whose party are you going to?"

Icarus shrugged and put the cigarette out. "Luca's. He's a good friend . . . It's my first."

Helios looked like he was about to throw a fit.

"What? No kissing, no parties?? What the fuck?" he hissed. "What are you, a Jehovah's Witness?"

Icarus smirked.

"You're the second person to ask me that this month. But no, I just can't have anyone getting too close. And I'm kind of Catholic, if you care much about that."

"What?! Why?!" Helios cried.

Icarus's smirk widened into a grin. "Helios Black. I am a filthy cat burglar with a house full of money, priceless art, and stolen goods. If someone gets even a glimpse through our windows, Interpol will tear our home apart. I definitely can't have friends coming and going all the time."

He put the cold cigarette in his pocket and brushed the remaining ash down into the yard. "And I'm Catholic because—"

"Oh, shut up!" Helios turned around and hopped back inside.

HUSH

They slid back into the linen closet, dark and warm.

"Open your mouth." One last time.

Icarus placed an unlit cigarette between Helios's teeth.

"Contraband," he murmured. "For when things get rough and I'm not around."

"Fuck, dude . . . Fuck," Helios hissed, pinking delicately. He looked hungrily, but still didn't touch him.

They spent the rest of their time in the library, at Icarus's request. He'd spent a decade in this building looking at books he couldn't touch. If Icarus never got to roam freely in this space again, he was going to satisfy this urge once and for all.

Helios went back to whatever he'd been doing on the floor. The books he had open were all about plants, and he seemed mildly reluctant to talk about it. So Icarus didn't ask.

At the end of the night, Helios walked him to the back door, leaned against it to watch him put on his shoes.

"See you again, my friend?"

Icarus looked up into Helios's face, searched his eyes. "Icarus."

"Icarus?"

Icarus smiled.

STUN

Icarus could hear the party long before he saw it. He wasn't the only one walking down the street toward it, either. It wasn't anyone he knew, but he could tell where they were headed because they were all talking loudly and some people were carrying drinks. Everyone looked like they had found the time to quickly tear off all their homecoming clothes and get into something more casual.

Icarus rolled his shoulders and widened his stride. He knew he could wear anything as long as he carried himself like it was on purpose.

The music was loud enough to make his ears hurt when he opened the front door. Luca's house wasn't big and it was crammed near to bursting with people.

Icarus wondered for about one second why no one had called the cops on this yet, before remembering that Akeem had said his dad was the captain. Typical.

He eyed the ceiling warily, wondering if there were this many people upstairs as well.

"Ayyy! *Twelve Angry Men*!" Some guy Icarus had never seen before in his life slapped him hard on the shoulder. "Looking good, short stack! Beer's in the kitchen, Luca said to send you out back." He gave Icarus a push to the right, then turned back to what appeared to be a wrestling match in the middle of Luca's living room.

Icarus forced his way through the crowd and into the kitchen.

Some of the cheerleaders were gathered around the island, and he could see a drink table behind them. Icarus took a deep breath for confidence and started edging around the perimeter.

"Icarus!"

Celestina jumped down from the counter. The crowd parted for her as she rushed across the space, slamming into him hard.

"You came!" She squeezed him, long arms around his neck, body pressed against him tight.

"You look so pretty," she gushed, tipsy and free.

Icarus gently pulled back to take her in. She was still wearing elaborate, gaudy homecoming makeup. She looked radiant. "I just got here," he blurted.

"Junie's making grilled cheeses!" one of the cheerleaders shouted. "You want some?"

It took Icarus a moment to realize she was talking to him.

"Nah, I'm looking for Luca?"

Celestina hooked her arm around his neck and dragged him across the kitchen with her. Her power of making people get out of her way was intoxicating.

"Ooh you look like one of the guys from *Some Like It Hot*!" Mina Silvestri said, and skittered her nails across the curve of Icarus's chin. It took everything in him not to flinch. Were all popular girls so grabby?

"Aw, you're too sweet," Icarus said. He leaned away from her and toward Celestina as subtly as he could manage.

"Where did you find him?" Jenna Davis cooed. She pulled up the bandanna that she was wearing as a tube top and crossed her long tanned legs, looking down on them from her seat on the counter.

"He's one of Luca's friends," Celestina said. "And he's my sweetheart, so keep your claws out of him." She nuzzled into Icarus's neck, and he curled his hand into a fist with an effort to remain still.

Jenna reached backward and waved her hand until a grilled cheese was put into it. She tore it in half and gave the other half to Mina.

"Are you sure you don't want any?" Mina said, leaning closer to him with her piece.

"He already said no," Celestina said firmly. "Luca's in the back with the rest of the boys. I'm gonna take him. Pass me that bottle of honey Jack. We'll bring out some ice."

Celestina tugged Icarus out of the circle. He squeezed her hand gratefully.

PROOF

It was much quieter outside. It was still pretty crowded, but people were clumped up in groups, smoking, talking amongst each other, and drinking.

Luca, Akeem, Patrick, and the rest of the guys he would have expected were crowded together on a couch. What he didn't expect was Julian, standing next to the couch with his arms crossed.

He could hear the lecture Julian was giving from twenty feet away.

"—help you clean up because it's not going to be me, that's for sure. You should be fucking lucky I'm not taking pictures," Julian griped at Luca.

Icarus almost dropped the ice Celestina had forced him to carry. "Julian?"

"Oh . . . well, look who decided to show up," Julian snapped. "What the hell is this . . . this *Singing in the Rain*–ass fit."

"Shut up, Julian," Icarus said immediately.

"Oh my god."

Luca, who'd had his head in his hands during Julian's tirade, got up immediately. "Oh my god dude, wow. You should have gone to the dance; you *definitely* should have gone wearing that. Don't listen to Julian. Holy shit."

He pulled the ice out of Icarus's arms and set it on the ground. Then he dragged Icarus into a hug.

Luca was . . . compact, lean in the way Helios was. He smelled like sweat and, interestingly, a bit like girly perfume. Helios had hugged him carefully, like he thought he might be pushed away. Had wrapped his arms around the top of Icarus's shoulders, held him close to his chest.

Luca hugged him like he had every right to. Like they had *ever* done it before. Swept his arms under Icarus's arms, wrapped one around his upper back, curled the other around his waist. Pushed his chin into the curve of Icarus's neck. Held him full and sweet. Tears sprang to Icarus's eyes without his permission.

"Come, sit." Luca pulled back from him. "Let's do shots once my cousin stops screaming at us."

"I'm not screaming!" Julian shouted over Icarus's horrified, "Cousin?!"

"Yeah," Luca said, like it wasn't tearing Icarus's mind in half.

Akeem moved over so Icarus could fit, while Celestina draped herself over all of the boys. She put her feet in Patrick's lap and her head in Luca's, leaving her chest and stomach draped over Icarus and Akeem.

Luca placed a gentle hand over Celestina's box braids and continued arguing with Julian about taking the couch out of the living room and putting it outside.

Eventually, Julian threw up his hands. "Whatever! I'm not going to tell, but if Aunt Margie asks, I'm not covering for you," he hissed, then turned to Icarus. "See you later, punk. Don't get too fucked up."

Luca shook his head. "He's not going to tell. He loves me." He wiggled his eyebrows at Icarus.

He reached to the side and grabbed a lime. Unhingedly, Luca bit the top off and spit it into the night, then started passing shot glasses down the couch.

"Who wants tequila?"

HAZE

Icarus liked parties and he liked tequila. He liked this couch and he liked sitting next to Akeem, who spread out his knees to survey the party like an emperor.

This was his fifth shot.

Luca's face swam before him, soft and friendly. Celestina's hands were in his hair.

"There's stuff in it," he mumbled. Warning her.

"I like seeing you try, like this," he heard Celestina say.

Suddenly, Akeem and Patrick weren't next to him anymore, and it was much quieter than it was before. Luca's arm was around his shoulder and Celestina was in his lap and his hands were on her waist and his skin felt so strange. Like everything was muted. Finally, he knew what it meant to feel normal.

"I can't sleep here," Luca huffed into Icarus's neck. "It's so loud. I just want to sleep."

"Where are you going to go? It's your house."

Icarus giggled. "We're neighbors you know. Five blocks or so."

Luca pulled back, grimacing. "Five blocks isn't neighbors."

Icarus closed his eyes. "It's close."

"Here, here." A vodka-soaked lemon wedge was pressed against his lips and he opened them, licking the juice.

"You're supposed to bite it!" Celestina laughed. She pulled it away from him, then leaned back in a beautiful arc, her braids brushing Icarus's knees as she bit into the lemon and took a swig of the half-finished bottle of rye.

"Wow," Icarus breathed. "I wish I could paint that."

"You could." Luca lay his head on Icarus's shoulder. "She'd let you. Would you paint me? You have to be nice to your friends."

"I . . . I am nice. I try to be."

BLOOD

The wind blew through his hair as they ran.

Celestina whooped loud into the night, galloping beside him.

The streetlights blocked out the stars, and they streamed as they flew by. Beams against the black of the sky, and they were beautiful.

Luca was so strong.

Icarus's arms could barely hold anything, the world was so dizzy, but his thighs were clamped round Luca's waist and he knew he was being carried.

It was Luca's hair that smelled like girl perfume. It must be his shampoo.

The ground found his feet, and his keys found his hands, and they were stumbling up the stairs, fast and clumsily. Celestina fell down a few and they had to tug her up.

The neighbors were yelling. Sorry. Sorry. I can't help it, I'm too happy. We're too happy.

The house was warm.

Celestina looked incredible on his bed, in his room, her smile hitting him like a big brass band. Luca was pushing in behind him. Closing his closet door, stumbling down into the soft mattress. His hands so big as they tugged Celestina closer to them both.

His nose was cold as it nudged in behind Icarus's ear.

Luca sighed. "You smell like lavender here."

EDEN

Icarus woke up to the sound of loud snoring.

His head felt like it had been beaten with a bat and his mouth tasted terrible. He rubbed his eyes, then let his arm flop down.

"Ow." A soft voice.

Icarus's eyes snapped open.

"No. Nononononononononnono." His heart was going to burst out of his chest. He was going to throw up.

"Dude, please talk quieter," Luca panted. "My head is killing me."

Celestina turned away from the closet door, where a sliver of light was peeking through.

They couldn't be here, they couldn't be in this house, in this room, in his bed. He didn't know what to do. There was no way to get them from the closet to the front door without them seeing at least fifty things they shouldn't and he didn't have answers for these kinds of questions. He was so stupid. So fucking stupid. He wanted to die.

Icarus could feel his chest tightening as he fought to breathe. He couldn't even run away without making this worse.

"Fuck. *Fuck*."

"Hey, are you okay?" Luca shifted in the dark and a hand landed on his back.

The reprieve that last night's drinking had given him had worn away, and he felt the touch like the crack of a whip. It was the last straw.

Icarus hid his face in his hands and sobbed.

EGGSHELL WHITE

Celestina and Luca sat at his breakfast table while Icarus cooked eggs and hash browns. Celestina kept her eyes on his back, while Luca took the opportunity to drink in everything around him. Icarus couldn't decide which was worse. His father's art looked so obsessive under these circumstances: a thousand of his mother's eyes watching them.

The kettle whistled and Icarus pulled it off the fire.

"I've never had tea before," Luca mused, clearly trying to lighten the mood.

Icarus didn't respond. He placed steaming plates in front of them and went to get sugar and cream.

When he finally settled and the table was full, milk, water, tea, orange juice, and Advil spread out before them, Celestina reached across the table. She didn't touch him, she just put her hand out flat on the wood like it was a substitute for his arm.

"Are you okay, Icarus?" she asked.

"I need you to promise me you won't tell anyone about this."

"We don't know what 'this' is," she said softly. "Is . . . are . . . do you think . . . is this a hoarder house?"

"It's too clean to be a hoarder house," Luca said, starting to eat. "My grandma is a hoarder and her house is full of mice."

Icarus stared hard at Celestina's hand on the table until it began to get blurry again. He covered his eyes and took a deep breath, pressing his palms into his skull. Okay. Okay.

He had to explain some things, but he didn't have to tell them all of it.

"My dad does art restoration. Most of . . . this is his work. A lot of it isn't. There . . . there are things in this apartment that are worth more than all the buildings on this block put together. I'm not supposed to have people in here, I'm never supposed to bring people here."

"Oh." Celestina pulled her hand back. "We're the first people you've brought home . . . ?"

Luca looked up, sharply. "We're the first friends he's ever *had*," he corrected.

Icarus wished the floor would drag him straight to hell.

"I don't even know what to do now," he whispered. "It's been . . . my whole life. Everything is ruined."

Luca shook his head. "It's not ruined. As long as we don't tell anyone, nothing has changed. As long as we don't do anything about what we know, we'll be all right."

Celestina glanced at Luca, then turned back to Icarus. "What are the rules?"

"What?"

"What are the rules . . . for your life?"

Icarus had had enough of crying in front of these people, but being asked this? In that soft of a voice?

"I . . ." He took a deep breath and willed himself to stop shaking. "I'm not supposed to bring people over or go to their houses. I'm not supposed to do things that make people too interested in me . . . adults mostly, but kids also. I'm not allowed to talk about his work or mine. I'm not allowed to be . . . too good at certain things."

Luca gripped his fork hard in his fist. Their food was getting cold.

Celestina hadn't touched hers. Icarus put a spoon of sugar in his tea and took a sip.

"You shouldn't have to sleep in a closet," Celestina said.

Icarus shook his head. "We need the room."

STING

He walked them through the house, so they could understand with sober eyes.

Celestina dragged her fingertips across the door of Icarus's small bedroom as they passed it.

The storage room opened with a hiss and Luca couldn't contain a gasp. Icarus had been looking at these things his whole life, but with Celestina and Luca beside him, it felt like he was seeing it all for the first time with them. The blue LED lights, the floor to ceiling temperature and humidity-controlled containers. The vast wall of tools, the large porcelain worktable.

"No one else has been in here since it was built," Icarus murmured. "Most of it is my dad's, but this area over here is mine."

He opened a cabinet and pulled out the rack so they could look at some of his own restoration work. Celestina leaned in close to inspect the detail of the paintings. She held her hands tight behind her back, straining not to touch.

Luca just stared at Icarus. Looked at him hard like he was memorizing his face.

"Where do you get this stuff from?" he asked.

"Museums. Private collectors. Occasionally a library, but most of the time my dad will send me in person for something low-profile like that."

"How much do they p—"

"A lot," Icarus said, vaguely. "But storage and supplies cost almost as much. I . . . work for myself now though. I pay for anything I need and get a percentage of whatever I work on . . . "

Luca rubbed his temples and walked out of the room. "This is so much more complex than I thought. I thought he was just beating your ass or something. I was going to call CPS."

"Please don't do that, Luca," Icarus begged gravely. "I only have a couple more months left under this roof." Less if he got his gold anytime soon.

Luca whirled around. "You shouldn't have to have *any* more months—" he shouted. Then stopped. "I'm sorry. I'm sorry. This is just a lot to take in."

"Promise me you won't tell," Icarus whispered.

Luca stormed back into the room with his arms wide, ready to pull Icarus into them, but Icarus flinched.

"I'm sorry, but please don't touch me. I can't handle it right now. It's too much." Icarus wrapped his arms around himself tight.

Celestina closed the storage room door.

"Icarus. We won't tell anybody, but you need to promise that you'll talk about this with someone. With . . . us now, I guess. I'll make time for you; we'll figure something out. You don't have to be by yourself anymore."

Luca looked devastated. "I'll tell Akeem that you have everything handled. That you have a getaway plan or something."

Then he shook his head and laughed mirthlessly. "God. If you knew what we were all planning to do if you eventually asked for help. I mean I know *now* that it would have been a disaster, but we were going to go nuclear for you."

Icarus covered his eyes so he wouldn't cry. He barely even knew Akeem. Why did they care? Why did they care so much? "Fuck."

"Yeah, fuck." Celestina echoed. "It will be okay, though. You'll be okay. We've got this."

FILTH

Icarus scrubbed the dishes, dried them, and put them away. He got on his hands and knees and scrubbed the evidence of their footprints from the wood floor.

Wiped down the stairs all the way to the front steps, wiped them away from this house.

Then he rushed back upstairs and baked an apple brown Betty, with brown sugar, bourbon, and caramelized butter. Went two flights down, crossed his fingers, and knocked.

After a moment he knocked again.

SCRUB

"God, what is it?" a woman answered. She had a toddler in her arms and his older brother clinging to her leg. Her hair was a mess and she had bags under her eyes.

"Hi, I'm from the third floor. I wanted to apologize for the noise last night—"

"Some people are trying to sleep. You need to be more considerate," she scolded, then started to close the door.

"Wait!" Icarus cried. "Wait, I made this for you. It's like an apple pie sort of thing. I . . . don't know how to make a lot of desserts, but I'm really sorry. You can keep the pan."

The woman looked at the pan, then over at her son, taking up all the real estate in her arms.

"Come put it on the table," she said, ushering him in.

Their house was messy with toys and smelled a bit like milky throw-up. Icarus followed her through the din to their kitchen at the back of the house.

"It's got bourbon in it. And brown butter," Icarus continued.

"You don't look old enough to drink." His neighbor glared at him.

"I . . . figured *you* would be, though. My dad . . . doesn't let me have . . . friends. Things got a bit out of hand, but I promise they won't again. Ever."

The woman looked concerned. She put her baby in his high chair and peeled the tin foil off the tray to glance at what Icarus brought.

"You guys did get quiet pretty much as soon as you got up the stairs . . ."

"Please don't tell him," Icarus whispered, staring at the linoleum beneath his feet.

"Hey . . . hey, are you okay?" She stroked her fingers through her baby's hair, concerned.

"I'm fine. I just wanted to apologize and let you know it won't happen again. I hope you have a good rest of your afternoon. I'll see you around."

Icarus backed out of the kitchen and out of their lives and fled back upstairs into his tower.

SANCTUS DEUS

Angus Gallagher came upon the house like a thunderstorm.

"Where did you go?" Icarus asked.

Angus eyed the flowers on the table and the empty dish rack and Icarus thanked God that he'd decided to put everything away instead of letting them sit there and dry.

"Genoa."

He placed his bag next to the door.

"It's time to pray."

Icarus knelt. He could smell travel on his father's coat: the stale airport air, the salt of the sea, even the stink of fish if he strained for it.

"Ave Maria, gratia plena, Dominus tecum. Benedicta tu in mulieribus, et benedictus fructus ventris tui, Iesus—"

The house felt new and dangerous. Like Angus would magically know there'd been people here, would feel it in the air, would feel it in the way Icarus moved and looked at him.

The wafer Angus put on his tongue tasted like ash and the wine was sour.

"Eternal Father, I offer Thee the Body and Blood, Soul and Divinity of Thy dearly beloved Son, Our Lord Jesus Christ, in atonement for our sins and for the sins of the whole world."

Icarus opened an eye, but his father was resolute in his devotion, still as stone. One gray eye cracked a slit, slid in his direction, and Icarus froze like the prey of a snake.

"Do you have any confessions?"

Icarus paused.

"Greed. I have been wanting things I cannot have. Things that can't be bought or sold."

Angus never asked him to elaborate on his sins.

"Blood or prayer?"

Icarus eyed the switch that hung on the altar. He was always allowed to choose.

"Prayer."

"Three Hail Marys, for heavenly consolation."

"Yes, Father."

He remained kneeling as Angus rose, went to his workroom, and shut the door.

RIPE

There was an early frost Monday morning. Julian brought him a spiced cider. Icarus brought Julian a piece of brown Betty in a Tupperware container.

"You bake?"

"Occasionally," Icarus replied, closing his eyes against the steam from his cup. "And if I'm already baking, why not bake for you?"

Julian sniffed it and peered at him curiously.

Icarus realized that he hadn't brought Julian a fork at the same time he turned around in his seat and started eating it with his hands.

"Good work, man," he said, between sticky bites. "They'll make a homemaker out of you yet."

Icarus snickered and then took a sip of his own drink. "You never told me you and Luca were cousins."

Julian shrugged without looking back at him. "It would literally never come up in conversation. I wouldn't have even known you guys were friends if he hadn't been all *'Icarus this Icarus that oooo Icarus'* at my aunt's birthday party last month."

"Luca does what he wants, mostly. I'm surprised he mentioned me at all," Icarus said resolutely.

Julian snorted. "Don't I know it. I *did* help clean up the other night. In case you were wondering."

"Thanks."

Julian shook his head. "Pshh. Don't thank me for him. It's not *your* house." He placed the empty Tupperware container on Icarus's desk.

"Really ace, Icarus. You could sell those." He licked his fingers loudly, not even flinching when Axel next to them hissed "gross" under his breath.

"Mmm. Maybe one day."

PLUM

Icarus's heart kicked up as he walked through the hallways. He passed other people, sliding between them efficiently so they never touched, weaving through the crowd toward gym, toward Luca.

A hand reached through the rabble and clasped his, pulling him in another direction, and he didn't have to look to know it was Celestina. He knew the shape of her now.

Luca materialized like magic, like he'd been waiting, and joined them. He and Celestina parted the crowd together, dragging him with them to the side door and out into the cold.

Neither of them said anything. Luca looked determined, and Celestina looked worried. Icarus didn't complain like he usually did, though his eyes did dart between them.

They pulled him off school property, across the baseball fields and into the surrounding woods. Deep enough into the forest that it was quiet and private. The leaves crunched beneath their shoes. They were still frosted this deep in.

Celestina stopped walking where the trees were the thickest, then turned to him.

"What happened after we left?"

Icarus shrugged one shoulder, uncomfortable. "He came home. He hasn't said anything, so I don't think he noticed. I cleaned up everything, wiped the floor—"

"Are we allowed to touch you again?" Luca interrupted, urgently.

Icarus sighed and looked up at the canopy of branches above them.

"I just got overwhelmed, Luca. I was feeling . . . It's not your fault, it's mine."

Luca shook his head. "I asked my mom about it and she said that people should ask after someone tells you no the first time."

Icarus closed his eyes for a moment at that image. Of Luca asking. Then he did something he'd never done before.

"Come here."

Luca fell into his arms, shaking. Icarus tried to mirror Luca's arm placement from the party. To do it right.

"I think what you had built up in your head was much worse than what's actually happening," Icarus said. "I'm sure it's definitely weirder though."

Celestina wrapped her arms around both of them and squeezed really tight. "I'm making this weird," she crowed. "I'm making this weird so it won't be so tense!"

Icarus laughed, and let her sway them all back and forth.

FEATHERS

"You scared me. You scared everyone."

Icarus thought about Luca's words while he sat next to Sorrel in art class.

"You're so nice and normal until anyone asks you to go anywhere with them and then you get cagey. You're always covered in bruises and small cuts. You're out of school a bunch randomly. You look like you never sleep. What was everyone supposed to think?"

He brushed ocher into the highlights of Sorrel's hands.

"You thought no one noticed?" Luca had scoffed. "Yeah, I mean teachers might not notice, they're too busy. But everyone else does."

He'd asked if Luca had started trying to be his friend just because of this. He had been starting to get angry at the thought, but Luca shook his head.

"I think it's because you're so ... popular that a bunch of people noticed anyway," Celestina cut in. "If you were more of an actual loner it might have taken longer."

"Too long and too late," Luca had said, looking out into the woods.

Icarus painted like Vermeer, in dark layers of discordant color with glazes of true color on top. The shadows of Sorrel's hands were purple and the midtones were turquoise green.

"Did you get to dance with her?" Icarus asked Sorrel, breaking the silence.

"Huh?" Sorrel looked up.

"The girl. The one you wanted to dance with at homecoming," Icarus finished.

Sorrel flushed delicately. "Mm-hmm. But only for a little while. She went off with her friends after."

"Who was it?"

Sorrel paused for a bit, then continued painting.

"Mina Silvestri. I know she doesn't like me back, but it was nice."

Icarus stopped painting and spun around to face Sorrel. "Don't say that. Girls are just . . . people, like everyone else. Just talk to her."

"But—"

Icarus shook his head. "They may have their own tastes about what they're into, and you can't change it if you're *not* their type. But you don't even *know* what Mina's tastes are. So don't count yourself out before she does."

He went back to painting, putting sky blue in the ridges of Sorrel's cuticles.

"I'll introduce you to Celestina," he murmured, leaning in close to get the detail right. "Then you'll have a bridge."

Icarus could feel Sorrel looking at the side of his head.

"Thanks, I guess . . . " Sorrel replied softly. "Do you have any time this week to come over to my grandma's house?"

"Oh shit, yeah, the portrait. I almost forgot." Icarus rubbed his forehead, streaking paint into his hair. "I can do it Wednesday. Is Wednesday okay?"

Sorrel nodded. "Yeah. Thank you, Icarus."

"It's nothing. No problem."

TOY

Angus didn't say anything to him that night, but he did get into some kind of fight on the phone that he went into the nearly soundproof storage room to have.

Icarus lay in the middle of his bed, where he'd been squished between Celestina and Luca. It still sort of smelled like them. He knew he should change his sheets, get the drunk sweat out. But it felt indulgent, greedy to leave them here.

He didn't know if all friendships were like this. He had nothing to compare it to.

He wanted to roll around with them like fox pups in a warren. He wanted to nip and get nipped in return.

He understood now, the difference between that and what he felt with Helios.

Celestina, Luca, and Sorrel were so easy. Helios was hard.

Being with Helios felt like chess or a waltz. Icarus was surefooted in many ways, but not this. He didn't know how to play. But it was thrilling.

BLIND

Icarus pulled his pillow from under his head to turn it to the cool side, when he spotted it.

Chicken scratch in the corner on the wall.

He eyed the shelf behind his head. A pencil had definitely been pulled from his collection: #1 lead too soft to write with, really.

Luca Gallo had written his phone number, and Celestina's and Julian's for extra credit. The soft lead had smeared and was half rubbed away by the sheets.

THE BEGINNING

Icarus brought Helios more coffee. His hands were cold from the climb in October air, so he held the thermos while Helios drank.

"The party itself wasn't too bad. I like loud crowded places, but Luca's house was groaning under the weight of all those people. There was this frenetic energy there that smoothed out the more we drank. Is it always like that?"

Helios smirked. "Most of the time. It starts out a bit spiky feeling, then the more you dance, the more you drink, the world gets blurry."

"Like going from kaleidoscope to abstract watercolor," Icarus commented curiously. "I liked it. But, again, things got pretty out of hand."

"What did it feel like to have them in your house?" Helios took a sip and closed his eyes. "Before you woke up again, obviously."

Icarus sighed and rolled the thermos from hand to hand. "It was good. It was really good," he said quietly.

Helios clicked his tongue. "So eloquent."

Icarus shrugged. "It was such a private feeling . . . I don't really have words for it yet. It was just good. And then, in the morning it wasn't. I don't think I've ever felt so horrible and scared and upset."

Helios placed the mug on his nightstand, then reached forward to cup the thermos with Icarus.

"If it hurts so bad, why do you do it?" Helios asked.

"What?"

"Why do you come here to take this stuff from him?" Helios tried again, but Icarus shook his head.

"No, no that was rhetorical. Pause. How much do you know about all of this? Just everything relating to this?" Icarus said.

Helios just stared at him.

"When we met—" Icarus started to raise his voice. "—You called me by my father's name. How much do you know?"

"Shh," Helios said urgently, glancing quickly outside the curtain. "I don't know, dude. Our parents were friends for a long time, so there's a picture or two of your dad in my house. Like, group family pictures. When I was a kid, I thought he was an uncle I'd never met. I just asked my mom and she told me his name."

Icarus dropped the thermos and dug his fingernails into his thighs. His head was buzzing and he felt a bit like he was about to throw up.

"She never talked to you about any of it?"

Helios was starting to look a bit panicked. "You just look so much like your dad, Icarus. I'm not sure what—"

"Stop. Give me a second."

Icarus closed his eyes and controlled his breathing. He unclenched his hands and smoothed his palms over the marks, and let himself settle until his heart was back to a normal pace and the acid retreated back down his throat. He swallowed a few times, then opened his eyes.

"It's okay," he said. "I'll tell you."

SEVENTEEN YEARS

They lay side by side, back to back, because Helios thought it would be easier, not having to look each other in the eyes.

Icarus was quietly thankful.

"Our dads met in college," he started. "They'd been friends since freshman year. It was one of those situations where your dad was a legacy entry whose parents donated millions and my dad was a scholarship kid who could barely afford room and board. The Art Institute of Chicago wasn't even expensive back then. But, you know how it is."

"This isn't starting positively," Helios said darkly.

Icarus couldn't help the huff of laughter that escaped him.

"Dude, shut up. Anyway, my dad was an art major and art history minor, and yours was an art history major and art minor. My dad was the artist and your dad was the art collector." Icarus waved a hand, encompassing the house around them.

"They were cool with each other all the way through school, through graduation. Then they found our moms and got married. They were definitely friends after that for a while, because I've seen a picture of your dad holding me as a baby."

Helios turned onto his side, facing Icarus, but he closed his eyes.

"Keep going."

Icarus bent his knees and rolled onto his back to get more comfortable. "Around when I was one, and you were probably still baking, my mom got really sick with some kind of blood cancer. So, my dad—who was still pretty early on in his career—went to your dad and asked him for money to help."

Helios's eyes snapped open. "There is no way that went well. He pays my child support into a locked trust and I'm his own kid."

"Stop interrupting," Icarus snapped, crossly. "Anyway, they had a huge fight and eventually your dad conceded to pay for medical intervention if my dad painted him a commission. My dad is . . . very good. He was considered a rising star back then. So, I'm sure your dad probably thought of it as an investment of some kind. Either way, their relationship was pretty much ruined at that point.

"Your dad asked for a six-foot by nine-foot painting. Paid to have the canvas brought in and kept in a room here big enough for my dad to work on it."

Icarus could feel Helios opening his mouth to talk. "Yes, here in this house, don't ask. Anyway, my dad was allowed to come every night after work to paint it. But my mom was dying faster than he could paint and eventually he had to ask your dad for an advance on the money. He said no, of course."

Helios made a soft, sad sound.

"So, in the last days, my dad was painting to outlast my mom's illness. And he didn't succeed. He didn't even get a penny before my mom died." Icarus sighed. "Nobody had good insurance in those days. He was a free-lancer and even if he got an office job, company insurance wouldn't kick in for months."

"Jesus fucking Christ."

"So, I don't know. My dad had some sort of breakdown and figured out how to get in here so he could destroy the half-finished painting. Once he did it the first time, he realized how easy it was and decided to keep doing it. Your dad got new security after the first break-in of course, but Angus is nothing if not determined . . ." Icarus drummed his fingers on his chest. "He said that your dad only loved one thing, and he was going to destroy it. Even if it took the work of his entire life."

Helios was quiet.

"Oh."

Icarus turned over to face him. "You can open your eyes now."

Helios didn't. "I'm sorry, Icarus."

"Hmm." Icarus didn't want to say, "It's okay," because it wasn't, or, "You're forgiven," because it wasn't Helios's fault.

So he just let silence be for a while.

BOILED

"After that, it was just normal. He got better at breaking in here, and by the time I was old enough to know what was going on, he started training me to do the same," Icarus said. "I've been doing this since I was twelve."

"That's so fucked up. You do know that's fucked up."

"I mean, of course. But at the same time, complaining about this feels so . . . petty. Like, *'Oh Dad, I don't want to exact emotional, philosophical, and economic vengeance for your dead wife and my dead mom because I wanna go to school parties and have sleepovers.'* It just sounds stupid." Icarus rubbed his temples.

"It's *not* stupid, Icarus. That's more than half your life that you can't get back. That's developmental opportunities ruined. No wonder you were ready to beat me to death to get out of the basement that one time. You never got to be normal."

"I would never have hurt you," Icarus promised, searching Helios's eyes. "I just wanted to scare you. I was scared."

"Don't worry about it at all, seriously," Helios muttered. "You looked so hot that day I almost passed out. All of your black gear really does something for me."

Icarus laughed. "Jeez. Okay. Well. What was happening on your end that whole time?"

Helios flicked a glance at Icarus before allowing the subject change.

"If I'm managing my timelines correctly . . . basing this on our ages, my parents must have gotten their divorce about two years after your whole situation, and he kicked my mom and I out off and on until it stuck. When I was almost eight, we moved to New York and lived in a roach-infested apartment until my mom finished law school. But it was pretty much smooth sailing from there. He's big into the whole 'leaving people without a penny' thing, I'm beginning to realize."

"Hmm," Icarus said again, looking at the anxiety on Helios's face. He chose mercy. "That explains why you give off rich kid vibes but not like . . . generational wealth, own multiple million-dollar paintings vibes."

"You are so mean," Helios griped, as Icarus snickered again.

He could feel the joy ricocheting off his bones. He reached over and curled a finger in Helios's hair.

"I like when you look at me like that. Fond," Helios said, soft and true.

"Fond," Icarus echoed.

THROUGH

Before Icarus climbed back down, Helios caught him by the laces of his sweatshirt.

"My dad has been acting weird. I didn't want to talk about it because it's making me nervous. But he's going to New York again. He'll be gone for a week and a half, though. So you could maybe come and actually stay over."

Icarus was too wrapped up in worry about the first thing Helios said to understand the last bit. He took long enough to respond that Helios began to deflate.

"No, Helios," he said, gently. "I would love to come. I'll . . . I'll ask my dad if I can take a trip somewhere, but I'll stay here. With you."

"Mmm." Helios darted forward and pressed their foreheads together, so quick, so soft. Then he let go of Icarus's tether.

"He'll be gone by eight p.m. on the nineteenth. See you then."

Icarus flowed like water down the side of the house and floated home.

TAUGHT

When Icarus came inside, Angus was sitting at the kitchen table, waiting for him.

"Where do you go in the evenings?" he asked plainly.

Angus didn't even say hello. There was a glass of water next to him and a notebook that was worn and well used.

Icarus didn't even pause. He'd practiced for this.

"The diner across from Black mansion. I used to go for walks before to deal with stress but it's a bit easier to be walking somewhere in particular, and I like the coffee there."

Icarus gazed across the room. Then his eyes locked on the coffee making supplies over his father's shoulder. Coffee supplies he'd bought recently, of much higher quality than any diner would have. His hands went numb with anxiety. "Uh . . . and their late-night breakfast is nice too."

Angus, thankfully, didn't follow Icarus's attention to the counter, and instead stared back at him.

"It . . . " Icarus continued. "It also seems like a good idea to create a habit that makes it make sense for me to be in that part of town? In case people see me . . . around."

Angus took a drink of his water and placed the glass carefully on the wood.

"You are nearly a man grown. You are allowed to make most choices and be most places," he said quietly. "Make sure you choose correctly."

"Yes, Father."

Angus looked back down to his notebook and picked up his pen, finished with the conversation.

"Also, make sure you get enough sleep," he muttered and waved a hand.

Icarus took the out and retreated to his bedroom.

The cell phone photo of that new piece, the one near the back door, burned in his pocket. Angus probably knew about it. Icarus knew Angus tracked Mr. Black's purchases. But like the discovery of Helios, something didn't feel right. He still couldn't face him about this.

CHECK

Class with Aspen had been uneventful of late, but Icarus couldn't help thinking about Luca's and Celestina's words in the forest when they saw him last week.

"People only noticed because you're so extroverted. If you were more of a loner, it would be too late."

It had been said with the kind of effortless cruelty that only someone popular would use while trying to make someone feel better. The intention was kind, but it was burning a hole in the back of his brain.

Next to him, Aspen was drawing circles in her notebook.

"Hey."

She looked up. "Are you doing okay?" Icarus asked. He was worse at this than Luca and he knew it.

Aspen scrunched her nose up. "You mean generally speaking, or like right now this second?"

Icarus looked around, but no one was paying attention to them. It was group work time, so their teacher Mr. Shadid was reading a book at his desk, and it was loud enough for them to talk without people overhearing.

"Generally speaking," Icarus said. "Like, is your life going okay? It dawned on me that I've never asked."

Aspen's face went through a series of emotions. Confusion, amusement, resignation. And then it went blank.

"Not really? But whose life *is* going okay," she said, deadpan as ever.

"Besides, most of us can't do enough to tangibly make each other's lives better, so, like . . . calm down."

Icarus huffed. "I just figured I'd ask."

Aspen stuck her eraser on the paper on an angle and flicked it so it spun around quickly.

"I was getting Ds in math, but now I'm getting Bs because you sit here. We're good, dude." The eraser stopped. "Speaking of, you do know that Celestina and Luca are a thing, right? You and her seemed close."

Icarus grinned. "We're friends."

Aspen nodded. Then she went back to drawing circles.

Clearly she'd decided the conversation had run its course.

"If you need anything, though, let me know," Icarus insisted.

"Sure." Aspen didn't look back up.

LINE

"Beautiful, beautiful. Lighter on the border between body and space." Mrs. Sims crossed the room, observing their pieces.

Icarus could see that Sorrel was extremely nervous. He kept rolling a pencil back and forth on the chair. It was a quiet but irritating noise.

"It's fine."

"Easy for you to say," Sorrel snapped, then looked contrite.

Icarus smiled back at him. "Don't worry about it. Already forgiven. We still on for the portrait tonight?"

"Yeah, we can go straight after."

Mrs. Sims glided in their direction, standing behind Sorrel's chair while he cringed.

"The metaphor is a bit heavy-handed, but overall a very solid piece. Try adding a bit more dimension to the shadow on the table and it should be A-plus work."

She gazed at Icarus's painting. "Beautiful work as always, Mr. Gallagher. Any interest in putting this one up in the hall or submitting it anywhere?"

"Nope!" Icarus said chipperly. "It's going straight in the trash. Unless you have any objections." He glanced at Sorrel, and Sorrel shrugged. Icarus always threw school art projects in the garbage. He didn't need them. When you drew all the time, you really didn't get attached to stuff you didn't design with purpose.

Mrs. Sims shook her head. "Bring a horse to water," she muttered and continued on her way.

"She hates when you do that," Sorrel said.

Icarus started peeling the tape off the borders of the canvas. "She's going to have to get over it."

DRAFT

He followed Sorrel out into the parking lot and down a shady street with pretty bungalows. This part of town wasn't the nice area where Mr. Black lived, but it definitely wasn't anything to sneeze at.

Sorrel kept up a quiet conversation about the giant party they were planning for his grandmother, and Icarus listened. Asking him leading questions to make him talk more.

He was calm with Sorrel. It was like being in a Beatrix Potter novel with little squirrels doing laundry and rabbits mending fences. Sorrel didn't ask anything of him, and as delightful as it was with Celestina and Luca, Sorrel didn't pressure Icarus to do anything, he just trailed next to him timidly. It was relaxing.

Sorrel lived in a house that looked like a cottage, with white shutters and brown wood slats. It smelled like baking bread when they went in and ivy was climbing the windows.

Sorrel's grandmother was ornery and demanding, but she had Sorrel's dishwater eyes.

She sat, large and imposing, swaddled in a crochet blanket on a pink seersucker couch. Her white hair lit orange in the golden hour sun.

"Where did you find this one?" she asked her grandson, voice soft as the rushes.

Sorrel, who was sitting behind him eating chips and watching, just shrugged.

Icarus spent an hour filling in her hollows and crests in lead, then sprayed the paper with some heavy-duty hairspray borrowed from the bath-room.

Then he gently placed the paper in her trembling hand.

Her eyes flicked up at Sorrel, who went to the back of the room to figure things out in the kitchen.

"Salieri," she said, jutting her chin at Sorrel.

One of Mozart's rivals. A cruel word.

Icarus urgently didn't like this woman.

"Haydn," he countered. "It was lovely to meet you, ma'am."

Sorrel's grandmother leaned back to glare at him, but didn't say another word.

AMBROSIA

Sorrel's mom worked nights, but before she left she had prepared a small tea party for them. Finger sandwiches, a few shortbread cookies with jam, rolls of ham and cheese, cream in a little carafe, water just boiled on the stove. The choice of Earl Grey or English breakfast, both decaf of course.

Sorrel seemed a bit embarrassed, but not so much that he wasn't grateful.

Icarus, on the other hand, was thrilled. It was adorable. If this was Luca's house he would have begun making fun of him immediately, but he couldn't do that to Sorrel, so instead he just glowed with delight.

They moved to the back porch to eat, leaving Sorrel's grandma inside.

"She's not very nice," Icarus said immediately.

Sorrel just shrugged. "I think she thinks she's being encouraging. Tough love generation and all that."

That would make sense. He wished he had as easy of an excuse for his dad.

"So . . . Mina Silvestri . . . ?" Icarus started. He felt nosey about it, they would be a weird couple.

Sorrel made a few expressions before taking the bait. "She used to live a few houses down from me. I like her energy? She's full of . . ."

"Pep?" Icarus suggested.

"Confidence. I wish I had her confidence," Sorrel said, popping a cookie in his mouth.

"She's . . . certainly something. She was at the party I went to. She dragged her nails across my face and tried to hand-feed me a sandwich."

Sorrel laughed and Icarus realized it was the first time he'd heard him do that so openly.

"Hmm. Yeah," he said when he finished. "That's what I like about her."

Icarus gazed at Sorrel and the lavender glow on him from the setting sun.

He pulled out his phone and texted Celestina for the first time.

Icarus: *Hey Celestina, this is Icarus. I made a new friend and I want you to meet him. Is that ok?*

Celestina replied immediately.

Celestina: *What? Yes. Omg yes. Who is it?*

Icarus: *Sorrel McAllister. Sorrel's into Mina, so he'll probably want to talk about that."*

"What are you doing?" Sorrel asked, peering over Icarus's shoulder.

Icarus let him. "I'm setting up a hangout with Celestina, you, and Luca maybe, if you want."

Sorrel locked eyes with him. "You don't have to do that for me," he said seriously.

Icarus leaned back and met Sorrel's resolve equally. "Would you prefer I didn't?"

Sorrel broke their connection and looked out toward the grass, the wildflowers at the edge of his yard, and the sun glowing red in a sea of indigo.

"I don't like to owe people," Sorrel said.

That, Icarus understood.

He picked up a cookie. "You don't owe me anything. Consider it payment for this."

CHOKE

Sorrel was busy every day of this week, but would be available while Icarus was busy at Helios's. Luca and Celestina decided they would meet up without Icarus, then do something together when he got back.

Now all Icarus had to do was figure out how to ask his dad about taking time off.

He had missed school pretty regularly for years, but it was always for something his dad wanted to do, never him. And even then, not for vacation, only work trips.

Even without the torque, Icarus had enough money saved up to buy a plane ticket to anywhere in the world, twice over. Not needing to ask his dad for money or help before leaving wouldn't be suspicious.

He waited until Friday to bring it up, watching his father's temperament closely.

COTTON

Angus was in the workshop doing something noisy, again. Perhaps making paints.

They had rows and rows of shelves of paint and dye, oil, latex, acrylic, watercolor, gauche, encaustic. But historical paints, *organic paints*, would occasionally have to be made from scratch the hard way.

They'd had plants drying in the sun for weeks, packages showing up from China, Egypt, Brazil; the room smelled sharply of piss from the Indian yellow sitting innocently in a lump. Somehow still making the space reek from inside a sealed box.

Angus was grinding for aquamarine when Icarus approached him from behind.

"Respirator, Icarus," he called, somehow hearing footsteps over his own noise. Icarus put the regular hospital-style paper mask down and picked up the heavy-duty respirator mask with big plastic filters on the sides and the accompanying goggles. He also slipped on a pair of gloves. Icarus hadn't been planning on assisting, but he knew his father's wrists were starting to hurt. He had begun wearing his braces again.

"Vine black, if you're helping," Angus grunted.

Icarus crossed the room and opened the fridge. Vine black was charcoal made from grape vine twigs, and they only made it in small batches. He pulled out a large Tupperware container and removed a few tablespoons. Then he grabbed the glass muller, a large piece of sheet glass, and the linseed oil Angus had made a few months ago.

He set himself up, sifting the powdered charcoal until he was left with a fine dust. Icarus poured the charcoal onto the glass pane and introduced it to the linseed. He didn't begin to speak until he and his father were both mixing at the same rhythm.

"I want to take a trip next week," Icarus said. "I need you to sign me out of school."

The charcoal was still gritty beneath the glass muller, but it would be smooth soon. He rubbed it faster.

Angus was quiet for a bit. "Do you have any work or projects that would coincide with this absence?"

"No."

They ground together while Angus thought. Icarus looked down at his work, refused to meet his father's eyes. The charcoal needed more linseed, but if he ground it like this, sticky and black, it would go faster. It was a cheater's technique.

"Do you need to take anything with you? Any weapons or gear?"

"No, sir."

Icarus's goggles were fogging, he must be sweating beneath them. He could feel his father watching him.

"I . . . need some time away. I'll be back by Sunday morning for church."

Angus had stopped grinding, but continued again.

"You are nearly a man grown," he said, echoing his earlier words. "There aren't many places where you haven't been. Or many places where you couldn't go."

Icarus stayed quiet.

"You've never asked for this," Angus continued. "You've also never let me down."

The pestle swirled like a metronome. Icarus added more linseed and swirled the paint counterclockwise.

"You can go. Bring me back something beautiful if you can."

"Thank you, Dad." A drop of sweat from his hair landed on the glass pane and he swirled it in with the rest.

They sat in silence for the rest of the time, until Icarus bottled his paint in a small silver tube.

Until his glass pane had been washed, rubbed with alcohol, and washed again. Until he had brought the pane, linseed oil, and glass muller to his father's side. There, he lingered for a moment.

"Can I . . . buy something from you?"

CHATEAU LATOUR BORDEAUX

Icarus carried the bottle of wine from his father's workroom to his closet. He wrapped it in gauze and placed it at the bottom of his backpack.

RUSH

It was midnight when he arrived. Backpack full of clothes and proper climbing gear.

Icarus thought for a moment about using the front door, wished this once he could. But he didn't.

Helios was sleeping when he got there, back to the window and snoring lightly. Icarus slipped into his room, quiet, thief-like, and took off his climbing gear. He put on a T-shirt and black sleep-shorts.

"Helios."

Helios didn't move, just sighed in his dream.

Icarus crawled into bed beside him, close enough to touch but not bridging the divide. Curled toward his warmth and closed his eyes.

"I'm here," he whispered.

Helios turned over and breathed into the dark.

ORION

The light was different, behind his eyelids. Icarus's room was always dark in the mornings, but Helios's room in the Black house was awash with sunshine. More than he ever imagined this room would get. He could almost smell it in the air.

Icarus stayed heavy and lax, sinking into the blankets like a warm snowdrift. The mattress was too soft beneath him, but the difference was good. It was how he knew he wasn't home.

"Sweetheart."

Icarus opened his eyes all the way.

Helios was brilliant in this sun. He had to shield his gaze against it. Had to look at the space beside him through the shadow of his own hand. Helios's hair spilled across the pillow, violent, sanguine, eyelashes flaxgold. He was blood in milk, he was the skin of a Pink Lady apple, he was honey warmed in a hot spoon over tea. He was looking at Icarus lazy and indulgent. Not surprised in the least to wake up not alone.

He was three and a half inches away from Icarus's shoulder.

And like a rush, the thought occurred to him: he had never seen Helios during the daytime.

"Here you are," Helios whispered.

He reached across the forbidden space, fingertips hesitant. Icarus held his breath. Helios's lips were chapped, he had a hangnail on his index finger, his T-shirt was gray, he had sleep in his eyes, and he was still . . . so much.

Icarus could feel himself breathing too hard. Being embarrassing, as Helios grazed his cheek.

"Am I allowed?" Helios asked, voice still rough from sleep.

Icarus closed his eyes for a moment, then nodded.

THE SKY

Helios touched him tentatively. Brushing the pads of his fingers, kitten-like, over Icarus's face.

He smoothed down Icarus's eyebrows, over the crest of his nose, tapping just once on the tip. He skimmed the paper-thin skin beneath Icarus's eyes, lilac with lack of sleep. He fit his index finger into the hollow beneath Icarus's cheekbone, thumbed the generous swell of it. Dragged his hand down Icarus's jaw, felt the cleft of his chin.

And Icarus, doing his part, tried his hardest not to vibrate clean off the bed.

Every gesture was like a crescendo in strings. His bones ached, settled like steel. His skin was so raw it nearly felt bruised. He wanted to arch his back and cry out, but he couldn't do something like that for something as small as this. The reaction was too much.

"Oh. Don't do that, please," Helios whispered.

Icarus opened his eyes, confused, and saw a bit of scarlet on Helios's finger. Helios reached out again and wiped the blood from where Icarus had been biting his lip.

"I . . . I don't want to be loud," Icarus admitted.

Helios wiped again, the edge of his thumb nearly touching Icarus's mouth.

"Why not?" he said, effortless.

Why not.

Helios started again, trailing his finger from the peak of Icarus's chin to the valley of his throat, and watched, riveted, as Icarus tilted his head back and panted. He curled his fingers in the sheets, twisting them, pulling them off Helios's shoulder in his fervor.

"Good god. How do you even go outside?"

Icarus let out a helpless whine. "It's . . . it's . . . " *not the same,* he wanted to say, but he couldn't.

Not with nails scratching against his collarbone, pulling at the neck of his shirt. Helios skipped across the cloth and started again at the gap of soft space on the inside of Icarus's bicep. Strained tight.

Icarus let go of the sheet, and curled close around his arm, as if to protect it, but left it outstretched: hand open and shaking. Patient for exploration.

Helios settled his fingers into the hollow of Icarus's inner elbow. Swirled around that spot to figure out the noise Icarus would make, then traveled farther down.

"Please please please—" Icarus found himself muttering, eyes growing wet, aching *aching*.

Helios hummed curiously and drew his fingers away.

Icarus took a moment to catch his breath. Sweat was beading on his hairline. No one had ever taken liberties with him like this. Even *he* couldn't test his own limits like this.

"What does it feel like?" Helios asked.

Icarus looked up into Helios's brown eyes and stayed—caught to the quick.

"Holy."

Helios sat up in the bed, his broad back to Icarus, and wrenched his hands through his hair.

"I don't deserve this," Icarus heard him mutter.

Helios looked back at the mess he'd left behind. "I want to make you breakfast. Are you okay to get ready up here?"

Icarus nodded.

Helios got up, rolled his shoulders, and left the room.

STARK

Icarus' brushed his teeth and washed his face in the bathroom nearest by. He had never seen this room before. There was never any need to be inside a bathroom when he visited this house.

He looked at himself in the mirror and just felt . . . insane.

His skin was still prickly and strange. He expected to see the trails Helios's fingers had left reflected back at him. But there was no trace except in the flush of his own cheeks.

Icarus splashed them with cold water until that was gone too.

He got dressed quickly and followed the sounds of cooking down to the kitchen.

BURNISHED

Helios was making pancakes. He'd set the long breakfast table with plates and cutlery, putting his plate and Icarus's next to each other instead of across from each other. There was milk and juice and empty glasses.

Something in Icarus's gut tightened at the sight.

"Do you like bananas? I'm making like a caramel thing for them," Helios said.

Icarus sat down to watch him. "Yeah," he replied quietly.

Helios took their plates to the stove and brought them back steaming.

"I'm not amazing at cooking," Helios said, sitting down. "But I'm amazing at this specifically. I can make a waffle and French toast version too."

Helios's bananas Foster pancakes were rich and buttery; the bananas were mellow and spiced with cinnamon and nutmeg. There was even a dollop of fresh whipped cream.

"Is this homemade too?" Icarus asked, poking his spoon at the topping.

Helios immediately looked bashful. "I made it yesterday before you came."

Icarus smiled and sat back in his chair. Helios, clearly anxious, turned his attention away from him and ate a bit faster, so Icarus decided to let this one go.

"I usually go back to sleep for a while after breakfast," Helios admitted.

"You can still do that. I'll make myself busy," Icarus said. The storage room was waiting for him.

"Will you leave?" Helios asked, warily.

Icarus reached out to finger the edge of Helios's sleeve. Helios turned toward him, bending down, close enough to touch but just far enough that they didn't.

"I'll stay," Icarus said.

STRESS

Icarus ran his finger over the banister and thought about his own finger-prints. He sat on the stairs and wondered why Mr. Black didn't have cameras inside. His eyes scraped the corners of the ceilings, but like always, there were no telltale glints or hunks of plastic.

He remembered the first night he'd felt like he was being watched, felt the air disturbed, because Helios was here. Like everything had shifted to follow his orbit.

Icarus left Helios to sleep and went to the back stairs. He couldn't steal the gold torque during this vacation. After his brutal lie about only stealing art, Icarus couldn't chance the likelihood that Helios would catch him steal-ing something for money. Or worse, find it stashed in his bag. He would have to come back.

More, he wasn't exactly sure how to break it to Helios that he was leav-ing. Or how to ask him to come with him. Or if Helios even could. He had been planning this escape for himself for so long that making major reno-vations to it seemed unwise. Icarus really wasn't the reckless type, he was cautious. Always.

But even thinking about disappearing and leaving Helios here in this mess made him feel so guilty he had been avoiding thinking about it whenever he could. Even the torque hadn't crossed his mind in—

Icarus was halfway down the stairs when he saw it.

The disc was gone. *Orpheus Losing Eurydice.*

Heart racing, he flew down the stairs to the table it had been sitting on. It was a messy job. There was a small scrape on the wood, like the person who had lifted the disc didn't have a sure grip.

Icarus didn't touch anything. He held his hands up to make sure of that and backed away from the table. He abandoned his plans for the torque and left the foyer. There was something going on that he didn't understand, but it felt dangerous. Even being in this part of the house felt . . .

Icarus looked around the edges of the walls, in the corners, around every individual object, searching for changes or reflections, looking for the camera he was *so* sure was there. He didn't see anything. But he wasn't perfect.

He had been walking around this house with his balaclava off this entire time, but he hadn't done anything illegal in here yet. Even if the entire house had cameras, Helios was near him visibly acting like he was a guest. Even if Mr. Black threatened Helios into confessing about the break-ins, the same tapes that would show him here would also show Helios enjoying his company. It might mean some kind of punishment for both of them, but it shouldn't land him in a cell.

If there was surveillance in here that was older than the arrival of the disc, it would show a man the size and shape of his father, face covered, silently moving around the space.

As long as Icarus relaxed, he would be fine.

He would be fine.

Even the diner owner had assumed he was visiting a "girlfriend" and laughed it off as boyish mischief or whatever. So even if he got caught on camera in here, it wouldn't be the worst. He could figure out a way to work with that.

But the missing disc? A huge problem.

Icarus walked the house, looking for it on every floor in every room. Even risking Mr. Black's private wing, standing in the doorways with the lights off and his phone beam on.

It wasn't in the house.

Icarus crouched down in the middle of a hallway to think. It had arrived after a trip and disappeared before a trip. Maybe Mr. Black had acquired it to resell. He had brought it into the house, but it was too heavy to bring all the way upstairs, so he just left it there in the back foyer. Something like that. It made sense.

Icarus pressed his forehead to the carpet and willed himself to calm down.

When he finally sat up, he could hear music. Classical piano, and a series of small thumps. Helios was probably upstairs practicing after his nap.

Instead of following the sound, Icarus did something else he'd never done here before.

He went to the living room and sat on the couch.

The expensive knobby white fabric looked easy to dirty. It was too dense and bouncy for his tastes. It was like nothing he would have in his own home. But Icarus relished this anyway. Taking a rest, any kind of rest here, had always been unthinkable.

A normal kid would feel comfortable here. Icarus was supposed to do what a normal kid would be doing, after sneaking in to hide away with his . . . someone.

BLUE SMOKE

Icarus woke with a start.

Helios was sitting next to him on the floor, with a book in his hand. The entire house smelled creamy and succulent, rich with herbs and a little smoky.

Helios turned a page.

Icarus stared at the back of Helios's neck. At the sharp angles of his hair shaved thin at his nape. He had a freckle close to the collar of his shirt.

"If you're not allowed to leave, who cuts your hair?" Icarus asked, voice rough from sleep.

"My dad. He insists on it every other week," Helios replied, turning another page.

Icarus sat up and leaned close. Helios smelled different, freshly washed, and he had changed clothes to something more casual. Maybe he'd been working out or something. Icarus wanted to bury his face in the curve of Helios's neck. But he didn't. He just memorized the angle, to keep for later.

"Lunch will be ready in fifteen. It's just a casserole," Helios explained. "We're getting dangerously close to the limit of my cooking abilities, though, so you might have to pick up some slack before the week is finished."

Icarus hmmed low in his throat. "I'll cook for you," he said.

They sat in soft silence for long minutes.

"Later," Helios said and turned his face to the side, enough for Icarus to see the curve of his eyelashes. "Can you tell me about the painting in my room?"

Like before, he was trying to be casual. But his fingertips pressed the sides of his book and his spine was too rigid, too still. Icarus knew when he was being seduced. He knew that Helios was being brave now.

"I will."

HAYSTACK

Icarus touched the edge of the frame and looked back at Helios.

"Ready?"

Helios turned off the lights and there they were again, in the dark like the first time they'd met. Helios turned on his flashlight and set it on its side on the windowsill so that it pointed to the painting, like Icarus's headlight must have that night.

Icarus waited until he could feel Helios come up beside him.

"It's harder than doing a traditional reproduction," he started. "This canvas is from a painting a bit larger than this one, and it had to be cut down to size. But it's from the same region and same year that this was painted."

He dragged his fingertip along the edge of the canvas. "We stripped it down to the bottom, took off all the paint with turpentine and mineral spirits, then we washed it very gently and re-stretched it to frame."

"It took twenty days for my father to paint this. He's so quick, much quicker than I am. He uses many pictures taken with different light sources, brightness, and shade to figure out the true colors. It's easier with pieces that have a bit of fame because there's so many pictures taken of them."

He glanced at Helios, but Helios kept his eyes on the piece before them.

"After he's finished painting it like new, he checks my own photographs to assess the damages. All paintings have them. This one had sun damage, dust damage, general lacquer aging, crayon damage of course . . ."

"I was four," Helios murmured.

"It was a Malachite Crayola Gem Tone crayon. The color was released in 1994, but was permanently retired," Icarus said with a smirk. "He made me scour eBay until it turned up."

Helios finally turned to him. "That's insane."

Icarus shrugged. "To a thief, the work is worth it." He touched the crayon smear. "My dad replicated your drawings though. It would have been fun to be able to say I did, but I didn't."

"I would have believed you," Helios said, "if you'd lied."

Icarus hmmed.

"After he was done painting this, he shaded over it in a transparent gold and then covered that with a clear lacquer. A tinted lacquer would test positive for modern interaction if the painting was appraised. The only thing I did help with was adding the cracks. We put each one in with razor blades and X-Acto knives. That took four days."

"Then he dried the painting in a vacuum environment and dusted it with one layer of fuller's earth. I was supposed to add a second layer on location, but . . . well."

Icarus shrugged.

Helios touched the painting along the edge where Icarus's fingers had been. Tracing his path like a man in a desert.

"One of the others from this collection sold for one hundred million dollars," Icarus finished. "A Haystack by Monet."

"It sounds . . . harder to make a forgery than to make the original," Helios said, letting his arm fall to his side.

Icarus shrugged. "I guess. It's like two artworks in one. But it's not . . . worth anything. You could probably argue that it isn't even art."

"It's still beautiful."

Icarus shrugged. "It's a job. My job, sometimes."

Helios's eyes were hard and dark when he faced him. "That doesn't mean it's worthless."

STREAM

Helios's weight beside him in this bed felt like a stone pulling the mattress down.

If Helios was Celestina, he might have wrapped himself around Icarus, twined their arms and legs together, let Icarus shake until he drowned.

But he was not. There was space between them, careful and deliberate. And Helios's eyes were closed. He was being terribly polite.

"Helios," Icarus whispered.

"Hmm?"

"Can you do it again?"

Helios gazed at him for a while.

"What do you think about, when this happens to you?" he asked, first.

Icarus cringed. Nothing. He couldn't think of anything.

"It's . . . complicated."

"Have you ever let someone just touch the same spot over and over again? It might be different than what we did before." Helios propped himself up on his elbow and pushed his hair out of his face.

"No. We could . . . we could try that." Icarus turned on his side and offered Helios the inside of his wrist.

Helios let out a sigh, but the look on his face was inscrutable. Icarus didn't know what it meant.

Then, Helios licked the tip of his pointer and index fingers and pressed them to the center of Icarus's wrist.

"Gross," Icarus hissed reflexively, fighting the urge to tug his arm away.

Helios laughed dryly. "Many things are gross."

Like earlier, in the morning light, soft prickles shot up Icarus's arm. Then buzzing got brighter and rougher until he had to curl around his arm again, pull his knees up tight, wrap his other arm around his waist to withstand it.

Helios was steady, dragging his fingertips down just one inch before starting at the top again. Each time the sensation stopped it was like a vacuum until it began again, and the rhythm of it was beating behind his eyes.

Icarus knew he was breathing hard. He knew when it tipped over into whimpering.

"What are you thinking about?" Helios asked again.

"I . . . I can't," Icarus panted.

"Your eyes, when you're like this . . ." Helios murmured. "It's like watching you dream awake."

Icarus didn't know what to say to that, so he just pressed his face deeper into the pillow and tried to keep quiet.

"Can we try pressure?" Helios didn't wait. He stopped the soft stroking and rubbed his thumb hard into the same space.

Instead of increasing the feedback, it muted it. Icarus was finally able to catch his breath.

"Oh god . . . oh my god? I think that turns it off," he said, in wonder.

Helios hummed and rubbed the shivery feeling away until Icarus could feel the skin getting raw and his heart slowing back down.

"That's amazing," Icarus said. "I didn't even know—"

Helios dragged his fingers over the red patch of skin, soft like he had before, and Icarus shouted, doubled over, and snatched his arm out of Helios's reach. Something like pleasure lanced itself deep in the base of his spine and Icarus pushed himself to the edge of the bed to tremble it away.

"Make it stop again make it stop again make it stop again—" The words fell out of his mouth without his permission.

Helios grabbed Icarus's wrist tight with his whole hand.

Icarus fell still with a sob of relief.

"I'm sorry! I didn't know that would happen," Helios said, panicked.

"This shit is so fucking embarrassing." Icarus wiped his eyes with his other hand, and laughed, shivery and pained.

"It . . ." Helios took a deep breath. "It doesn't have to be, I don't think. It could be good if someone cared to try and understand it. And I want to try."

"But it's . . . gross." Icarus wanted to sink through the bed and down into the floor.

"It's not. But even if it was, some gross things can be good too," Helios said. He began letting go of Icarus's wrist, but Icarus stopped him.

Please.

Helios understood. He reached across the bed and carefully, carefully, pulled Icarus closer. And didn't let go.

HUE

"You are my strangest friend."

Luca had said this to Icarus once, closer to when they first met. He'd laughed it off then, but he was beginning to understand what Luca meant now. Helios was . . . weird. But in a fun way.

Helios woke up in the middle of Icarus sketching him and instead of complaining or calling Icarus names, he sat up, took off his shirt, and draped himself across the bed more attractively, letting his arm hang off the side. Fingers lax but delicately posed.

"How long have you been awake? Is this your first drawing of me or have I been asleep long enough for you to make more?" Helios asked.

"Third," Icarus said, leaning back in the child-size rocking chair he'd pulled from the corner of Helios's bedroom. "And it hasn't been long."

Helios grinned. "I've been drawn before, but I'm curious to know what you think I look like."

Icarus raised an eyebrow. "Given enough time, I could draw you exactly. Paint you in your colors."

Helios chuckled and dragged his knuckles across the dusty wood floor. "Hmm. What are my colors, then?"

Icarus stared at Helios hard. "In Pantone, your hair is PMS 717, mostly. You blush from PMS 705 to PMS 708. Your eyes are harder—they're PMS 4695 in this light, PMS 478 in the sun and PMS 440 at night in the dark."

Helios closed them for a moment, then sighed.

"That's hot and creepy at the same time."

Icarus laughed. "The inside of your mouth is PMS 178. . . ." He smirked, then went back to his drawing.

Helios made a series of offended and scandalized noises for Icarus to chuckle at, then settled back into his original pose.

"Since you like looking at me so much, are you finally feeling like watching me dance?" Helios asked.

Icarus had felt shy about asking. "Sure."

RUST

After they had cereal, Helios scampered back upstairs to "do something in the dance room" and told Icarus to "find his own fun."

So Icarus decided to start on dinner.

The inside of Helios's fridge was massive and filled with takeout containers. He gazed at them warily and resisted the desire to throw them away. If it was out of character for Helios to do so, it certainly wouldn't be good to disrupt that ecosystem for Mr. Black to discover upon his return.

He did manage to find some frozen pork in the freezer, a few shrimp, peas, a red pepper that had seen better days, half an onion, rice, oil, and some tomato paste. So he was intending to make something that should turn out a bit like paella.

He scrounged the kitchen for a bowl, a saucepan, and a cast-iron skillet and got started prepping ingredients. He defrosted the pork and shrimp in vinegar, salt, and water. Then, after an unusually difficult search, he found knives.

The pork needed to marinate in orange juice with salt, sugar, vinegar, and half of a taco seasoning packet he found in the back of their horribly lacking spice cabinet. The shrimp, he boiled until they were just turning pink, then popped back in the fridge.

He was planning to smoke the marinated pork in the cast-iron skillet on broil until the outside had a fair amount of char to it. But that should probably wait until they were ready to eat.

The rice he could do now. It was . . . definitely *not* how this was supposed to be done, but he dumped the rice, water, tomato paste, and a few Maggi cubes all into the same pot. Tasted the broth to make sure it was appropriately salty, then put it on to boil.

Then Icarus settled across from it all, at the kitchen table, and put his head in his hands.

This . . . house, felt homey the way his house did when Angus was gone. Not nearly as much, because it was impossible to make big houses really feel that way. But it was close, with Mr. Black gone and Helios here.

The rain had finally come in overnight and was persisting through the day. It was darker in here than it should be.

Icarus wondered if a younger Helios had ever sat in this room, maybe reading or coloring while his mom cooked dinner.

He looked at the stove and wondered whether Helios thought about what Icarus lived like, when he was gone.

EUPHORIA

Helios had leaned against the kitchen doorway to watch Icarus as he put away all his prep work for dinner. Didn't say a single thing, just stared in that meaningful way he did. When Icarus was finished, Helios nodded up the stairs.

The dance room was big. It was the length of Icarus and his dad's entire apartment with many individual mirrors tacked up against one side of the wall. It looked like it had never been intended to be a dance room but had hastily been transformed into one. The light in here was dim lamplight: dark where Icarus was sitting, bright in the front of the room where Helios was meant to dance.

Helios was fiddling with an old tape player in the corner.

"This piece was choreographed by Alvin Ailey for *The Lark Ascending* by Ralph Vaughan Williams," Helios said. "I'm going to do the girl part, because it's more interesting for a solo dance. Men's solo parts are mostly about jumping really high, which is fine. But I'm sure you'll like this better."

"I don't mind having to watch you jump around."

"*Getting* to, not *having* to. But shhh." Helios forced down a smile.

He settled into position. Feet arched, arms outstretched above his head, bent like a willow, strained and taut.

The tape crackled a bit, then swelled out with its rendition of the classical piece. Icarus folded his knees up so he could rest his chin on them, as Helios fluttered his arms and bowed, lark-like.

It was a terribly sad song, sweet and light despite it. Icarus's eyes tracked Helios's feet, thinking about the calluses and bandages. He hadn't known that men could do pointe.

Helios was wearing a T-shirt with the sleeves torn off, and athletic shorts over leggings that ended at the knee. He looked vaguely like he was about to play basketball, which would have been kind of funny, if it weren't stunning in its contrast.

Helios stretched and spun and reached out his hands, and now that Icarus could see his arms moving in the way they were meant to, he felt so foolish for ever thinking he could have beaten Helios at arm wrestling.

Helios was an athlete. Brilliant in motion, gold in the light of these mid-century modern lamps. It made Icarus want to sigh, long and wistful.

Suddenly, Helios stopped and turned to him.

"This is where the girl part ends and then there's supposed to be a lift and it turns into a couples dance," he said, panting. "It's a beautiful lift, too. You'd have loved it. I can show you later when I get out of here—"

"Can you lift me?" Icarus asked.

"Uh . . . probably?" Helios looked back at the tape player. The song was soaring into some kind of crescendo and it was feeling a bit loud for the space. He jogged over and turned it down very low until it was practically a whisper.

"I can definitely pick you up, but you have to be in a really specific position for a lift and you have to stay very stiff. I . . . won't let you hit the ground if you wiggle, but we could still get hurt."

Icarus shook his head. He wanted to know just how strong Helios was. He wanted to be a part of this. "I can do it. Show me how to stand."

Helios looked a bit doubtful, but he stood next to Icarus facing the mirrors and posed. He put his head back and flung his arms straight behind him at a gentle angle, then turned his feet out and lifted one knee with a foot arched sharply inward.

Icarus looked at him for a moment, then arranged his body the same way. He twisted his hips until he could feel them loosen enough for the turn out and pushed his foot until the ache felt right.

"Like this?"

Helios broke position to check Icarus's form. He circled him, correcting with soft touches.

"You've never done this before?" Helios asked.

"What? No, of course not," Icarus said crossly. "This is starting to hurt."

Helios made a sad sound. "Your turn out is perfect. Your arch is . . ."

"Are you jealous?" Icarus joked.

Helios didn't answer him.

"Usually you would run into this position and I would catch you, but I think we could do it the opposite way. You stay here and I'll run and catch you up."

"Okay."

"Watch yourself in the mirror," Helios said, backing away.

Helios waited a minute for the song to catch up, then Icarus heard the sound of pounding feet and then . . .

He was aloft.

STRAIN

Helios clamped his hands firmly beneath Icarus's arms, spanning the width of his ribs, so tight that it hurt. But Icarus was frozen, staring at himself in the collage of mirrors.

Head thrown back, arms bent and solid, but placed in exactly this way. *Arched* in exactly this way, he looked fragile and graceful and vulnerable in Helios's grasp.

He looked, for the first time in his life: pretty. Icarus stared back at himself desperately trying to sear this image into his mind.

Helios's chin was pressed to the cut of Icarus's stomach, using Icarus's own musculature for balance. Helios took the momentum of the lift and turned it into a spin so he could let Icarus down gently.

Icarus slid down Helios like a silk scarf falling from his shoulder until his feet were on solid ground. Helios was breathing steady, but Icarus was panting like he'd been running.

"How do you not get dizzy?" He laughed.

Helios still didn't look happy.

"I need to talk to you about something," he said, rushing to turn the music off. "Can you do this with your hand?"

Helios stuck his arm out and bent his thumb close to his arm.

Icarus did it too, a little farther than Helios could. "Yeah, why?"

Helios let out a sharp breath. "Do you know what Ehlers-Danlos syndrome is?"

Icarus shrugged. "No. Why?"

Helios rubbed his eyes. "Okay. Okay. EDS is a connective tissue disorder that impacts how flexible you are, and it has a lot of other side effects. Your turn out was . . . too extreme for someone who hasn't broken their body in for this. Sometimes . . ."

Helios paused like he was trying to figure out how to continue. "I've taught the little ones, a few times. At my school, we're taught how to pick up on signs that they might have something like this going on so we can inform the parents. A girl comes in who can do the front splits on her first try. A boy comes in with arms that bend in unusual ways . . . I just. There was probably never an opportunity for you to learn about this."

"What does it mean?" Icarus said. "What does it do to you? Is it bad?"

"It *hurts*, Icarus!" Helios cried.

"Oh."

"Do your hands hurt? Does it hurt when you climb the wall of my house? Does it hurt so much sometimes you need to take baths to make it stop?" He sounded frantic.

Yes, it did.

"It hurts all the time," Icarus said, starting to feel uncomfortable with how emotional Helios was getting. "Does it eventually kill you? If those are features of it, I think my dad might have it too."

Helios nodded and squatted on the floor, sitting on his heels. "That would make sense, it's genetic." He looked up at Icarus. "And no, it doesn't usually kill you, but it doesn't feel good. Your joints and connective tissues move that way because they're weaker than everyone else's. If you keep doing this you'll have to go to physical therapy, wear special rings and braces. You might have to do that stuff anyway."

Icarus looked down at Helios and thought about what he was saying. Thought about his father rubbing his wrists and the joints of his fingers, the braces he wore every day. He thought about how he liked to soak his own hands in the hottest water possible while washing dishes, the ache that sometimes woke him up at night.

Then he knelt on the floor next to him. Helios immediately hid his face in his own arms.

"I'm not going to stop climbing your wall until the year is over," Icarus said simply. "I've been doing it for almost six years. And that was without you being inside waiting for me."

"How could you do this? Your entire body must feel . . . must feel . . ." Helios's ears were bright red.

"It feels like an ache, everywhere. Like a good stretch gone too tight. I always thought it was because I was moving in ways that other people often didn't." Icarus chuckled. "EDS, huh."

Helios sniffed. "It might not be that specifically," he said wetly. "There's other kinds of connective disorders, but that one seems most likely."

"Dude, are you crying?"

"Shut up."

The water didn't bead on the unfinished wood floors. It just sank in and made the planks dark and spotted.

"Why does this mean so much to you?" Icarus asked, softly.

Helios took a shuddering breath and looked at him, eyes PMS 176, cheeks PMS 708.

"How should I feel, to know that coming to see me hurts you every time? That if we didn't meet, you might have gone your whole life not knowing? Fuck you, Icarus," he said, without heat. "Fuck you."

Icarus knew Helios was upset, but he wanted to grin and grin and grin. His heart sang at the fact that something meaningless like his discomfort brought Helios to tears. No one had ever felt that way about him and it was so fresh and new.

"I'll keep coming if he keeps you in here another year," Icarus declared.

"Fuck you."

"And another year and another year."

Helios pushed Icarus over with one strong arm and Icarus collapsed onto the floor next to him, giggling.

"You're such an asshole."

Icarus laughed until the feeling centered itself in his chest, warm and comfortable.

"If he lets you out, though, that will be the last time I ever come back here," Icarus admitted.

Helios pulled his arm down and gosh he was so pink and splotchy. He looked terrible. He looked delicious.

Icarus gazed up at him until Helios reached over with one finger and dragged it down the bridge of his nose.

"You grew up in here, didn't you," Helios whispered.

Icarus's smile faltered.

"This is my home, but I didn't grow up here. You've spent your whole life in this house," Helios said. He caressed the tip of Icarus's nose again and Icarus shivered.

"Have you ever seen the grand baths?" Helios asked.

He did it once more and Icarus arched up into his touch, helpless. "What is there to steal in a bath, Helios?" he purred.

"Nothing. I'll take you then. After dinner."

FOAM

The back of his neck prickled with the weight of Helios's gaze as Icarus shredded charred pork. He mixed the meat with the rice and transferred everything to the deep saucepan. Drizzled it with oil. Turned the flame on low. Covered it. Gripped the edge of the counter and let his head fall until his chin touched his chest.

"I want you to tell me when something you do hurts you," Helios said behind him.

"All of it does, in its own way," Icarus murmured into the soft fabric of his gray sweater.

Helios made a noise of disgust. "You know what I'm talking about, Icarus."

Icarus rolled his eyes and glared at Helios over his shoulder.

"What are you gonna do about it? You gonna do everything for me? You gonna come home with me and do my chores and do sports for me in gym class? Just . . . leave it alone. We can't do anything about it right now."

"If I was at home," Helios started, "I'd buy you rings to stop your fingers from aching. The only towels you'd use would be cashmere. Did you know people with EDS sometimes have sensitive skin? Not as sensitive as yours, but, well . . . " Helios laughed dryly. "Now that I'm putting things together, that sign should have been more obvious."

Icarus turned around completely at that, but said nothing.

"You would sleep when you want to sleep. No light would touch you when your head hurt. I would do all the chores. You would only move if it . . .

if it made you happy," Helios whispered. He scratched his nails across the wood, light, but agitated.

"I could . . . carry you . . ." He trailed off.

"You've only known me for three months," Icarus said.

Helios's eyes were very dark now. He brushed his fingers through his red hair and leaned his cheek on his palm.

"I know you work hard. I know you're loyal and talented. You're funny and the way your brain works surprises me every time we talk. I know you don't have to be here, but you are. I know that it meant something for you to bring me coffee. I know free climbing up the side of a building regularly isn't something to joke about. And now I know that it *hurt*. I know what you look like when you're sad, when you're scared, and when you're coming undone," Helios replied. "It could have been three days."

Icarus felt like he was about to fall to his knees. But he didn't.

"Why do you say things like that to me? How did you learn to talk like that?" He turned from Helios and opened the lid of the paella just so he'd have something to do with his hands. The room filled with fragrant steam.

"I know what to say when it's important." Helios stood up to begin setting the table. "I rehearse it."

SATURNALIA

The grand baths were like nothing Icarus had seen in his entire life. Cream tile from floor to ceiling, like a Roman bathhouse, mosaic in red, brown, onyx, jade, and gold.

The overhead was bright. But Helios turned it down until it was just dim enough to see, and turned on a couple lamps instead.

The bath itself was a circle nearly fifteen feet across. There were eight brass spigots all around the edge, and when Helios turned the knob by the ladder, they all turned on at the same time.

"Who designed this room?" Icarus asked.

Helios smiled. "My mom. She's an ancient history buff. There's more stuff in this style in our house, but nothing this crazy. We could never afford to build it in New York, much less fill it up with water. No one ever took me in here as a kid, so I didn't even know this room existed until I stumbled upon it while snooping around my first week."

"What is your mom like?" Icarus asked.

Helios grinned. "She's fun and nice. She'd love you if you guys ever met. She's nothing like my dad. I can take you to meet her when this is all over if you want."

Icarus shrugged, then leaned to look down at the edge, surprised at how fast the tub was filling.

"This is crazy."

Helios stepped out of the room and returned with some black bathroom towels and a few bottles. Icarus sat on the edge of the tub with his pants rolled up, as Helios tossed some oils and eucalyptus leaves in the water.

"The knob by the ladder controls the temperature. It's a bit stiff so pull hard. You won't break it," Helios said. "When you're done, you can just leave it as it is and I'll come and rake out the leaves or whatever. In the bathroom next door there's more bath stuff, so if you want anything feel free to raid it. I'm the only one who comes in here."

Helios scratched his neck and stood there, watching as the water got closer to the top.

"Is there anything else you need before I go?" he asked.

Icarus kicked the water gently.

"Can you stay?"

Many emotions flew across Helios's face in quick succession before he settled on something like resignation.

"Okay."

TAZIENKI PARK

It was less frightening than many things, to be naked in this room.

Icarus put his clothes in a neat stack against the wall and slipped easily into the bath. It was a little over five feet deep, good for standing in. The water was warm enough for him to gasp on contact.

He looked up at Helios, who had his back to him. Helios seemed to be having some kind of struggle. He had the large bath towel draped over his shoulders as he got undressed, kicking his pants messily to the side to keep a firm grip on the cloth. Even holding it close with one hand as he wrestled his shirt over his head.

It was curious.

Icarus ducked under the water and scratched his fingers through his hair, then popped up, wiping the drops from his eyes.

At the very moment when he could see, Helios dropped his towel and moved to quickly get into the water.

"Wait."

Helios froze. Crouched on the edge, his arm tight across his chest, knees pressed too close together. He looked scared.

Icarus crossed the basin in a few short strides until they were near.

"I want to see you," Icarus said plainly.

Misery, then determination, and Helios slowly stood with his toes at the edge of the pool.

From this angle he was as large as a god, backlit and gleaming, goose-bumped hair glowing ember. He was hard in some places and curiously soft in others. The curve of his chest was unusual, his hips were trim from dance but still, unusual. He looked different, where he should look the same as Icarus. Not like a girl, exactly. But . . . different. Unique.

Icarus's gaze passed Helios's shoulders and he stared up into his face. He could see shame there starting to turn to defiance, then into anger. So, he placed a hand on Helios's ankle. Slid it up until he was holding Helios's calf. Ignored the way it made him feel and persisted.

"There is a statue like you in Warsaw," he said.

He wondered at the picture they made.

Icarus dark and small, in the water, head tilted back in devout wonder. Helios, red like the sun, gold in the light, standing above him.

"You were made the same way as the angels."

Icarus would know.

Helios looked away from him, still nervous. But he stood there, like he wasn't sure what to do.

"I can't be the only person who's seen you," Icarus breathed.

Helios shrugged and put his arm across his chest again. "I used to get around a lot. People like it, if that's what they're looking for."

"Did you think I wouldn't like it? Fuck, you're trembling." Icarus was starting to feel bad for asking for this. "Come here. Get in."

Helios crouched immediately. Icarus took a step back, let him slide into the water. But he stayed close. Close enough to feel the heat radiating off of Helios's humiliated skin.

"Intersex," Helios said, stubbornly. "I'm not trans. I was born like this, though it shouldn't matter either way."

"There's no one to fight here. It's just me." Icarus raised a hand and traced the edge of Helios's shoulder in the air above it. Near enough that water dripped from his fingers to Helios's skin, but not enough to touch.

He reached, stroking the warmth of steam across the dark hidden place of Helios's under arm, then across his collar and up to his throat. Helios tilted his head back, giving Icarus more room.

"I didn't think you'd hate it, it's just . . ." Helios huffed.

Icarus hummed, tracing the shell of Helios's ear, then skittering his fingernails over the sharp heavy curve of Helios's jaw. Helios fell quiet, but the violent flush was fading from his skin.

"You think I'd know art, and not know this?" Icarus said.

He pressed closer, still. "There have been men like you before we had words for it."

And even though it hurt, Icarus stood on his toes to gain an extra inch, and brushed his lips against Helios's cheek.

Helios cried out.

Lifted his hands to hold Icarus, forgetting himself.

Icarus caught Helios's wrists in his grasp before he could, and trailed his mouth across Helios's face. Soft, staccato kisses, because they were easy and he knew he was untalented.

Helios's mouth, when he found it again, was sticky and hot. He wondered, in the grip of madness, whether his own mouth felt the same.

Icarus let Helios fall back against the wall of the pool, to look at him hazy eyed, flushed and waiting. Breathing fast. But Icarus pulled away and let the cool air fill the void between them.

"I haven't gotten to shower in two days and I really want to. After, we can float a bit if you want."

Helios let out a shuddery noise.

"Was that your first kiss?" he asked.

Icarus turned around and started walking determinedly toward the bar of soap Helios had left on the edge of the tub.

"Icarus, seriously, was that your first kiss?! That shouldn't be allowed! You're not supposed to be good at it! You're supposed to be slobbery and gross. Ugh, fuck you," Helios ranted.

Icarus's laughter echoed off the tiles, filling up the room.

BUTTERFLY

Even though there was no other place *less* like the woods than this, Icarus thought about Celestina's pond: drifting with her together and apart.

He'd scrubbed until all of his skin felt brand new, and watched Helios wash his hair as though it was a performance. Then he drifted on his back until they made contact.

Icarus noticed that the shock of touch was lessening the more of it he had. The sensitivity was still there, but it wasn't a roar unless the experience was something new. The brush of their shoulders in the water felt striking enough to make his heart race, but the hand Helios outstretched and wrapped around his own was firm and ran a comfortable pleasure up his arm.

Icarus opened his eyes and took a bleary glance down Helios's body from this impossible angle. He was all swells and valleys with water lapping at the sides, like a great island. The lamplight gleamed off the tracker around his ankle. There were more small healing bruises beneath his clothes than Icarus had imagined.

"Can I draw you like this?"

Helios was quiet for long minutes, thinking.

"No," he said, finally. "But not never. Maybe in a few years."

SILENT

The night was blue again, in Helios's room. The moon must be close to full for the shadows to stretch so far across the ground.

This was the closest they'd ever been. Helios was tucked beneath Icarus's chin, forehead pressed against his chest. His breath warming the hand Icarus had draped over his own side to lie between them. Helios held Icarus's wrist; firm like he had the previous night so that he could do it as long as they liked.

"Can I tell you why I'm here now?" Helios whispered.

"You don't have to if you don't want to. I don't need to know," Icarus said. He uncurled his fingers until they brushed Helios's lips.

Helios kissed them softly, but shook his head.

"I should," he said into the dark. "It's been long enough that it's started to feel like lying and I don't want it to anymore. I came straight here from rehab. Things got out of control."

"What was it for?"

"Opioids," Helios confessed immediately. "For about a year. Then methadone treatment for a year after that. Then I relapsed. I had been six months sober."

It felt like a stone had landed in Icarus's chest, and he fought the desire to jolt them out of this comfortable position so he could sit up and face Helios properly.

"What happened?" he asked carefully.

Helios shivered. "Partying at first. It's . . . when your friends are doing things . . . after a while, living that way becomes normal. It's worse if you're responsible with it. It takes people a long time to notice something is wrong if you're showing up to school, keeping up with your grades, keeping up with dance, working out. But my mom noticed. Eventually. And it stopped.

"I lost a few friends who didn't like that I wasn't partying much anymore. Who thought I was abandoning them. But after methadone treatment, things were looking up. I felt like I was in control of my life again. Then, I had a friend come in from out of town. Someone I was really close to back in the bad days, and I thought . . . I don't know. I missed him."

Helios sighed. He let go of Icarus's wrist so he could wrap his arm around his own stomach.

"We got coffee and coffee turned into lunch, and lunch turned into dinner, and dinner turned into drinks, and drinks turned into clubbing, and then things got out of control again. It was only one night.

"Then I woke up and I was in a house I'd never been to, surrounded by people I didn't know, and he was dead next to me. And I was dying too. And I was fucked up and I was scared. So, I called my mom."

Helios sat up. He pushed his hand through his hair and rubbed his eyes. Icarus sat up too and shifted until they were pressed together, knee to knee.

"There were . . . police involved. I was in the hospital for days. His mom, Roger's mom, came there and screamed at me like I was the one who did it to him. Even though I had been clean and Roger was in active addiction—but I couldn't even blame her. I was too busy sweating and hurting and feeling guilty and ashamed. It felt disgusting—I was disgusting."

"You're not disgusting," Icarus interrupted.

"I was. Icarus, you weren't there," Helios said.

Icarus stayed quiet.

"Anyway, when I'd finally sweated everything out, my mom showed up with my dad to check me out of the hospital and back into rehab for a week.

Since the police were involved, and I'm a minor, she had to have him come and sign some paperwork. I hadn't seen him in almost ten years . . ."

"When he finally arrived, he . . . hit me. Then, he told me what was about to happen to me and then dropped me off at rehab. The day I was discharged, he sent escorts to pick me up and fly me here. I just remember my mom standing next to him in the hospital crying and crying."

Helios stopped talking and stared up at the ceiling.

"I've always been a disappointment."

Icarus couldn't say that Helios wasn't, he couldn't say it was going to be okay because he didn't know if it would be, he didn't have a paragraph of loving words that he'd rehearsed the way Helios did. He only had the truth.

"I want you anyway."

Then, softer, "I'll want you still, all the same."

Helios sobbed and threw his hands down in his lap.

"Do you even understand what that means?" he spat.

Icarus didn't know the particulars. But he didn't like the way Helios was talking about himself.

"Stop being mean to yourself. You just lost a friend and you're basically in jail. This entire day has been extremely stressful and we're learning way too much about each other way too quickly. But that's fine. If we have to do a speed run getting to know each other that's fine. I don't think you're disgusting. I just think something really bad happened to you, and you're dealing with it, and you're trying your best. Are you trying your best?"

"Yeah, but—" Helios started.

Icarus shook his head. "There's nothing more than that, then. The only thing we can do is try our fucking best and pray that it's good enough for everyone around us. This is good enough for me. In the future, if something happens, we'll figure it out. But right now, this is fine. It's *fine*."

Helios was quiet. He rubbed his face again.

"Hey, hey, look at me," Icarus said. "Do you have any more horrible secrets to spring on me, because we have about two hours before midnight and if we're trying to do this all today I'm going to need a cigarette or something. Do you have wings? Is your favorite food licorice? Do you have a foot fetish?"

Helios snorted.

"Are you afraid of clowns? Do you sing horribly in the shower? Come on, give me something to work with here, man." Icarus nudged Helios with his shoulder, hard. "I'm grasping at straws."

Helios began to laugh. "No no, there's nothing."

"Oh no, it's gotta be something," Icarus said darkly. "We've already gallivanted through medical trauma, abuse, addiction, my weird joints, extracurricular genders, almost getting off from your touching my face, a dance recital, Roman baths in the middle of Michigan—"

Helios was laughing hard now.

"There's nothing else!" He gazed up at Icarus, eyes crinkled with fondness.

"Are you sure?" Icarus demanded.

"I'm sure!"

"Okay, good. I have a surprise for you."

SWALLOW

Helios looked at the $800 bottle of wine Icarus pulled out of his back-pack.

He rubbed the last of the tears from his face and shrugged helplessly.

"I can't have that. I . . ."

"Oh—oh shit. Well. It was gonna be a gift or whatever . . . Do you want to go pour it out with me instead, then?" Icarus asked, shaking the bottle at him like that was more exciting than drinking it.

Helios went downstairs to grab a bottle opener and they reunited in the bathroom next door.

"I had to buy this from my dad, otherwise I knew he wouldn't give it to me. He's a bit of a tight ass about anything besides art, art supplies, and clothes," Icarus admitted, while Helios twisted the cork out.

"We should really make a Horrible Dads club. I'm sure it won't be hard to find members." Helios tossed the opener with the cork still attached into the sink.

"It smells good."

"It should, it cost me almost a grand."

"*What*?" Helios shouted.

Icarus grabbed the bottle and upended it into the sink before anything else could be said about it. They watched the wine gurgle out in spurts, red, rich, and fragrant.

Icarus turned on the faucet and rinsed it away. Then he swirled a bit of water in the bottle, poured it out, and stuck the cork back in.

Before Icarus could turn to head back into the bedroom, Helios caught him by the cheek and kissed him on the forehead, long and sweet.

"Thank you. This was . . . a very nice gift."

NIGHTSHADE

Helios fell asleep eventually, but Icarus couldn't.

He watched the rise and fall of Helios's chest and thought about the horrors he'd heard tonight.

He didn't know if he could handle the responsibility of this, but he wanted to try. Besides, Icarus was sure that someone else, in this same position—hearing about the life *he* lived—would be awake while Icarus fell into a fitful sleep.

It didn't feel fair.

Earlier, Helios had thought hard about what he would do to make Icarus comfortable. Icarus could do the same. Together, they could do the same.

He'd save up more money. Their house would be sober. They'd pick friends who respected that and ditch the ones that didn't. Maybe they would live somewhere more rural. Not in the middle of nowhere, because that might actually be worse. But maybe a township or something. Somewhere with a detox center nearby . . . a good hospital.

If they tried, maybe it would be okay.

Even if a real relationship didn't work out, they could look out for each other. Help each other heal from everything that happened before they went their own ways.

Icarus was almost eighteen. He'd be a man in less than a month. He trusted himself to figure it out.

WHISPER

The morning found him soft and bright, curled toward the edge of the bed.

Icarus stretched and yawned and turned over to find Helios awake and looking at him. Helios's eyes darted away quickly.

Fear, again.

Icarus had never had someone look at him like this so often. Like he was bigger than he was, like he was dangerous.

He reached across the space and brushed his thumb against Helios's cheek. Skittered his fingers over the arch of Helios's eyebrow, brushed his wrist against Helios's jaw as he pulled his hand back and away.

PANT

They kissed again in the pantry.

Helios apparently having reached the limit of his politeness and composure somewhere between Icarus putting milk on the table and getting a box of cornflakes.

He pushed Icarus farther into the dark warm room, begged him down to the floor, and clambered into his lap, long legged and heavy, asking to be touched.

He ran the bridge of his nose up the side of Icarus's neck, teased his teeth against Icarus's ear, and flicked the tip of his tongue at Icarus's bottom lip until Icarus caught him with a firm hand on the back of his neck.

Shook him once. "Less." Instead of more.

He leaned up into Helios's space and brushed their mouths together. Holding Helios back until he keened. Icarus was sure Helios wanted something much more elaborate, but this alone made Icarus feel raw, feel flayed open. Helios scrunched his hands into Icarus's shirt like he understood that Icarus couldn't take gestures bigger than this and Icarus was grateful.

So he cupped his hand behind Helios's head and lowered him backward down to the floor.

"Give me anything," Helios asked.

"I'm trying." He thought a bit, then curled his arm under Helios's thigh, lifting to rest it on his hip. Shoved his knee beneath him, until they were twisted like girls.

Helios grinned. "Really?"

Icarus rolled his spine like the crack of a whip and Helios slammed his head back on the granite.

"Stop underestimating me."

He turned Helios inside out. Rested his forehead on Helios's knee until Helios clawed at the floor and said a litany of beautiful and rude things about him.

Then, because he was technically still a guest, Icarus cleaned up his mess.

CHECK

Icarus had never spent so much time with another person in his life, so he begged off to be by himself for a while to recharge. He walked through the backyard and to the edge of the trees while Helios went back to sleep.

Icarus stuck his feet in the fence and climbed over to sit on the wood. He pulled out his phone and texted Celestina:

> **Icarus:** How are you? Anything interesting happen in class?

He didn't even have to wait a moment:

> **Celestina:** !!!

> **Celestina:** We're ok how are you?? We had lunch with Sorrel! Me and Luca! He wants to have us over for tea this week too. He's so cute.

> **Icarus:** haha. That sounds really good. I'm glad to hear you guys are hanging out.

> **Celestina:** Yeah yeah yeah, matchmaker. How's your trip 👀

Icarus: It's . . . going really good. I'm happy. How is Luca?

Celestina: He misses you, keeps going on and on about how gym is boring when you're not there.

Icarus smirked.

Icarus: tell him to keep his pants on, I'll be back on Monday.

Celestina: mmmkayyy I'll tryyyyyy. I'm about to start a test. Try to text more often. I'll talk to you later byyyyyyyyyeeeeeeee. 💝

Icarus turned off his phone again and pressed the hunk of metal to his chest.

COMET

It was just a window, just a glimpse out of this enchanted place, but it sobered him a bit, rubbed the dust from his eyes.

When Icarus got back to the house, he asked Helios to help him clean his presence from this place. To wipe out two sets of footprints on the rugs in each room. To wash all their dishes. To take out all the trash from any room they'd been inside.

They scrubbed out the Roman baths together too, after Helios mentioned he didn't usually use the scented oil when he was alone, and the smell of it was still lingering in the walls.

Icarus packed up the drawings he'd done of Helios, packed up the errant clothing spilling from his backpack. Compressed his climbing gear as much as possible, and tucked it deep under Helios's bed.

They ate the leftovers of what they'd cooked that week for dinner, hand-washed the containers, dried them, and put them away in the cabinets.

Icarus even went by the white plush couch and picked any hairs he'd left on it from its fibers, one by one.

The torque called to him, from its home in the dark, and again Icarus turned from it. He could not answer until he was ready to never come back here again.

HOME STAR

"There are places in this house where my dad rarely goes. We can hang out there so it doesn't mess up our work." Helios held his hand, pulling him along, the way Celestina liked to. Icarus loved how it felt so solid and familiar.

Helios tugged him up the stairs and past his bedroom, through a door that opened into another small wing of rooms. He turned on the light in the room closest to the door to reveal its dark red walls, comfy beanbag chairs, a massive globe, and a messy scattering of books.

Icarus toed at one of the beanbag chairs and it let out a visible puff of dust.

"Oh. I guess that's to be expected," Helios said. "Whatever, that's not where I was planning for us to sit anyway."

He led Icarus to the huge globe and fiddled with the side until it opened up, letting down a small staircase. Inside was a little bench with a bit of cushion on the back, just large enough to fit three people. Closed inside the globe as it was, the bench wasn't at all dusty.

"It's a model of the Atwood Sphere. They have one in Chicago at the planetarium, but the outside of theirs isn't painted like a globe, it's just silver," Helios explained, ushering Icarus inside. "Grab that strap so we can pull the door closed."

As the stairs went up, the inside of the globe got darker and darker until it was pitch-black when it latched.

"Whoa," Icarus whispered.

There were pinpricks all over the steel. Little dots of light from the room around them that—in the dark of the Atwood Sphere model—looked like stars.

"It's a sky map," Helios explained. "There are six hundred and ninety-two holes cut into it. My mom had it made when she was pregnant because she couldn't go outside much. It's not the real thing, but it's almost as good."

"This is incredible. I wish my dad could see this."

Icarus felt the air shift and understood that he was being looked at, though it was really too dark to tell.

"What's your dad like?" Helios asked quietly.

Icarus shrugged though he knew Helios couldn't see it. "He's like me, I suppose. He's shyer, though, and a bit more . . . stern? He's hard to please, but I can usually manage to do it. He focuses more on his work than anything else." Icarus looked up at the stars. "I get the feeling that he's a shadow of the person he once was. A person I've never met."

"What do you mean?"

Icarus grinned. "You know how every so often you'll meet like a teacher or some other adult and you can tell that they were like . . . really cool in college. Just really get the vibe that they were a handful and then eventually cooled off?"

"The 'I used to smoke a lot of weed' vibe?"

Icarus laughed. "Kind of! I mean, there are other versions of it, but yeah. My dad gives off this vibe that he used to be really happy and interesting once upon a time, but it was a long time ago and now 'interesting' is all he has left."

He shifted around until he could feel Helios's breath on his face.

"I know he loves me but it's more like a master and an apprentice situation than a dad. Not at all like I assume your mom loves you. He used to let me walk around by myself at night when I was like twelve, which is fucking ridiculous."

"Wow."

"Right now he thinks I'm on vacation, barely asked me where I was going."

Helios shifted until his head was on the bench by Icarus's thigh. His legs were propped up on the wall of the sphere. Icarus could see his position in the void left without stars, feel he was there by the dusting of hair near his arm. Helios turned his face to press into Icarus's elbow in the new firm way they'd learned worked for him.

"You said . . . the other day, that after I'm let out of here, you would never come back to this house. Does your father know?" Helios asked.

Icarus reached across his lap and curled his fingers into Helios's hair.

"Not yet, but he will."

"What will you do?"

Icarus sighed. Now was as good a time as any.

"I want to go to school, but I might start working immediately if anyone will have me. In the short term, though, I was wondering if you wanted to come with me?"

It was quiet for longer than was comfortable.

"Where?" Helios asked. He sounded sad.

"Anywhere that will have us. Anywhere I can work and you can dance." Icarus tugged Helios's hair gently by the root. "We can figure out the logistics some other time, but I wanted to offer. We don't even have to stay in this country if there's anywhere you want to travel to."

Helios arched back, following the grip of Icarus's hand.

"I don't want you to feel like . . . You don't have to feel responsible for me. I can handle myself, Icarus, I don't want you to feel bad."

"I need to look at you while we're having this conversation," Icarus interrupted. He unlocked the sphere's door and gently lowered the stairs.

Helios looked up at him from the bench, legs still propped against the wall.

"Helios, we share history," Icarus continued. "I don't feel *bad* for you, I feel like we're similar. I like waking up to you with me. Is it bad to want that all the time? Is it selfish for me to want to know that you're away from your dad in a way that matters? To know that you're okay because I'll see you every day? We don't have to *be* together to live together. I was going to leave this town soon anyway and I can't imagine planning to leave and just ditching you here."

Helios took a moment to digest that.

"I want—" Helios swallowed hard. "I want you to stop acting like you're not an option. For me. That way. Just because I have experience doesn't mean I wouldn't be faithful. To you."

He spoke in fits and starts, like each phrase cost him dearly. Icarus scooted toward the edge of the bench as Helios sat up to face him properly.

"Unless. That's not. What you—"

"Helios." Icarus placed his hands around Helios's face, pushed his thumbs into the soft warm space beneath his ears. "Helios, would you like to be with me, and come to live by my side?"

"Yes, I'll come," Helios breathed, eyebrows knitting with emotion.

Icarus grinned. "Will you brighten my house with your light, Helios? Will you bring your heat to my hearth? Do you need me to say things poetically for you to take me seriously? Because I will."

"Okay, you can stop now," Helios laughed. "You love ruining intense moments."

"I do," Icarus confessed sweetly, pulling his hands back to tuck them under his arms and stop their shaking.

"Come on. I want to show you something else."

ROUGH

At the back of the red wing there was another storage room, not dissimilar to the one in Mr. Black's personal wing.

Unlike Mr. Black's, which was a cyclonic mess, this one was more organized. It was just very densely packed. Large metal shelves of paint and supplies lined the wall; canvases were stacked into unwieldy piles. The larger canvases were practically slipping, held up only by a crate of notebooks.

"It was her studio," Helios said, dragging a hand across the top of a jar of paintbrushes. "My mom was an art major like your dad. I think they met before our dads did actually, but not by a lot."

"Cool. So is this mostly old work?" Icarus asked. "Does she still do this?"

There were a few unfinished landscapes around. They weren't anything to write home about. Helios's mom was an average painter.

"Not really. The stuff on the walls is older work, but I'm sure the rest of it is from right before we moved out," Helios replied. "But that's not what I wanted to show you."

He paused. "Please don't be mad," he said, softer.

Icarus followed him to the very back of the room. There was a desk stacked with notebooks, a door that was cracked open to reveal a small bathroom, and in the corner across from the desk, a large canvas covered with muslin next to a small stool.

The canvas was one of the biggest Icarus had ever seen outside a museum. The hairs on his neck stood on end.

"What is this, Helios?" he asked, but Icarus already knew.

How could he not?

Helios reached for the muslin, but Icarus put up a hand. He closed his eyes and took a deep breath. Then he strode across the space and pressed his forehead to Helios's shoulder.

"I'm not angry at you. Not for this."

Then he stepped away, grasped the muslin, and tore it down.

The canvas was . . .

Anyone could still see that it had once been breathtaking.

The splashes of acid had stripped away most of the middle of the canvas, even forming a few holes big enough for Icarus to crawl through. But it wasn't a perfect job.

Angus hadn't brushed it evenly over the whole thing, he had thrown it recklessly. So you could still see the sky, the trees, and the water at the edges. It looked like someone had burned a hole in the world.

Icarus backed away from it, disturbed. He accidentally bumped into the desk behind him, unable to tear his eyes away. Notebooks and loose paper spilled to the floor. Helios crouched to pick them up.

Icarus tore his eyes away from the painting that had taken his mother's life, to apologize and help, but found himself looking back at his own face.

"What the fuck?" Helios mumbled.

Instead of picking up the drawings, Helios spread them out wider to look at them. "It's you."

"It's my father," Icarus whispered. "Your mom was drawing him."

BURN

"What the fuck . . ." Helios breathed. "What the fuck."

He muttered it over and over as they pulled out more and more pictures of Angus. Pictures of him painting, pictures of him laughing. Pictures of him by the water or reclining on the same sofa that sat downstairs. Pictures of only his eyes, only his mouth, only his hands.

It was worship, Icarus knew. But he didn't say it out loud.

Helios's mom had drawn Angus Gallagher with such longing, it was obvious and embarrassing.

Drawn the wrinkles next to his eyes like she wanted to run her fingers over them. Drawn his tired bruised gaze like she wanted it to look back at her forever. Icarus's own features romanticized, his Roman nose, his crooked grin, the way his ears stuck out too much. He remembered the dance, the lift from the other day and wondered—violently—if this beautiful creature was what Helios saw when he looked at him.

"Was she stalking him?" Helios pushed the notebook to the side with disgust and no small amount of fear. "This is so creepy."

"I think . . . she was in love with him." Icarus picked up a picture where his dad looked mischievous. An expression he had never seen on his dad's face in his entire life.

"She was in love with him, quietly, I think," Icarus continued. "Because there is no art of your mother in my house, but there are a thousand paintings of mine."

Icarus looked behind him at the half-dissolved painting and then at the stool next to it.

He let the drawing fall from his hand and pulled the stool to the center of the canvas and sat in it. The painting loomed above him, impossible, like a thousand-yard stretch. Angus must have cried to see so many inches before him.

"What would you do, if I was sitting here every day?" Icarus asked.

Helios was still on his knees.

"You couldn't touch me; you couldn't even look at me too hard. And I was in love and I was in pain and I was working fast, frantic, and you loved me. And it wasn't appropriate to."

Icarus turned to pick up another drawing. A different one of his father's face half turned, arm outstretched, his jaw and back and wrists, strong and delicate as he knew his own were.

"This is fucked up, Helios, but you should try to be kind to her about it," he finished.

Helios climbed to his feet and flew down upon Icarus with terrible purpose. Kissing him hard, and fast, harder than Icarus would have liked to allow. But the ringing in his ears and the jangle of his nerves left him too helpless from the onslaught to protest.

"Be kind?" Helios said, between bites. "Fuck, Icarus. She probably *named* me for you, and you're worried about me being *kind*?"

Helios shoved a hand under Icarus's shirt, scrambling to get closer. Winding his arm behind Icarus's back and pulling him, shoving him, pushing a thigh between his, like he had the right to do it.

"I was made for you; I was born for you, and you're still standing before me acting like you're not worthy," Helios hissed, ignoring Icarus's whimpers. "Questioning your looks like it would ever matter. Even if you *were* ugly I wouldn't care, I wouldn't care."

He bit Icarus's throat, licked a hot line up to Icarus's ear, sucked his earlobe into his mouth and Icarus couldn't make a sound. He was blind, from this. A raw nerve echoing with each scrape against it. He couldn't even breathe.

"Climbing into my house, into my bed, touching everything except for me. I was yours before we even met and I'll be yours until we die," Helios continued against the curve of Icarus's neck and Icarus was helpless, lost in the sharp fantasy of such a thing.

Helios sounded like he was a second from tears, but his hands were broad against Icarus's back. He'd lost the fight against discipline and was picking Icarus up off the floor, wrapping his legs around his waist.

"If you're such a good thief, then why haven't you stolen me yet?" The words tore themselves from him and Icarus didn't know.

He wanted to tell him, wanted to cry out that if Helios was made for him, then Icarus had learned to steal just for this. The years of agony and loneliness were worth it, just for *this*. But he couldn't make a sound.

Icarus's eyes rolled back in his head and he scrambled for something to hold on to. An anchor. He grasped the side of the shelf nearest to them and a bottle dropped to the floor.

"Helios?"

Helios tore himself away from Icarus so fast and violently that he slammed into the shelf beside them. Bottles of paint rained down, plastic bouncing and rolling; glass shattered and sent color across the floor like an arc.

Icarus and Helios looked at the door, then back at each other, panting and terrified.

Mr. Black was home early.

WHOLE

"What was that noise?"

Mr. Black was headed up the stairs.

Icarus looked helplessly at his only exit. In order to get back to his stuff, he would have to go out into the main hall to duck into another wing. He couldn't do that without passing Mr. Black, or at least being seen.

"Into the bathroom," Helios said urgently. "There's a window there. Come back for your stuff later."

Helios wrenched the door open and pushed Icarus inside. As Icarus went, he snatched another drawing off the floor and shoved it in his pocket.

Icarus tugged at the window, but it was sticking. He could probably get it open but definitely not quietly enough while Mr. Black was in the room. So, instead, he just stood there shaking, listening to the sound of paper being hastily shuffled as Helios tried to clean.

"Why are you in here?" Mr. Black shouted.

"I'm sorry!" Helios cried. "Don't come in, there's glass!"

The sound of things crashing filled the room from the front to the back of the room where they were, as Mr. Black crossed it.

"Please, I'm sorry!" Helios begged.

Icarus could tell the moment Mr. Black reached Helios from the hysteria in his screams. Icarus crouched down near the ground and pressed his palms into his eyes, trying desperately not to cry. His back was wet with sweat.

"You've ruined everything," Mr. Black hissed, and Helios sobbed.

Icarus could hear him scrabbling on the floor. Hear the crunch of glass, hear the breath Helios choked out as Mr. Black's fist connected with his skin. It got quiet and Icarus's heart stumbled.

He put his hand on the doorknob.

"No. Nonononononononono."

Mr. Black was whispering something to Helios and Icarus couldn't hear it.

"No, *please!*" Helios shrieked and there was a terrible racket as Mr. Black dragged Helios across the floor, glass and all. Icarus pressed himself against the door and sobbed silently. Curling his fingers into the wood.

"—ish I could just go. I wish I could just go. *Just go.*" Icarus's eyes snapped open. Helios was talking to him.

He took one last beat to listen then followed orders, wrenching the window open with a whine.

This was the third floor. Normally, he'd be anxious about climbing down without his gear—without his shoes. But adrenaline is something special. He scampered over the side of Helios's house like it was what he was made for, and he sprinted down the sidewalk in his socks. He didn't look back.

He just fled.

WEEDS

Icarus's socks were torn to shreds by the time he made it to his street.

He collapsed into his front yard, gasping.

He started to climb up the stairs, but his throat tightened and he ran back down them to vomit neatly into the hedge.

Then, he clung to the side of the building, brick cutting into his hands, and cried like a child.

HOUSE

Icarus didn't have his keys so he was forced to knock.

It took almost twenty minutes, but eventually Angus came to the door. He took in Icarus's tear-stained face, his bare feet, and the way his arms shook, and guided him into the house with a palm on the back of his head.

"Why are you home so early? Where are your things?" Angus asked, gently. He didn't ask if Icarus was all right, but Icarus didn't expect him to.

"I left them there," Icarus said.

Angus shook his head. "Are you hungry? Have you eaten?"

"I'm not. I don't think I can."

Angus pulled out a kitchen chair. "Come and sit. I'll be back."

Icarus settled down, wrapping his arms around himself, and waited. Angus came back with a large wooden basin filled with steaming water and their medical box. He knelt on the floor in front of his son and began peeling his socks off.

Angus dipped Icarus's feet in the bath, and with the very soft cloths he mostly used for smudging charcoal, he began to rub the dirt from his feet.

Icarus looked down at the top of his father's head and thought about the drawings hidden in his pocket.

"Are you hurt anywhere else?"

"No."

"Are you safe, are there people chasing you?" Angus pulled up Icarus's foot to see if there were any cuts.

"No. I . . . I have a girlfriend. I was staying with her while her dad was

279

out of town, but he came back unexpectedly," Icarus lied.

Angus paused.

"I won't be bringing her here or telling her about any of this."

Angus sighed and continued to wash. He patted Icarus's feet with a small hand towel, then rubbed the tops with linseed oil. He daubed Neosporin into the many small injuries Icarus had picked up and covered them with Band-Aids.

"If you love her, don't be a coward. Introduce yourself to him," Angus said, and it was all Icarus could do to not begin hysterically laughing. What an awful idea.

"I have to go back and get my things. Maybe I'll do it then." Icarus gave his father a smile. Like he would have done in a normal situation.

To his surprise, Angus returned it.

GUT

Icarus had never wished so badly that Helios had access to a phone.

Long after Angus had gone to bed, Icarus got up and walked to the police station. He asked the receptionist about what he would need to do to report a domestic abuse situation.

They wanted more information about him than he felt comfortable giving and told him that after he filed a report, they would send a social worker to investigate. But since they were so rural and caseloads were backed up, it might be a month or so before anything happened.

That was far too late. Icarus was going to get Helios out of there as soon as humanly possible.

Before they could ask him to fill out any paperwork, he backed out, thanked them for their time, and left.

Icarus wondered if you could hear the screams from the street.

Icarus wondered if, because he'd come here tonight, police would give the Black house a visit whether he made a formal complaint or not.

He wondered if them asking questions might alert Mr. Black that someone had been in his home to witness him.

He wondered if Helios would survive Mr. Black knowing that.

SHROUD

Angus let him sleep the whole day.

When Icarus awoke, there was a dumpling stew freshly made in the fridge for him. The whole house smelled like chicken and herbs.

Icarus ate his share and went back to bed.

WINE

He knelt, in supplication, took the flesh and the blood. Whispered desperation.

Asked for strength and bravery and cleverness. Asked for luck.

Saw the sky through the roof with eyes unseeing and kissed the cross with unclean lips.

Ave Maria, gratia plena, Dominus tecum. Benedicta tu in mulieribus, et benedictus fructus ventris tui, Iesus. Sancta Maria, Mater Dei, ora pro nobis peccatoribus, nunc, et in hora mortis nostrae.

Angus Gallagher looked weary as he asked, "Do you have any confessions?"

Icarus pressed his forehead to the floor.

"Lust, Anger . . . Greed."

The silence lasted long enough for Icarus's heart to slow. Angus sighed and put a hand on the back of Icarus's neck.

"Your sins are yours to decide. But love is never a sin, and the rules of men who don't understand that don't matter," he said, gently. "Do you have any other confessions?"

" . . . no."

Angus took his hand back. When Icarus finally had the strength to pull his face up from the wood, he was alone.

THAT NIGHT

Helios's bedroom window was nailed shut, but the window of the bathroom wasn't. What a ridiculous power play from an insecure and abusive man. To make this room feel like more of a prison.

Icarus slipped inside and soft walked down the hallway. He could hear the TV downstairs blaring sitcom garbage and took advantage of the irregular sound.

He found Helios curled in a ball, fast asleep. Closed the door tight behind him and locked it.

Icarus's gear was still under the bed, against the wall in the darkest corner. He pulled them out and quickly checked to make sure everything was there.

Then he knelt at Helios's bedside. Tucked his hand beneath the blanket to curl around a warm shoulder.

"Helios," he whispered.

Helios's eyes snapped open and he tried to scramble backward before recognizing Icarus beneath his balaclava.

"Jesus fucking Christ, how did you get in here?" Helios gasped.

"Bathroom window," Icarus said, soft and reassuring. "I wanted to check on you, grab my stuff, you know . . ."

Helios glanced nervously at the door.

"Icarus, it's not safe here."

"Let me see you, please. I haven't . . . I *need*—tell me what happened?"

Helios laughed and pushed a hand through his hair in anguish. "He tossed me around, dragged me for a bit. My ribs still hurt a lot on one side."

He got out of bed and let the sheet fall from his shoulders so Icarus could see him. Helios's legs were peppered with small Band-Aids, though no horrible gashes like Icarus had imagined in his nightmares. He had bruising around his arms, up his sides, and around his throat, where Mr. Black had grabbed him. There was a scratch across his back that was shallow and healing. Icarus took pictures, quiet and solemn, for proof if they needed it later.

Then, he touched each one, gauging their severity by the quiet noises Helios made. The only one that seemed dangerous was the mottled yellow and purple bruise across his ribs.

"Icarus, you have to go. Things have been weird around here—my dad is acting different. Suspicious. It's much worse than before. You shouldn't come back here for a week, maybe two. Even for stealing," Helios said firmly.

Icarus brushed his lips across an abrasion on Helios's hip and Helios hissed.

"I'm not kidding. He's been going in rooms he never goes into and picking up things he rarely touches. You're not safe here." Helios shuddered as Icarus tongued a purple mark at his collar.

"He goes in his office for all his phone calls, and he used—he used to take them in the living room where I could overhear."

This couldn't be allowed to go on.

"I'll give you your two weeks," Icarus said, running his nose up the length of Helios's neck. "But when I come back, do you want to leave with me?"

Helios was frowning when Icarus pulled back to see his face.

"Icarus, I'm wearing a tracker made of fucking steel. How are you going to—" Helios started.

"Then I'll have two weeks to figure that out." Icarus pushed Helios backward, and he sat on the bed hard with a small gasp of pain.

"My ribs." Helios wrapped an arm around them. "They feel like they're broken."

Icarus sank to his knees and lifted Helios's shirt again for a closer inspection. "I think they're bruised. I broke one of mine when I was learning to climb. If they were broken, you would be screaming right now. That's not to say it doesn't hurt though. Can you take Tylenol?"

Helios shook his head and looked so very sad. "Where are we going to go?"

Icarus ceased his attentions and sat back on his heels. He picked up one of Helios's hands to hold. "Helios. I have some savings and . . . a plan to get more. I'm not going to wait around for this maniac to kill you."

"Can . . . can I tell my mom?"

Icarus rolled his eyes. "Of course you can tell your mom. The only reason we aren't going straight to her is because he'll probably go there first. The goal is to get you out of here, get her on the phone, send pictures of your bruises and cuts so she understands why you had to leave. Get her blessing to go dark for a bit and then run off. I don't want there to be like a national manhunt."

Helios swallowed.

"I want her to know you," Helios said, earnestly. "I want her to *see* you. I think she would love you so much."

Icarus leaned up and brushed their lips together, soft.

"Don't kiss me so hard next time," he said with a smile. "I almost died."

Helios beamed back, and wiped his eyes. "You have to go. You really have to go."

Icarus squeezed his hand just once, then crawled under the bed to get his things.

"Two weeks," he said seriously. "I'll be back for you."

WEAK

The morning came gentle and light.

Icarus got out of bed and got ready for school. He pulled on his softest, warmest clothes, laced up his boots, and ran a comb through his hair. He didn't feel ready to join the real world again, but he had to. He had to.

On the kitchen table, still steaming beneath an upturned dessert plate, was a bowl of oatmeal. There was a heaping spoonful of his favorite blackberry jam in the center. Cinnamon sugar sprinkled over the edges. Angus was nowhere to be found.

Icarus leaned his head against the top of the wooden chair and willed his tears to stay in his eyes. He was loved, he was loved, he was *loved*, in spite of his father's strangeness. He had almost forgotten that.

He ate it slow, even though it made him late.

BACK

Julian looked at him with curious eyes. Icarus had missed him so.

He placed a hot cappuccino in front of Icarus.

"Luca said you'd be back today." Julian crossed his arms on his desk and leaned his chin into the hollow.

"Thank you."

Icarus took a sip and calculated the time between when their project was due and when Helios had said he could come back. He knew he would be gone before the day of their presentation.

It would only be a betrayal if he didn't finish the work before he left. Julian might forgive him for leaving only if Icarus came to him with his half of the paper in hand.

"You seem different," Julian said. "Where were you?"

Icarus shrugged. "I was visiting family."

Julian nodded like he understood.

"Family's not always what it's cracked up to be, huh." He turned around in his chair.

Icarus held words about that behind his teeth, and said nothing.

MUD

Celestina popped her head up underneath his arm, tugging his jacket around her on the other side.

"You ready to ditch another day?" she asked, beaming up at him.

Her box braids had been exchanged for a curly bun, fuzzy, lovely, and soft.

"I can only skip gym. Or they'll call home and get weird," Icarus said, squeezing her shoulders through the denim. "I missed you."

"Let me get a real hug." Celestina shoved her other arm under his jacket and squished him hard and tight. There it was, Icarus thought, as he nuzzled into her hair. That was why this was easier. Celestina and Luca only ever applied pressure, while Helios stroked and brushed. Nervous, gentle.

She pulled him up the hill, where Luca and Sorrel were waiting for them. Luca half ran down the hill and slammed into him, nearly knocking him off his feet.

"Luca!" Celestina shouted in playful warning.

Luca lifted him into the air and swung him around. He caught Sorrel's gaze out of the corner of his eye. Sorrel looked confused, worried, and a bit embarrassed.

"I'm glad you're back. Things were starting to get dire," Luca said, finally letting go. "I walked the mile with the goth kids and they started doing astrology on me so I decided to walk faster but they kept catching up."

Icarus laughed. He wanted to spin around and shake off the joy in his bones. He turned to Sorrel. "Hey, man. You talk to Celestina about your whole thing?" he asked.

Sorrel nodded. His eyes darted between the three of them.

"So . . . any movement?" Icarus pressed.

Sorrel shrugged.

"I subtly asked Mina about him and she was like *he's nice*," Celestina said, sitting down on the crunchy hard ground. "Which is better than *'ew gross'* or *'who?'* so I figure he has a shot."

"That's better than nothing."

Icarus sat down in front of Celestina and lay back into her lap so she could get her fingers in his hair. Then he closed his eyes and listened to them talk around him.

He'd never had this. More than two people he liked being together around him, it felt so easy. It was worth it. It was all that he imagined it to be.

DETAIL

Aspen nodded when he walked into math class but didn't say anything.

Icarus looked up at the teacher droning and figured this would be as good a time as any to start working on his plan.

First they would have to handle collateral damage:

Icarus would be leaving school before graduation, so he would have to either transfer to a school in their new area or get his GED. He'd heard getting a GED was more difficult, and he'd have to find out if they could travel internationally. He and Helios had never discussed school, but he obviously wasn't going to class. So he'd either have to continue with whatever he was doing already or get his GED too. Technically he should only have six more months of school left to finish, so it wasn't a huge hurdle. But, it also wasn't something he could just rashly ignore.

He would have to drain his bank account, where roughly half of his money was. He would have to make time to do it the day of their escape. Just in case Angus was so overwhelmed by fury that he tried to freeze Icarus's assets.

Next, he needed to figure out how to get the security anklet off Helios. He had no idea how it worked. It would be foolish to assume it just sent an alert if Helios left the property. What if it was electrified? It would have to be cut off, and he would have to do research about how.

He would have to work on the actual choreography of escaping the property. He was strong, strong enough to probably pick up Helios for a moment. But he couldn't carry him all the way down the wall. But if he bolted hooks to the roof, and had Helios in some kind of harness, he could handle the weight of him on his back.

He would have to pack his most precious items and bring them with him. But he couldn't bring them on the climb itself. He would have to stash them somewhere—maybe the diner across the street. But the idea of all that money sitting somewhere he didn't trust made him uncomfortable.

Between now and when he left, he would have to finish all his homework and the project he was working on with Julian.

Last, he would have to tell Luca and Celestina, eventually. Which was the hardest part. No one else had to know, but the two of them were important to him.

The leaving, at least, should be easy. They could take a bus and a train to Detroit. Sit where they were for forty-eight hours to wait out the initial panic search, then buy plane tickets. If Helios had access to his passport, they could swing by New York, grab it, and go immediately, but if not they could head elsewhere and have a new one expedited. With the new account with his savings and selling the gold, they could be out of Mr. Black's reach completely in a month.

He looked down at his quick list, just a few words—*Leave, GED, Account, Steal, Lift, Pack, Work, Friends*—and felt more secure than he had in months.

Aspen glanced over at it too.

"You shouldn't drop out," she said. "We've only got half a year left, and the GED is much harder. Took my brother three times to get it and he's not stupid. They make it like that for . . . classist reasons."

"I'm not dropping out," Icarus whispered. "I'm *moving*."

Aspen didn't look impressed. "Do what you want, dude. I just thought someone should mention it. Alfie said he wished someone had mentioned it to him."

Icarus frowned and folded the paper up.

"Thanks."

FLUTTER

Today was the last day for their final projects. Sorrel was glazing his still life when Icarus walked in.

"How did you meet them?" Sorrel asked him immediately.

Icarus sighed and started scraping wax off his own piece.

"Luca sat next to me on the first day of class, and Celestina needed a pencil and no one else around her had an extra," he said. "Something wrong?"

Sorrel shook his head. "No . . . I just. They're a bit much for me. They're nice and all, I just can't keep up with them."

That . . . was disappointing. Icarus slid his eyes over to Sorrel without turning his head. "You know Mina is more like them than she is like us," he warned.

Sorrel shrugged. "With her, it's worth it."

Icarus sighed again. It was for the best, probably. He was going to try to keep in contact with people from here when he left, but he didn't know if Sorrel was brave enough to help him flee. Their relationship would have to go back to the way it was before. Impersonal. Isolated.

Icarus fought a wave of grief about it. But said nothing.

"It's like they're too bright for me," Sorrel continued. "They suit some-one like you though. Luca literally wouldn't shut up about you. I think he has a crush on you."

Icarus smirked. "Nah, he's just a sweet guy. He's like that with Akeem too."

"You know Akeem?" Sorrel gasped.

"We don't hang out or anything. We're in different . . . friend groups."

Sorrel made a displeased noise and fell silent.

"You don't have to hang out with them again for my sake," Icarus said quietly. "Do what you need. I'm just rooting for you to get what you want."

"Why?"

"Why not?"

Sorrel made a face, but didn't ask Icarus anything more about it.

In the second half of class, they were graded on their paintings. Sorrel got a B plus, and Icarus got an A minus for oversimplicity of technique.

As he walked out of class, Icarus dumped his painting in the garbage.

LOWER

He headed straight from school to the big-box hardware store one town over.

Sometimes Angus would send him here to pick up small things: wood, light bulbs, batteries. Icarus liked the way it smelled. He stood in the front door to inhale. Sawdust, chemicals, steel, dust, dirt, paint.

He strode through the aisles until he was in the section he needed, then waited until an employee was walking by.

"Can you help me? I'm looking for a type of saw."

The man was older, with hands that were swollen from use. He paused and looked at Icarus.

"You need it for an art project or summat?" he asked. Icarus clearly wasn't dressed like he worked in construction.

"I'm looking for a handsaw that can cut through steel," Icarus said.

The man gazed at him; a bit contemplative. "A circ saw would be better, more stability."

"The steel is close to skin. A table saw won't work for what I need it for."

The man narrowed his eyes. "You're not tryna cut off handcuffs, are you? You'd be better off with a bolt cutter. A handsaw's overkill."

Icarus closed his eyes for a second and asked God for patience.

"The steel is about one inch thick, with about a centimeter and a half of space between the skin and the steel. Can a handsaw cut through that or not?" he asked.

The old man held up his hands and chuckled. "Aw, don't get your gym shorts in a bunch. We can find you one that will work. But you gotta put something in between that skin and the blade. Won't stop an accident, but could stop something bad from being something worse. Follow me."

He took a few steps, then looked back over his shoulder. "Nothing illegal, now?"

Icarus shook his head. "My friend got stuck in a trap. Just trying to get him out, sir."

He left with four sheets of sound-dampening foam, a Worx 4.5-inch electric compact circular saw, self-adhering bandages, steel mesh gloves, and a 1.25-inch-thick roll of rubber for the precious arch of Helios's ankle.

GRIEF

He was home an hour later than usual, and again it smelled like cooking.

A chicken had been basted in heavy cream, butter, and spices and there were potatoes chopped on the counter. Some packaged lettuce had been left out on the table with a few tomatoes next to it.

Icarus could hear muffled yelling in the storage room.

So, he picked up where Angus left off. He checked to make sure the oven had finished pre-heating and put the chicken inside, then rinsed the potatoes and set them to boil for mash. Then he started chopping tomatoes for the salad.

By the time Angus was finished with his call, Icarus had fixed the salad, mashed the potatoes, and retreated to his room to start on his homework.

His father knocked on his door, and like always, opened it without waiting.

"I meant to have it finished before you came in," he said.

Icarus looked up at him, confused. Angus hadn't made this many meals in succession in ages. Definitely since his freshman year at least.

"Why?"

Angus made a tight expression. "Do your feet hurt, still?"

Icarus shook his head. "No. Can I . . . borrow the car? I want to go to the sports store; my harness is getting a little weak."

Angus nodded, looking relieved. "Keys are in the bowl by the door. I have some work to do, so I can't eat with you tonight."

Icarus nodded. "That's fine. Thanks . . . Dad."

Angus closed the door without another word.

THE REST

Icarus went to pick up his gear after school the following day. He rarely drove, but he knew how, thankfully. There weren't a lot of people clamoring for exotic sporting goods in their tiny town, or the one next to it. So he had no choice. It was at least a two-hour journey and on the bus it would have been five.

Angus liked old things, so his Ford only had a tape deck. Just some ancient cassettes, so Icarus was stuck listening to disco the whole way.

Icarus watched the sun slip down until the road was washed out in pink and orange.

The harness he was looking for was the kind pararescuers used to help people mountain climbing. He called twice to make sure they had it and were holding it for him by the front of the store.

Icarus wished he could talk to Helios about this. Could have him try it on for size.

He wished they had more time.

It was ready for him when he got there, even though the store was ten minutes from closing. The sales associate wrapped it up for him and slipped a few coupons in the bag.

"Good luck on your climb!" she said, perky and kind.

"Yeah, thanks."

SIN

Somehow Luca could tell something was wrong and pressured him into talking about it. Icarus wasn't used to people being able to do that.

It was one of the last days that they would be outside walking the mile instead of inside playing sports. The air was crisp and the grass was crunchy. Their breath steamed out in cloudy puffs.

Luca kept looking over his shoulder at the small group of goth girls following behind them.

"They're creeping me out," he hissed.

Icarus grinned. "They like it that way." He looked over his shoulder at them and waved. They giggled, bashful and sweet, and fell a bit farther behind.

"To answer your question, yes and no," Icarus said, picking up where he'd left off. "I don't think my dad knows you guys were in our house, but he has been acting kind of strange. He's been taking phone calls in our storage room and being kind of . . . nice? He made me breakfast and dinner a couple times this week. That hasn't happened in a really long time."

Luca rubbed his runny nose and Icarus decided to bring tissues to class tomorrow in case they had to be outside again.

"Do you really cook every night?"

"Yeah. It's less terrible than you'd think. Cooking every night means I also get to eat whatever I want every night as well. You just kind of fold it into the rest of your chores."

"God, I wish. My mom makes the nastiest casseroles and then cries if we pick at it."

Luca sneezed.

Icarus took off his jacket and draped it over Luca's shoulders.

"What? No, dude, what about you?" Luca said, trying to wriggle out from under it.

"You're almost blue. Just put it on. Wear more than a sweater tomorrow," Icarus said grumpily.

He stopped walking until Luca put his long arms through the sleeves. They stuck out like a scarecrow.

He looked at Luca hard again as Luca tried and failed to button the jacket up. He really was close to Helios's size.

"Do you mind doing me a favor? I have some equipment that I need to test and it looks like it would be about your size. Do you mind helping me with it?"

Luca shrugged. "Yeah, I guess. I'm free tonight? Maybe tomorrow? Friday is the—oh, wait! Has Celestina asked you yet?"

Icarus shook his head. "Asked what?"

"She wants you to come to dinner at her house on Friday," Luca explained. "She usually has the girls over every Friday, but this one is for us. Me, her almost boyfriend, and you, her . . . well. Her something."

Icarus grinned and stared up at the clouds. Her something. Well.

He would have to come back to this town, chase them down, huh.

"I wouldn't miss it for the world."

FRILL

Luca was the first person in his life who demanded more and stuck to it. Who looked Icarus in the eyes and said that he wanted more from him, even if it was embarrassing. It was only fair that he would be the first to know.

About this, about him.

About Helios.

Icarus came home and threw the makings for chili in the slow cooker before gathering up the harness. He knew his father was doing *something* with all this cooking for him. But after three and a half years of being responsible for dinner, he didn't feel comfortable not trying. It would be almost ready by the time Icarus was back and he could start baking some buttermilk corn bread to go with it.

He slung the harness into a black duffel bag and scampered out the door. The wind was picking up speed, cutting and dry as he walked the five blocks down to Luca's house. It felt so strange coming this way while it was still light out.

The only memories he had of Luca's house were fuzzy at the edges. The yard looked so much nicer when there weren't drunk kids lying on it. There were flowerpots full of withered plants, bushes turning red in the chill, small trees heavy with winter berries. It was probably picturesque in summer.

Icarus knocked and waited until Luca's freckled face appeared.

"Hey, man, come in!" He threw an arm over Icarus's shoulder and Icarus leaned into it, easily.

Luca pulled him upstairs into his bedroom, which was a bit messy. Clothes on the floor, sports paraphernalia on the walls, backpack slung across the bed, comics spilling out from a box under his desk.

It smelled richly of Luca. In the same way Helios's bed smelled of Helios. Was everyone's room like this? Icarus didn't know.

"What do you have for me to try on?" Luca asked, sitting down on his bed.

Icarus sat down next to him and took a deep breath.

BRICK

Luca looked at the pictures of Helios on Icarus's phone with a tight expression.

"How . . . did you meet?" he asked gently.

Icarus felt his heart beating out of his chest.

"Our dads know each other. His dad has something my dad wants in his house, so I was breaking in to get it. When I did, I found him. I've been visiting him in there ever since."

Icarus had thought this through. The exact words to use to not give *so* much away that it would put Luca in danger just for knowing, but enough that Luca would understand. He had rehearsed it.

"You know breaking and entering is a crime, right?" Luca raised an eyebrow. "How are you going to get him out?"

Icarus shrugged. "I'm going to climb up there, strap an emergency transport harness onto him, and carry him down."

Luca handed Icarus his phone back, then he stared down at his lap for a moment, processing. After a while he threw his head back and laughed.

"You're serious? This isn't a prank or anything?" Luca was smiling but it didn't reach his eyes.

"I can't leave him there," Icarus said firmly. "If you knew you could get another kid in this situation out, wouldn't you?"

"I would call the police," Luca said, standing up. He closed his bedroom door and locked it. "Did you try that?"

Icarus fingered the edge of the duffel bag's strap. "I . . . actually went in person to the police station. It's considered domestic abuse, which requires a visit from a social worker before any major moves can be made. They said it would take a couple months before anyone was able to come by. He can't stay there for a few months."

Luca covered his eyes and took a deep breath.

"Why isn't anything involving you easy," he whispered. "I feel like I'm an NPC meeting the main character at the very end of a game. I feel like we've had fifteen minutes together and you're about to die in an explosion."

Icarus just stared up at Luca as he paced, hands tucked under his armpits in obvious anxiety.

"Luca."

Luca shook his head and didn't answer.

"*Luca,*" Icarus tried again. "I need you. I can't do this on my own."

"You shouldn't be doing this at all," Luca hissed. "This isn't something for you to have to handle! This is a job for cops or like the FBI."

"I'll call them as soon as we get him out. *Please,* Luca."

Luca kept pacing.

Icarus hid his face in his hands.

"Are you going to tell Celestina?" Luca asked suddenly.

Icarus didn't look up. "She's important to me too."

Luca stopped pacing and leaned against his desk. He took a long, deep breath.

"Fine, let's do it."

FALL

Luca strapped himself in while Icarus watched, pleased that it was so easy. Helios wouldn't need his help.

Icarus pulled his arms through his own straps, buckled them close, pulled them tight.

"Are you ready?"

Luca scoffed. "Sure."

Icarus grabbed hold of the straps closest to his arms and took a deep breath. Then he crouched and, with a shout, lifted Luca off the floor.

He steadied himself, widening his stance and leaning forward. Luca pulled his legs up, shifting his weight so it was easier.

Icarus breathed fast, then, with a groan, pushed himself to standing.

He held Luca aloft for an agonizing moment, then leaned back and deposited him gently back to the floor.

"That . . . that could . . . have been worse," Icarus panted.

"I didn't think you'd be able to lift me at all," Luca said bitterly. "But wonders never cease with you, do they."

"I'll only have to lift him to jump down off the roof. Then gravity should take care of the rest," Icarus said.

"I hope so."

Luca unbuckled himself and slithered out of the harness. Icarus stepped from beneath his bonds and folded the whole thing back into the duffel.

"I . . . I have to go home. I left something cooking," Icarus said. "Please don't tell anyone."

Luca sighed and rubbed his neck anxiously. "Yeah. I guess. Yeah," he mumbled.

Icarus put the duffel back on the floor and crossed the room. He tentatively put his arms around Luca, tried to hug him. Do it the way he had been taught. Tucked his hands against Luca's shoulder blades and placed his face against Luca's chest.

"Thank you," he whispered.

Icarus began to let go, but Luca clung to him suddenly. Pushed his fingers into Icarus's hair, shoved his face into the curve of Icarus's neck.

"I wish you could stay," he confessed in a rush. "If it was just you and he didn't exist, we could have figured out a way you could stay."

Icarus closed his eyes. "I know. But he does and I can't . . ."

"Why is everything so hard with you?" He pulled back to search Icarus's gaze, devastated. "Why can't some things just be easy?"

"You're the only best friends I've ever had. I can't risk anything happening to that," Icarus replied softly. "Nothing can ever replace you."

Luca looked away. Let Icarus untangle them.

"You have to tell her," Luca whispered.

"I will."

Icarus unlocked Luca's bedroom door.

"We should practice a few times," Luca called as Icarus walked out the door and down the stairs. "You have to be ready; I don't want you to fall."

TECH

Halfway home, Icarus paused to lean against someone's wooden fence and catch his breath.

His chest ached. He pressed his hand over his heart.

He didn't want to leave.

He *had* to.

He could come back. After Helios turned eighteen, they could come back.

Maybe he could introduce Helios to his friends. They would like him and he would like them. More than Sorrel did at any rate.

Celestina would be mad at him for leaving, though. Maybe she would turn her back on him for the first time. Maybe she would hit him.

Icarus squatted down on the ground, forehead against the fence, and breathed slowly, willed his heart to stop racing before he slipped into a panic attack.

Breathed slowly.

Breathed slowly.

"Young man, are you all right?"

Icarus stood up fast and started walking. "I'm fine," he called over his shoulder, not looking back.

TITHE

When he got home, the chili was finished and the corn bread was already made, sitting on the counter. A slice had been taken from it.

A single bowl, spoon, and plate lay waiting for him on the table.

Icarus looked down the hall at the closed workshop door and grew even more suspicious. He ate his dinner quickly and put away his dishes.

The workshop light was off and the house was quiet, but there was no note. Angus never left without leaving a note.

Icarus opened the workshop door and slipped inside.

"Dad?" he called. His eyes slowly adjusted to the black of the room. When he could finally see, Icarus stumbled back, knocking into the door hard.

In the center of the table, with tools beside it and a soft cloth for cleaning, was the disc from Mr. Black's house.

Orpheus Losing Eurydice, staring back at him, dangerous and inexplicable. The empty space in the foyer haunted him, the scratches on the table and the mess.

There was a reason Angus no longer went to the Black house himself. His hands . . . their hands.

Angus was where Icarus thought he would be, curled up on the futon beneath a quilt, asleep. One of his arms was out and dragging against the floor, his wrist in a brace.

A wave of panic swept Icarus across the room, and before rationality could stop him, he found himself shaking his father awake.

"What is it?" Angus griped blearily.

"Why did you take that?" Icarus demanded.

"What?"

"*Orpheus*," Icarus said, louder. "It's bait. If I could tell it was bait, *you* could tell it was bait. Why did you fucking steal that?!"

Angus startled and sat up, pushing Icarus's hand away. He ran his fingers through his gray hair and then steepled his hands beneath his chin.

"I don't know what you were thinking!" Icarus hissed, starting to pace. "You put me at risk, you put everything at risk. Over that? It's not even famous or rare, it's just a random antiquity!"

Angus didn't speak.

"What, does it belong to a museum? Was it illegally smuggled? What was worth breaking into that man's house after five years of forcing me to do it for you?"

"I never forced—" Angus started.

Icarus threw his arm out, furiously. "*Asking, whatever*!" he shouted.

Angus closed his eyes for a long moment, but opened them before Icarus could start screaming again.

"It's a favorite of Ramona's. Mr. Black's wife. He . . . likes to buy pieces she is fond of and destroy them. Or display them, whichever he thinks would hurt worse. The piece is on loan from a museum and they will never get it back from him. Ever. To me, it's worth the risk."

Icarus stood in the shaft of light from the hallway and crossed his arms. The risk. Icarus *was* the risk. His safety was the risk. Icarus had been feeling so fucking hypocritical about planning to take the torque and leave nothing, but this was so much worse than that. At least Icarus was leaving the entire city directly afterward and saving a child abuse victim with the proceeds. Not sending his own kid in as some sacrifice, for a woman he hadn't even seen in—

"What does she mean to you?" Icarus asked dangerously.

"Icarus—"

"Were you fucking her while my mother was dying?"

Angus stood, fully awake now. "Watch your tone."

Icarus whirled around. He snatched the disc off the table. He was so furious he could barely feel his arms.

"*Icarus stop!*" Angus shouted. He grabbed it from Icarus's grasp, sinking beneath its heft. With a groan, he settled it back onto the table. "I owe her. She *helped* me. I owe her."

Icarus backed away, shaking.

"The commission. She painted from the bottom up and I painted from the top down. She was helping me. We were working as fast as we were able," Angus panted. "I owe her for *trying*."

Icarus pressed himself into the wall by the door as Angus pushed the statue away from the edge of the table, gritting his teeth at the pain.

"I was there every night, but it wasn't enough . . . She got up in the middle of the night, when Stuart was asleep, and filled in what she could. He broke her arm for it when he caught her, Icarus. That is on me."

Angus looked exhausted.

"I don't like talking about this," Angus said. "I am too old to keep reliving this."

"I didn't know," Icarus mumbled.

Angus rubbed his eyes, agonized. "I didn't tell you. How could you?"

That wasn't enough.

"Dad, you just *can't*. You can't do reckless things like this just because of your own fucking . . ." Icarus shook his head. "Look, I get it. I understand what it means to owe someone something. But, you also owe *me*. You owe it to me to not create fucking situations like this. Are you trying to go to prison? Do you want Mr. Black to catch me? To trap me? Do you think Ramona would

311

want that? Do you even know what she would want anymore?"

Angus shook his head. "Icarus—"

"It's been sixteen years. Can't this stop? Can't we all just stop?" Icarus wanted to scream this, but could hear the tears in his voice. The sound choked, quiet, in his throat.

"You have never asked for this before." Angus caught the edge of the table, put his other hand to his chest.

"I . . . I . . . it's not like I don't care anymore. I do care, and I still love her just like you do, but. Please, Dad. *Please.*"

Angus swallowed. He brushed the dust off his hands and crossed the room.

The weight of his hands, when they came, was heavy on Icarus's shoulders.

"You can stop. Icarus. My son. You can stop now."

Icarus looked up at his father.

"When will *you* stop?"

Angus turned from him and faced the dark of the room.

"When I am ready."

BREATHE

Icarus couldn't stop either. Not yet. He still needed the gold. Goddamn him, but he still needed to take something and leave nothing behind.

It would be the last thing Icarus stole from that house.

NOSE

Icarus fingered the cup of lavender Earl Grey tea Julian had brought him.

"Thank you for doing this for me," Icarus said. "I know I say thank you every day, but I mean it generally speaking. Not just for the drink."

Julian turned around in his chair to look at Icarus.

"Why do you sound sad?" he said, scowling at him.

Icarus shrugged. "I'm not. I just figured you should know that this has meant a lot to me."

"Okayyyyy . . ." Julian slowly swiveled toward the front of the room. "If you were trying not to sound foreboding, you definitely failed."

Icarus just laughed and looked out the window. The sun was shining bright and crisp.

"After graduation, do you think we could write each other letters?" he asked softly.

"Like, emails?" Julian said, quieter, as class began to start.

"No, like actual letters. Old-fashioned."

Julian gave him a look of such intense annoyance over his shoulder that Icarus couldn't help but laugh again, and was harshly shhed by Rebecca Smith next to him.

"Why?"

"I'll miss how mean you are," Icarus said, frankly, ignoring Rebecca.

"Can't you find a new bully?" Julian hissed.

Icarus finally did what he'd been wanting to for months. He reached forward and flipped the tag sticking out of Julian's sweater back inside. Julian arched hysterically and slapped his hand where Icarus's had just been.

"What the—"

"Your tag."

"I know! I know, I pull them up on purpose because it's too scratchy," Julian griped.

"You should just cut them out."

"What?"

"Here." Icarus dug in his bag and found his X-Acto knife from art class. He pulled back Julian's sweater and slipped the blade around the tag until it was free. Then, he patted Julian's sweater back into place.

"There you go."

Julian rubbed the spot from behind.

"Hmm. I'll write you letters, you big sap," he murmured. "You better write me back or I'll stop doing it."

"I will."

GREEN

These final days felt pale and flimsy. It was Wednesday and Icarus and Luca were forced to play dodgeball indoors for gym instead of walking in the cold.

Luca didn't look at him much while Icarus was in the position to look back, but Icarus felt the weight of his gaze all the same. They were on different teams, so they didn't get the opportunity to talk. And when it was time to get dressed, Luca slipped away so Icarus couldn't go after him.

Next period, Icarus sat down behind Celestina and put his face in the cradle of his arms. She turned around and reached over him to scrape her acrylic nails against the back of his neck.

She scratched him until he was shivering, loose-limbed and easy. Until the tips of his ears were hot. Then she traced the rims of those too.

Icarus made a soft noise and she immediately took her hand back.

"Luca said he told you about Friday dinner?"

"Mm-hmm."

"It's at six o'clock. I'll text you the address."

Icarus lifted his head so he could look at her. "Should I dress up nice?"

"Not unless you want my whole family to comment on it." Celestina grinned down at him. She'd braided gold beads into her hair and they shimmered under the fluorescent glare.

"Is Luca still coming? He's avoiding me, I think," Icarus murmured, burying his head back in his arms.

"He does that when he's embarrassed. Just talk to him, and it will be fine," Celestina said. She turned back around to pay attention to what was going on in class.

Icarus was afraid that it wouldn't be.

LIST

Icarus ditched his other classes and spent the rest of the day in the library finishing up his half of the paper for Julian.

He checked his bank account one more time, made a few calls to be sure the transfer to his new separate private account would land precisely when he meant it to.

He looked up hotels and transportation options along two different routes: toward Helios's mom and away from her.

Icarus even ordered a few pieces of clothing in what he was hoping was close to Helios's size, in case they didn't have time to pack.

He stared at the purchase button on the screen for a bit, his cursor hanging over it. Then he pulled out his phone and opened his photos for another glance at the pictures they'd taken of Helios's bruising. His chest tightened in pain again.

Icarus added a couple pairs of warm socks and a pair of tennis shoes a few sizes bigger than his to the cart and paid for it all with a click.

He looked over his shoulder at the other kids milling out of the library to head home for the day and felt strange. He didn't know why. This was just one more secret layered over his much older secrets.

He didn't know why it felt like it mattered that he was leaving these people. He didn't even know them. He'd never tried to.

Well—

Well.

LEAP

On Thursday, he went to the guidance counselor.

Icarus didn't have an appointment, so he had to sit outside and wait until whoever was in there decided to come out.

When he finally filled the doorway, Mrs. Drake's hammy face didn't look surprised.

"Take a seat, I'll be with you in a sec."

Icarus put his backpack next to the chair and looked down at his knees. He took a deep breath.

"So, what's going on? You doing all right?" Mrs. Drake was looking him up on her computer. He wondered if her notes on him had changed.

"If I were going to transfer schools, how would I set that into motion?" Icarus asked.

Mrs. Drake stopped scrolling. "Is there something going on at this school that makes you want to leave?" she asked.

Icarus steadied himself and tried again. "Everything's fine, I just want to know. I might have to move and I want to make sure I can pick up quickly and finish off the school year strong without having to do more time."

Mrs. Drake turned away from her computer to face him. "Well, it depends on where you're moving to."

God, talking to this woman was like playing chess.

"I'm sure most places would be a bit weird about taking someone with only one semester left of school. But this is kind of more like a backup plan.

I care enough about graduating to make it a priority regardless of what happens to me."

Mrs. Drake leaned closer to him. "They wouldn't be, it happens all the time. But more importantly, is something happening to you?"

Goddamn it.

"Yes, what's happening is that I might have to transfer schools," Icarus said. Then he stopped talking. Let the silence settle in the room for a while.

Mrs. Drake sighed. "Well, first thing you'll need is your father's signature on some paperwork. You're legally allowed to drop out at sixteen, but a transfer requires guardian approval. Let me just get him on the phone and we can have your transfer paperwork ready to go. If you wind up not needing it, then we can just discard it, okay?"

She picked up the phone.

"Stop!" Icarus cried quickly, standing up. "Please don't call him."

Mrs. Drake slowly put the phone down and crossed her arms. Then, she just stared at him expectantly.

"Don't . . . don't make me drop out just because I don't want to share this with you."

Mrs. Drake sighed and opened her desk drawer.

"I'm a mandated reporter, you know."

When Icarus didn't react, she explained. "Mandated reporters are compelled to report child abuse to the authorities. It's our job to make sure you're okay. Are you okay, Icarus Gallagher?"

Icarus shook his head. "I'm fine. It's something else. Someone else. I'm taking care of someone."

Mrs. Drake's face softened a bit. "Sometimes, having to take care of someone all on your own can be a kind of abuse, even if you love them. Parents can give you too much responsibility for you to handle. Even when they don't mean to hurt you, it still can hurt you a great deal. Is this how you feel?"

Icarus bit the inside of his mouth until it bled. He wanted to scream. He wanted to sob. He wanted to go back in time to freshman year so he could throw himself into this room. When it could have mattered, when it could have made a difference.

Icarus swallowed the blood. Misinterpreted her words on purpose, even though something inside him was weeping to hear them.

"I don't have any siblings to take care of. It's just me and my dad and he's fine. I promise it's not what you think, and if something was happening, I . . . " Icarus held his breath. "If something was happening to me, I would be okay. I'm going to be eighteen in three weeks."

He looked Mrs. Drake directly in the eyes. "When I turn eighteen, if I needed to, I could just leave."

Mrs. Drake's expression didn't even flicker. "When you turn eighteen, you can sign your own transference paperwork," she countered.

Icarus's gaze dropped to the desk. That was too much time from now, and he wouldn't be able to be here for it.

So, Icarus was going to do what he always did, when he was backed against a wall. He was going to be honest.

"Can you be kind to me?"

Mrs. Drake frowned.

"I'm not being mean to you, Icarus. There are just certain—"

"Please," Icarus interrupted. He placed both hands, palm side down on her desk and bowed his head. Begged. "I need help, and I need you to be kind to me. I promise I will come back to say thank you. Afterward."

Mrs. Drake sighed. "After what, Icarus."

"Just give me a year and I'll come back," he whispered.

Mrs. Drake was quiet. Then she reached under her desk into the drawer she'd opened.

"Sign this and postdate it for the next business day after your birthday. When you need it, write the school a formal letter requesting that it be sent to your new institution and we'll send it out for you."

"Thank you," he said. He quickly signed the paperwork and grabbed his backpack. "I won't tell anyone," he said, standing.

"You'd better not."

Mrs. Drake was looking down at his signature contemplatively. Icarus drummed his fingers against the top of the form, then backed away from the desk.

"I mean it. I'll finish school and come back here with something nice for you, so don't retire before that or anything." Perhaps he would give her a Vermeer.

Mrs. Drake scowled. "I'm forty-eight."

Icarus realized that he should get out of here while he was still ahead.

"Okay. I'm going to leave now."

"Close the door behind you."

AKEEM

Icarus stood in front of Mrs. Drake's office, head tilted back, eyes closed. He rolled his shoulders to throw off his stress and sighed.

"Ayy man. How you doing?" Akeem and Patrick were headed down the hall.

Akeem slapped Patrick on the shoulder. Patrick nodded goodbye and peeled off toward the main exit. Akeem continued toward Icarus.

"Been waiting for you. You got a minute?"

Icarus was uncomfortable and not really in the mood, but he nodded, and followed Akeem to a quiet spot by the back stairs. Akeem was at least a foot taller than him and Icarus could tell he was slowing down to match Icarus's short stride.

"You lookin' a bit better these days, not gonna lie," Akeem started with a grin. "Not happier, but, you know. Not a liability."

"I . . . I wanted to say thanks for your offer earlier," Icarus started. "I know you didn't have—"

Akeem cut him off. "And that's where you're wrong, man." He stopped walking and turned to face Icarus directly. "You got people looking out for you. You hear on the news about kids doing some fucked-up shit because no one was watching out for them. So now, we all watch."

He looked down at Icarus and Icarus felt so small and peculiar.

"Luca mentioned something about people calling CPS," Icarus started, tentatively. "I'm . . . really glad you didn't do that."

Akeem shrugged. "Luca said you got it covered. Next time I saw you in the hall, you looked different. I made him ask again just to double-check. You're not the only one whose old man is hard on him; I know what it looks like. Tough in the streets, tough at home, you know?"

Icarus rubbed his neck and laughed awkwardly. "Yeah . . . I guess . . . yeah."

"Mine was rough on my older brother and it didn't go how he planned. Now he's softer on me. But soft on a hard man ain't none too gentle either." Akeem shrugged. He adjusted his backpack strap over his shoulder. "I saw you in the counselor's office, so I figured I'd check on you myself before we back off completely. She got you covered?"

Icarus nodded. He felt his throat getting tight and his eyes start to burn.

"Ayy, none of that." Akeem sounded panicked at the idea that Icarus was about to cry. He looked over his back to make sure they were still alone. Then he slapped Icarus on the shoulder just like he had Patrick.

"You'll be all right," he said. "You have a good rest of the school year, man."

Icarus couldn't talk, he knew his voice would crack, so he just nodded again.

Akeem grinned and started to walk away. "See you round. And let me know if you change your mind on that football shit. Agility like yours? It ain't never too late."

Icarus laughed and wiped his eyes. By the time he was ready to answer, Akeem was already gone.

"Yeah. Okay."

BITE

The saw felt bulky and strange in his hands. Icarus couldn't afford to be unpracticed with it.

So, he went back to the hardware store and bought some steel rod. Spent an hour cutting it in the parking lot behind the store. Power cord hooked up to their external outlet.

He tossed the chunks of steel in the dumpster.

The blade was loud, but not much louder than an argument. The sound-proofing material he'd bought would definitely help, but it might not be enough.

He couldn't test it at home, or anywhere else really.

This would have to do. It would have to.

He had four more days until Helios would be ready for him.

SOFT

Luca was still shying away from him the next day, but Icarus couldn't take it anymore. They had to get it together for Celestina's dinner. They couldn't carry this into her home.

He pulled Luca from his corner in the boys' locker room and into a stall. Pushed him against the wall and locked the door.

"Stop running from me."

Luca's cheeks were stained red, and he twisted to avoid Icarus's gaze.

"Have you told her yet?" he mumbled.

"I haven't had time; I'm doing it tonight after dinner," Icarus replied.

"Why is it so weird to you that I'm uncomfortable?" Luca griped. "There are so many things to be uncomfortable about."

Icarus backed away, created room between them in this small space.

"You said you wanted to know me, and here I am." He stretched his arms out. "Here I am, Luca, and you know me now. You and Celestina are the only ones."

"Except for Helios," Luca mumbled.

"Helios is . . . he's . . . He's like my birthright, it's not the same," Icarus said, and he wasn't ashamed of it. Helios wouldn't be either, if he were here. He would *understand*.

"I've never had a best friend before," Icarus admitted. "I don't know how it works. Is it supposed to be like this?"

"Icarus, I just . . ." Luca closed his eyes. "I wish I could be angry at you. It feels like I'm not allowed."

Icarus leaned back against the stall divider and rubbed his eyes until lights sparked behind them.

"I'm sorry, Luca," he said, at last.

"It's fine, I'll get over it. But now you're leaving and I just . . ." Luca sighed. "Everything is happening very fucking fast."

Icarus let his hands fall to his sides, and he stepped closer to Luca again. Luca looked skittish, glanced through the slats between the door out into the bathroom.

"Can I come back home to you both," Icarus asked, "after Helios and I figure this out?"

"Stop talking to me like that," Luca begged. "I'm going to college. I got in to Penn State."

"Are you going to still be dating Celestina when you're there?" Icarus asked.

Luca blushed, pink this time. Not the angry red Icarus seemed to inspire in him. "I. Well, I hope so. I don't want to break up or anything. We just got together."

"Okay." Icarus nodded. "So she can visit you there. Can I visit you too?"

"As friends?" Luca asked.

Icarus shrugged. "Whatever. I'll make time for it. Depending on what happens, I might be in Paris, Milan, or New York. You're a plane ticket away."

"You'd fly from Paris to visit me at Penn State?" Luca wrinkled his nose in disbelief.

"I would fly from Antarctica to meet you at Penn State," Icarus said firmly. "I'd take a train, or a bus. I would walk if I needed to see you."

Luca made a wounded sound, and let his forehead drift down to rest on Icarus's shoulder.

STRAY CAT

Celestina's house was close to Sorrel's. They almost traveled the same route, except for a sharp right turn a bit early that led them down Celestina's block.

She'd gone home early while Icarus and Luca headed to his to try on the harness again. Icarus used some of Luca's dad's pomade to slick his hair back and pretended that Luca wasn't watching him. He'd squeezed Luca's arm in understanding as he'd walked past.

Celestina's home was in a big apartment building with a shared backyard.

They could smell the food cooking before they even made it to her front door.

Luca bounced on the balls of his feet, looking more anxious than Icarus felt. But when Celestina opened the door, he settled. Icarus watched Luca's shoulders drop in relief as he gave her a hug. Took comfort in it as Icarus was reeled forward for his own.

Celestina's dad was tall and round. He had a big smile and a bigger laugh, and he smacked Icarus hard on the back as he led them to the dining room. Celestina's mother looked just like her but a bit taller, more muscular. Icarus noticed a few medals and trophies on their living room mantlepiece. Celestina had a little sister, Bonnibelle, who looked about eight and who chattered boldly with all of them for the whole evening.

This house was loud and bright and full, and Icarus shivered into it like it was the first time he was being allowed in out of the cold.

MAPLE

The dinner table was round and large, unlike the small square table he and Angus ate at. They had a lazy Susan like a Chinese restaurant and the food was piled high in the middle. Black-eyed peas, sweet potatoes, roast chicken, corn and peppers, brussels sprouts, garden salad, shrimp and grits.

They sat down and held hands. Connected as they prayed. Heads bowed, together. Icarus's hand in Celestina's small one, and his other in Bonnibelle's even smaller. She gripped him back hard, unafraid, just like her sister.

When they started eating, Celestina's parents asked him questions. They were easier than he had imagined. Easier than he had spent his entire life preparing for.

"What are you planning to study in college?" "What's your favorite subject?" "Do you have any brothers and sisters?" "What's your favorite book?" "Do you play any sports?" "How did you and Stella meet?"

Stella! Oh! A nickname Icarus had never even thought about. A family name.

It was hard to swallow past the lump in his throat, but he managed.

After dinner, they cleared the table. They stacked their dishes by the sink and Celestina's dad brought out a banana cream pie, milk, coffee, and cinnamon-ginger ice cream.

Luca and Celestina were holding hands under the table and Icarus wanted to weep. He wanted to scoop this entire evening up and eat it with a spoon, taste it on his fingers, save it for later.

Was this what Celestina and Luca came home to every night? Maybe even Helios when he was with his mom? Maybe Sorrel and Aspen and Julian too?

How could he go home to his cold little bed now?

He understood more than ever the ghosts in Celestina and Luca's eyes when they saw his house. He understood, now, why Luca had been shaking.

BORN

The three of them went outside in the yard afterward. The night had fallen properly, the roads were blue and you could barely see the lights from the street.

Celestina sat down in the child-size swing that the whole building shared, while Luca gently pushed her. Icarus leaned against the wood beside them. He didn't know how to start.

"Luca said you had something to tell me?" Celestina kicked her legs to get more height.

Icarus swallowed. "Yeah. I . . ."

He fell silent.

Luca and Celestina waited him out, swinging in the dark.

"There is a kid locked up in a house across from Rudy's Diner, and I'm in love with him, I think."

"What do you mean?" Celestina asked, carefully.

"His name is Helios," Icarus said firmly. "His dad put a tracker on his ankle and he hasn't been outside in three months. I've been breaking in to see him and I'm going to break him out. Then I'll have to leave town for a while."

That was it. That was the whole thing.

"Get me down, get me down," Celestina said. She stopped kicking and dragged her feet in the dirt as Luca grabbed the chains to pull her back until the swing slowed to a stop.

"You're leaving? Leaving school?" Celestina exclaimed.

Icarus stared at the dirt. "I'm sorry."

"Don't be sorry, you fucking idiot," Luca said, exasperated. "Show her your phone and explain yourself properly."

Icarus pressed his lips together grimly, then dug his phone out of his pocket. He scrolled through his pictures and handed it to her.

Celestina looked at them in silence.

"He's already contacted the police, and they won't get to this guy for about a month. Icarus has to get him out sooner rather than later. He's not just leaving, he's rescuing someone." Luca looked up and right at him. "Someone he cares about."

"You said you're in love with him?" Celestina sounded angry. "You—" She looked up at Luca, then back at him. "How did you even meet?"

Icarus bit his lip. He went and sat down in front of the swing, so he was looking up at her through the gap in her knees. Looking up at both of them.

"You're my first friends. I didn't know how to talk to you about this or if I even should," he started. "But Helios . . ."

"Helios is like . . . He's—" Icarus stopped, and found himself without the right words.

Celestina tilted her head to the side curiously, then kicked her feet in the dirt.

"He's special," Celestina finished for him. "What do you like about him?"

Icarus shrugged, a bit embarrassed. "He's . . . beautiful. He has red hair, dark red. And he does ballet and he's so good at it. He's strong enough to lift me over his head. He's funny and mean and always saying surprising things and I know it's dangerous to break in to see him, but it's worth it. I feel . . . meeting him feels like learning about a part of myself that I haven't been allowed to understand until now."

Luca sighed.

Celestina reached out with one leg and pushed at Icarus's knee with her sneaker.

"It's cute," she said. "You having a crush."

Icarus sat back, even though it made the woodchips on the ground dig into his palms.

"I thought you would be mad at me," he admitted.

Celestina shrugged, then backed up until Luca got the hint that she wanted to be pushed again.

"Get out of the way, Icarus, can't you see I'm swinging?"

Luca heaved her up with a grunt and she flew up into the night sky. Icarus leaned against the wood again and watched her pretty hair sparkle in the streetlights.

"I forgive you. But only because this is your first time. No one is born knowing how friends work. You figure it out as you go along. And besides, you didn't 'not tell us,' you're telling us now."

Icarus smiled. His chest hurt in a good way.

"But I do gotta say, though. It *is* a bit strange that your name is Icarus and his name is Helios," Celestina remarked.

"Oh, that? It's not an accident."

"Oh?"

Icarus glanced at Luca. He hadn't told him this part. "His mom was maybe in love with my dad? And he got named that because my name was already Icarus."

"That's weird and gross?"

Icarus shrugged. "I know. I'm not even named after the guy from the myth. I'm named after the plant. *Icarus filiformis.* My mother was a botanist. She liked their shade of green. Our house is full of ferns. She wore the color all the time."

Luca rubbed his palms into his eyes. "I am going to split my head open against this pole."

"That painted lady from your house!" Celestina crowed.

"Dude, I don't even know. Figuring this out has been absolutely exhausting," Icarus admitted. "There's this big tragic story that has been really awful. Me and Helios getting away from all of them is pretty much the best-case scenario in this situation. I just really hope that I can pull it off."

Celestina flew backward, her braids flowing in front of her like she was underwater.

"Well. It's Friday. We have the whole night." She smiled and it was the brightest thing in the whole back yard. "Tell us your story, Icarus. The whole thing, from beginning to end. Then, we'll help you."

KISS

Celestina hugged him with her arms wrapped under his coat. Tucked her hands against his back and swayed from side to side, like he'd seen her do with her mother and sister earlier.

"Are we still friends?" Icarus asked.

"Why wouldn't we be?" she asked, like it was simple. Like it was foolish that he'd been afraid.

Luca held him too. Hesitantly at first, but Icarus wouldn't let him. Wormed his way closer, didn't let go early.

"You taught me how to do this, you know," Icarus confessed in a rush.

"Shut the fuck up, man," Luca groaned. "You can't just say stuff like that. Now I'm going to think about that for the rest of my life."

Icarus pulled back and looked at them both. This couple—his first friends—their hands clasped between them like a lifeline.

"Are you sure you're comfortable with this?" he asked.

"We'll be there," Luca promised.

"We won't fuck it up."

BURN

When Icarus got home, he was alone.

He checked the entire house to be sure, then went digging in the storage room and pulled out his family photo album. He sat down in the kitchen with the two sketches of Angus to one side and the album on the other. Telling Luca and Celestina the full story from beginning to end had made Icarus feel . . .

Wistful wasn't the right word. But it hurt, and he wanted to see if this would fix it.

There were pictures of them all on vacation together: Mr. Black grinning brightly with his new wife Ramona, thin and tan, hanging off his arm. Pictures of Angus and Ramona showing off their work. It was eerie to see them so happy. His mom was there too, dark hair shining in the sun, sleepy-eyed.

Icarus knew her face, knew the curve of her back, knew the shape of her hand from Angus's portraits. But she was better in a snapshot.

And Ramona was looking away from Angus in every one. Carefully looking away from him.

The keys in the front door jingled too quickly for Icarus to make a run for it, so he didn't. Stayed rooted to the chair and kept his eyes down.

Angus came into the room and hung up his coat; passed Icarus to put the shopping on the counter behind him while Icarus sweated. When Angus turned back around to head to his workroom, he stopped mid-stride.

"What is this?" he said, immediately reaching out for the drawing of himself. "Did you do this?"

Icarus swallowed. "Ramona did."

"Where did you get this?"

The shadow of the paper over his shoulder was shaking.

"There is a room in the red wing of the Black mansion. Helios and I found it. There are . . . a lot more."

Angus dropped the paper. "Helios," he breathed.

Icarus felt something shift inside him, from pain to fury.

"Yeah. Do you remember when I said that I felt uncomfortable going there because I felt like there was someone inside?" he said, bitterly. "And then you forced me to go back even though I was anxious?"

"How long has he been in there, Icarus?"

"Since the end of August." Icarus stood up and closed the album with a slam.

"All of this . . . fucking ridiculousness is probably because of this, you know. So like, thanks for that." He started to walk away, but Angus grabbed him by the arm.

"What do you mean?" He looked horrified.

Icarus snatched his arm back. "Oh, I thought you knew the whole story?" he said snidely. "Well, far be it from me to assume I would be the one to break this news when *I* wasn't even *there*."

He flipped open the album and shoved it to the first page he'd seen Ramona's face.

"She fucking loved you, for god knows how long. Mr. Black probably noticed and was pissed about it. He decided Mom's situation was the perfect opportunity to get back at you over it. Then he divorced his wife and abandoned his kid and then you *ruined my entire childhood*," Icarus shouted.

Angus reared back as if he'd been slapped.

"Icarus, I—"

337

"You stole so much from me," Icarus continued. "Time I can't get back, friendships I could have had, experiences I can never ever share. She died, and I get that and it was painful and it was horrible, but you never gave me a chance to *live*."

"You wanted it. You wanted to help. I never beat you, or forced you," Angus started.

But Icarus pushed him hard against the counter. He felt like he was going crazy. He couldn't control his body or his mouth anymore. It was all pouring out now.

"You didn't *have to*. You just *stared* at me with your sad fucking eyes!" he screamed. "You never . . . you never . . . I had to learn how to hug someone from a friend. No one had ever held my hand until this year! You're so fucking focused on yourself and your pain. You're the most selfish man I've ever known!"

He pushed him again, but this time Angus caught him by the wrists.

"Icarus, control yourself."

Icarus snatched himself out of Angus's grip and backed away so that he couldn't touch him again.

"I wish that I could hate you. I wish that I could. But I can't and that makes it worse. Understanding you has been the hardest thing I've ever had to do."

Angus's eyes were as deep as wounds.

"I . . . I'm sorry, Icarus."

Icarus could feel his eyes starting to prickle and he wanted to die.

He couldn't cry here. He could not handle that his body chose the humiliation of tears as a way to express his rage. He grabbed his jacket and snatched the keys out of his father's coat pocket and left the apartment.

And Angus let him go.

He walked right down the stairs and out of the house and up the street. He followed the path he usually took to Helios's house, but passed the diner and the mansion and walked until he'd gone past where the city paid for streetlights.

The thicket of trees grew denser until he was in the woods. He walked until he couldn't hear the noise from the town, in a straight line, so he'd be able to get out again. Until he was absolutely sure no one would bother him.

Then Icarus fell to his knees, took a deep breath, and screamed.

LOVE

When he got home, Angus was still at the table.

He was asleep. There was a glass of whiskey still in his hand, and the photo album still spread out in front of him. The drawings were gone, but Icarus found them quickly crumpled in the trash.

Angus had selected a small pile of images from the album and separated them from the rest. It was mostly pictures of him, Mr. Black, and Ramona, without Icarus's mom. The album was patchy with white spaces where they used to be. It was mostly an album of Evangeline now.

Icarus swept the pictures into a neat stack. He gently removed the glass from Angus's hand and rinsed it out in the sink.

Then, he went to Angus's cot, pulled his blanket from it, and draped it across his father's shoulders.

SATURDAY

Icarus was afraid to leave his room. He stayed in it for hours, longer than he ever had before, until he had to pee so bad and was so hungry he thought he was going to die.

But like always, his responsibilities were waiting for him.

Angus was still seated at the table, though his blanket had been put away. He had a notebook open in front of him.

"There's soup in the pressure cooker," he said.

"Why have you been cooking so much?" Icarus asked, choosing to be obstinate. If they were speaking frankly, he'd like to know.

Angus sighed. "You'll be eighteen in a week. That time goes by quickly . . . even quicker when I wasn't paying attention. I didn't know that cooking for you would be something worth missing until now."

That was pathetic. Icarus silently vowed to never become the sort of father who would have to come to that kind of conclusion.

"Okay," he said, and opened the cabinet to get a bowl.

"So, what are you going to do?"

"What?"

Angus looked over his shoulder at Icarus for a moment. "I'm sure Helios isn't having a good time in there. Stuart was rough on Ramona and he was rough on me when he saw fit to be. It's foolish to imagine that has changed."

Icarus was quiet, trying to decide if he would tell him.

"I'll be gone for a few months. Then, I might come back."

"The two of you?" Angus's eyebrows lifted. "Together?"

Then he made an unusual face. Leaned back in his chair for a moment, then returned to writing in his notebook.

"My girlfriend's dad came back unexpectedly," he said, repeating Icarus's words. "I'm assuming Stuart didn't see you. Otherwise there would have been cops."

Icarus opened the drawer for a spoon. "You're not disgusted?"

Angus shrugged. "You think I'd know art, and I wouldn't understand this?" Then he paused, comprehending what Icarus was actually asking. "The church has laws, yes. But the god I believe in would never embrace a man who turned his face from his son in shame. The god I believe in gave Titian and Donatello their talents and they used them to celebrate the world in His beauty. The god I believe in gave me you."

His pencil scratching stopped. "Is it illegal?"

Icarus was still processing his father's words. "What?"

"What you're about to do? Is it illegal?" Angus asked, finally meeting Icarus's gaze.

Icarus thought for a bit. "Is it kidnapping if he wants to leave?"

Angus shrugged.

"Do you need money?"

Icarus shook his head. "I have enough."

"Do you need me? Stuart isn't a fool; things may have changed between now and then."

Ah. And that was the question. Icarus considered it, really did, and then he smiled.

"I think having you there might make it worse, actually. I'm fine. I can do it on my own."

Angus put his hand over Icarus's, and it felt so strange to have anyone but Celestina do that. It took effort not to snatch his hand back in surprise.

"You're a good man. But please be careful. The higher you go, the more dangerous it is to get down. Try to leave out the front door if you can."

Icarus wouldn't. That was ridiculous. "I'll try."

SETTLE

Sunday came as gentle as spring.

The house was open, free of fear. It wasn't a home and never would be, but it didn't feel like a cage to Icarus anymore.

He looked at the back of his father's neck as he sorted paperwork at the breakfast table and thought about how, if a warden must live in a prison, then in some ways they are a prisoner too.

He let Angus cook for him again. Breakfast, lunch, and dinner.

When they held service, took the flesh and the blood, Angus didn't ask if Icarus had any confessions.

He caught Icarus by the cheek and squeezed just once. Then stood up and walked away.

Icarus glanced up, searching for the switch on the mantle, and saw that it wasn't there anymore.

EVE

His heart raced to think of leaving.

He brought Julian apple crumble again, just to see his face as he gobbled it up.

He jogged next to Luca while they were forced to play football, then stood forehead pressed against his shoulder in the bathroom stall for long minutes before they went to their next class.

Smiled when Aspen mentioned that she'd been accepted at Wooster. Icarus said he was proud of her and laughed when she made a face about it.

He let Celestina card her fingers through his hair with new meaning. Let her kiss his eyelids, like it was benediction.

Asked Sorrel about Mina and wasn't surprised that he'd chickened out. Sorrel asked him if he could do another portrait of his grandma, and Icarus turned him down kindly.

He walked past the guidance counselor's door and it was closed. She had another victim in there, probably.

When the day was over, he took the finished paper he'd written for Julian, folded it up small, and pushed it through the slats of his locker.

DAY

At 11 o'clock Icarus put the handsaw at the bottom of his backpack. He packed his favorite sweaters in one bag and more utilitarian pieces in the other: jeans, a few T-shirts, underwear, his warmest sweater even though it was itchy. He brought brand-new toothbrushes and toothpaste, hair pomade, a comb, deodorant, and better soap than hotels would have. He folded up his slip-on shoes and packed his Red Wing winter boots.

Then he brought the notebook he was currently sketching in, his favorite pen, a ring that had belonged to his mother, and a steel bracelet that belonged to Angus.

He looked at everything else in his room. Nothing left was small enough to carry.

At 11:45 p.m., it was time for him to leave.

Angus was on the phone in the storage unit screaming, furious. Icarus wanted to say goodbye, but he didn't have time and the door was too thick for knocking. He wrote his dad a quick letter and left it on the dining room table.

Then he went into the workshop. *Orpheus Losing Eurydice* was where they had left it after their fight. Sitting in the middle of the clean workshop table, shining, polished.

Icarus stared at it for a full minute. Then he picked it up and put it in his backpack.

When Icarus finally made it outside, Luca and Celestina were waiting for him.

"That's a lot of bags," Celestina said.

Icarus handed her the one full of his sweaters. "This one is for you guys to keep. I'm taking the one on my back up, and this last one is the one I need you guys to watch at the diner."

Luca took the bag off Icarus's shoulder and put it on his own, and they began their journey through the night.

"We should be down in about an hour. Can you order an omelet, some bacon, and coffee to go? I don't know if he's eaten much. Then we can leave. The bus passes by every thirty minutes."

"Sure."

"What do we do if the cops come?" Luca asked.

"Take my things home to my dad. He knows where I am and what I'm doing," Icarus said. "He's . . . stern but he's kind. Don't be scared of him."

Celestina giggled nervously. "You know, saying that makes him seem scarier."

"I know."

BOÖTES

Icarus looked back at the diner.

Celestina and Luca were sitting in his booth by the window, gazing at him. They seemed scared. He turned away toward the Black mansion and sank into the gloom of its trees to face his climb.

It was a clear night; the moon was bright and there was hardly any wind. But it was the coldest day this year and Icarus could feel it in his joints.

It wasn't ridiculous to assume that Helios's window was still nailed shut, and he was way too nervous to try any of the windows near it. So he entered the house on the third floor. It was easier, the climb and sneaking in. After months of free climbing and tiptoeing in gym shoes, getting to use his gear and socks was like taking off heavy training weights before a run.

He landed inside and froze for a moment, listened for the whine of extra electricity, new camera glare, objects where they shouldn't be. But everything was the same. The air felt the way it did when he was walking these rooms without his mask. Something about that felt off and it made him more nervous than if he had new security measures to face.

Icarus took a deep breath. He touched the edge of his balaclava to make sure it was on securely, then he gritted his teeth and began.

While starting high up was safer, he still had to make it down to the ground floor to drop off the disc and get his gold. Icarus could hear the TV on the first floor and knew Helios was probably in his room sleeping one floor below him.

This was the white wing. There weren't many valuable pieces here, so Icarus hadn't spent much time in this area. He didn't know the creaking of the floors or the best shadows. But he slid across the hallway anyway, slithering along the edge until he reached the first staircase.

The laugh track to *Seinfeld* was loud and disruptive and there wasn't any human noise accompanying it, so Icarus couldn't be sure where Mr. Black was, exactly. He could be in the kitchen near the living room just as easily as he could be on the couch, and Icarus didn't like those odds.

Icarus took a silent steadying breath and sat down on the carpet as close to the wall as he could manage. Scooting down the stairs like a child would spread his weight distribution and lessen the likelihood of a sharp creak. It wasn't dignified, but it was effective.

It took him three times as long, but he slipped down the first staircase on his bottom to the second floor, which was more familiar territory. Helios's room was about forty yards away. He had to pass the blue wing and the mezzanine over the living room to get there. But at least he knew where to step.

Icarus slid against the wall, putting one foot in front of the other. He couldn't press his back against it because of his gear. Even just the straps of the harness were making a hissing noise as they scraped the wallpaper.

His heart pounded in his chest as he slipped from the white wing to the blue wing.

"And don't get up in the middle of the night. If you need water, you have to learn to anticipate your needs and get it before you go back to bed."

The voice was loud and close. Icarus froze, covered his own mouth and nose, and checked the floor for his shadow.

Mr. Black slammed Helios's door shut and stomped back down the stairs in the opposite direction of where Icarus was standing.

Icarus felt light-headed. He pressed his temple against the wall and waited for the footsteps to retreat. He stood there in the silence and dark until he heard Mr. Black guffawing at the television again.

Icarus stepped gingerly through the blue wing. He brushed a hand across Helios's door as he passed it, brushed his lips against the wood.

ARIADNE

The mezzanine was worse. It was a chaos of bright openness.

Since the moment Icarus had entered this house, he'd been in a labyrinth of slender halls and quiet rooms. He could hear the hush of electricity in the walls, the wind shaking the trees when he passed a window. His path was closed on all sides and he could keep track of every inch of it.

When the blue wing opened up into the mezzanine above the stairs, Icarus's view was flooded with light.

The grand chandelier over the living room was at eye level, dazzling in its crystal brilliance—too small to obscure a body, but too big for the room. A decorative wood railing came up to Icarus's waist. He needed to cross the mezzanine to get down the stairs to the foyer where the stand for the disc and storage room were. But this part of the house was dangerously close to the living room, separated only by a short hallway.

If Icarus was standing where he intended to place the disc and Mr. Black stayed on the couch, he wouldn't be able to see Icarus. But he would absolutely be able to hear him if he did something awful—like drop it.

Icarus took a deep breath to calm his heart, then lay down on the floor.

Mr. Black was eating something; Icarus could hear it in his mouth as he laughed. The weight of the pack on Icarus's back wasn't silent, and he had to adjust for it. Icarus inched forward when the television was loudest, and that was irregular at best.

He could also see his own shadow stretching out to the edge of the mezzanine, and begged every god that would listen that there wasn't a twin of it somewhere across the way. He couldn't check from where he was.

By the time he was almost to the other side, sweat was making his neck itch and his hands slipped against the carpet. He paused and rested his cheek against the ground for a moment. There was a small tinkling sound, and a gasp.

"Great. Goddamn it." Mr. Black pounded his fist against the table in frustration and Icarus startled. He listened as Helios's father stood up from the couch and swept his hands over his clothing loudly.

"Fucking . . . paper towels." He strode into the kitchen.

Icarus seized the moment and scrambled the rest of the way across the mezzanine and into the red wing. There, he waited on the stairs until Mr. Black returned from the kitchen and wiped up whatever mess he'd just made.

He listened, straining, until he heard the couch sag with Mr. Black's weight. Then he sat back down on the red stairs and began crawling the way he did before.

To his dizzying relief, he managed to make it to the bottom silently.

Icarus froze and gave his eyes time to adjust to the darkness. The stand for the disc was still where Angus had left it.

Icarus slipped his backpack and harness off slowly and placed them on the stair next to him. He removed the disc he'd packed at the top and made sure he was holding it properly for a seamless deposit.

Just looking at it made sparks of anger come roaring back. Angus had always been more reckless than Icarus. He was a professional, of course, they both were, but Angus's anger was too close to the surface. This place was hateful for him.

With every step Icarus had taken at his father's heels as a kid, Icarus could see his desire to tear this place apart. It was in the quaking of his hands and the set of his shoulders.

They took small things first, then bigger pieces, *priceless* pieces. They took from Mr. Black with daring and impunity, with vengefulness and spite and pettiness. But they always replaced their thefts with replicas, they always put in the work to restore the home to its original state, never damaged anything or left a hole where a piece should be.

Each time they returned here, Icarus's grief lessened. It climbed down on a slow descent, safe and sound, until it landed on the shore and he became ready to walk away from this.

Angus's grief seemed to crest each time, climbing higher and higher with no real end in sight.

It left him with this: a problem and a solution.

In a house full of lenses that had seen his face, Icarus *had* to bring this back. There was no other choice; he would force this to work for him. If he got caught tonight, at the very least he could point to this disc and claim he had come to return it. Even if he got caught with the torque, he could claim he had come to return that too.

If there had been weeks, months, years of surveillance, he would *still* be able to spin the story that the first time he came was to replace the figurine and the last time to replace the disc.

He was his father's son; he was built in *his* shape. This was his tactical gear; these were his tools. They didn't update what had been working, and it might be the one thing that could save Icarus's skin.

Icarus's hands felt sweaty in his gloves. The rushing of his blood was drowning out the noise from the TV.

It was time for him to be selfish. They were getting the fuck out of here.

He sent a thief's prayer up to his god. Then stepped down from the carpet to granite.

METAMORPHOSES

The ground was cold and the chandelier from the living room cast a triangular shaft of light on the floor that Icarus had to slide around. He made it across the space and gently placed the disc back on its frame and froze.

He expected something: an alarm, a shout from behind, literally getting shot. But nothing. He held his breath, straining his ears for the sound of footsteps but it was quiet. The TV made an explosion sound, which startled him enough that he almost dropped to the ground, but it was followed by Mr. Black's laughter. Safely far away.

Icarus leaned against the table, fighting down his terror-vertigo. Then, he turned around to recalibrate.

From where he was standing, Icarus could see the storage room door, the staircase where his bag was sitting, and the living room down the hall. If he stretched, he could glimpse a sliver of the white couch he had slept on during his and Helios's vacation.

He couldn't bring his gear into the storage room. The aisles were too close together. The chance that he might accidentally bump into something was high.

Icarus was also wary of leaving his gear on the stairs, but there was nowhere else to stash it at this point. It had to stay.

He gritted his teeth and slid across the floor to the storage room door. Icarus waited until there was a burst of laughter and put in the code, then waited for another and opened the door.

He left the door cracked when he slipped inside.

The warm dusty scent of this place was soothing and familiar. It was too risky to turn on the overhead light, so Icarus used his headlight instead. But the beam was small and round, so he couldn't just sprint inside; he had to move carefully.

He picked through the shelves, heading toward the back until things began to look familiar. He spotted the small wooden statue first, before the torque across from it, and a thrum of fear went through him, so powerful that his lips felt numb.

There was no dust on the figurine. It had been moved by a naked hand; its base had been scraped across the dust circle Icarus had so painstakingly placed it back into.

Someone had moved it, had touched it, rubbed it clean. This didn't feel like something Helios would do.

So. Mr. Black knew they had come here. Icarus couldn't think beyond that. It was too dangerous to fall apart now.

Icarus's knees wanted to buckle and dots were swimming before his eyes. He took a moment to lean against the shelf and catch his breath. He didn't need to be careful about smudging dust in here anymore.

The laugh track from outside startled him and adrenaline jolted through him. Icarus stood up straight, shook his shoulders, rolled his neck, and shined his flashlight through to the other side.

The gold torque was untouched, still dusty and waiting for him. He rounded the first aisle and made his way toward the second. Icarus snatched the gold and shoved it messily inside his jacket breast pocket, like a common burglar.

There was a clatter outside and Icarus froze. It was too quiet. The television was off.

Icarus didn't hesitate. He sprinted straight down the aisle on his toes and scuttled into the crack behind the open door, just in time to hear Mr.

Black picking up the disc from its frame. He wasn't graceful like a thief: his fingers bashed the edge and the frame scraped the wood.

Icarus squeezed his eyes closed very hard, then opened them again.

"Angus?" Mr. Black called quietly.

Icarus stayed silent. His blood pounded in his ears so loudly that it was hard to concentrate. He bit his tongue trying to keep his breathing silent. There was no way Mr. Black wouldn't immediately see his bag and harness on the stairs.

"*Angus?*" Mr. Black shouted.

There was a terrible noise—Icarus's gear slamming onto the granite with a clatter. Faster than Icarus could have anticipated, Mr. Black shoved his way into the storage closet. The door slammed all the way open, hitting Icarus in the chest.

Icarus caught it by the handle so it wouldn't swing back and reveal his position. Mr. Black threw the light on and stormed down the first aisle.

"Come out and face me like a man!" Mr. Black yelled. "What, are the pieces on display not good enough for you anymore? Will it *ever be enough*?"

Icarus heard him reach the vault and begin entering a code. It was bright enough in the storage room for anyone to be able to see someone hiding. All aisles were perpendicular to the door—standing in the frame of it meant the entire room was immediately visible. Mr. Black had incorrectly assumed that "Angus" was somehow in the safe—the only place he couldn't see into.

Icarus rolled out from behind the door and slid into the main hall. His backpack and gear were far away from where he'd left them due to Mr. Black's tantrum, but he couldn't save Helios without them. He didn't have time to plan a new escape route.

He abandoned all pretense of silence and snatched his bag off the floor, throwing it over his shoulder, and ran to pick up the harness Mr. Black had tossed across the room.

"Shit. *Shit!*" Mr. Black shouted. Icarus could hear his thundering footsteps as he abandoned the vault and started running toward the noise.

Icarus rushed to the back door, taking the chance that Mr. Black would see him. He yanked it open and slammed it loudly, trying to create the illusion that he'd gone outside. Then Icarus threw himself back toward the wall next to the storage unit, in the shadow of the staircase, and froze.

"I swear to god. *Angus!*" Mr. Black roared.

Helios's father was so furious it made him careless. He took Icarus's bait, running straight out of the storage unit without looking around, and tore the back door open, dashing out into the night to give chase.

As soon as the door closed behind him, Icarus sprinted up the red stairs and toward Helios's room. He could still hear Mr. Black shrieking outside, but it was only a matter of time before he realized that Angus wasn't there.

Icarus dashed across the mezzanine to the blue wing and past it to the white. He ran into the closest room and opened the window. Then he snatched a porcelain figurine off an end table and threw it as hard and far as he could. All the way to where the yellow wing would be.

He heard it smash on the ground behind him as he ran in the opposite direction, back to the blue wing, and hurtled himself straight into Helios's room.

EURYDICE

He closed the door silently behind him.

"Helios," he whispered.

Helios's form was on the bed but it didn't move.

Icarus crept across the floor, relieved when he saw the shock of Helios's scarlet hair. Then immediately concerned again when he saw sweat beading on Helios's forehead. He pressed a hand to Helios's shoulder.

"Helios," he tried again.

This time, Helios startled and turned over to see him.

"You . . . came for me." The voice sounded so slow and his eyes didn't look exactly right.

"Hey, are you okay?" He wasn't hot, but he was sweaty and his eyes were blown out. Icarus pulled the sheet down urgently.

Helios started to sit up, but he was moving like he was underwater.

"I'm sorry, Icarus, it just hurt too much. I'm sorry."

"Stop apologizing. What did you do?" They didn't have time for this. Icarus felt panic rising in his chest, but he couldn't see any wounds on Helios's body. Even the Band-Aids had been taken off; all that was left were small silvery scars.

Helios leaned forward until his head was on Icarus's shoulder.

"I don't think my old dose works the way it used to," Helios murmured. "I only took half. I'm sorry."

Icarus was starting to tremble. He paused, clenched his eyes shut tight, and held his breath, then let it out. Listened for where Mr. Black was in the house. He could still hear him tearing about outside. They had time for this. This needed to be gentle.

He put a hand on Helios's cheek and put as much tenderness into his voice as he could manage.

"What did you take?"

"Methadone. Hid some in the lining of my shoes." Helios giggled. "For emergencies. Some emergency, huh? I think my ribs are broken, not bruised."

Icarus sighed in relief. Okay. Jesus fucking Christ. Terrible timing, but not nearly as bad as he'd thought. "That's okay, we can deal with that later. I'm not upset. But now we have to take the bus to the hospital," he said softly.

"I love you, Icarus," Helios said suddenly. "I love you so much."

The back door slammed and they both jumped.

Icarus gritted his teeth. "Yeah yeah, I love you too. Come on, we've got to go to your closet."

The last place he assumed Mr. Black would be searching for Angus was Helios's room. He could still hear commotion, but it was heading away from him, not toward him.

To Icarus's immense reassurance, Helios could walk unassisted, even if he was slow and kind of hunched over. Icarus took the flashlight from the bedside and put it on the floor, then unwrapped the insulation and began stapling it to the wall of the closet until it covered all the wall that he could reach. He pushed the remaining insulation under the crack of the door and pulled out the rest of the supplies.

"He never checked to see if I was okay afterward. He started leaving food outside my room instead of seeing if I could come downstairs," Helios said at a normal speaking volume.

"Please be quiet," Icarus hissed.

He cracked the closet door open and felt around on the wall outside of it until he found an outlet for the handsaw and plugged it in. Then he grabbed Helios's leg, pushed the tracker up as far as it would go, and started wrapping Helios's ankle in thick rubber.

"That hurts," Helios whined.

Icarus ignored him. He pushed the tracker over the protective rubber sheath and picked up the handsaw.

"Helios," he whispered. "If you move, I swear to god."

"What?"

He grabbed Helios by the chin, hard, meeting his hazy eyes. "I need you to stay still or I'll accidentally cut off your fucking ankle. Please for the love of god don't flinch," he said as loud as he dared.

Helios swallowed hard and nodded.

Icarus braced one knee against Helios's foot and steadied his arm against his thigh. He listened. Mr. Black was still in the yellow wing on the first floor. They had time and distance, but not nearly enough of it.

Icarus looked up at the ceiling.

"*Domine, exaudi vocem meam: Fiant aures tuae intendentes, in vocem deprecationis meae.* Please."

Then, he turned the handsaw on.

HELICE

Icarus tried not to speed up the process out of anxiety. Slow and steady was best. He tried not to think about Helios staring at him, the blood pumping through Helios's veins. His delicate ankles. Ankles that Helios needed to walk, to run, to dance.

The sparks were much brighter in this little dark room, the sound much louder than they had been behind the hardware store parking lot.

The whine of steel against steel gave way to another sound and Icarus turned off the saw immediately.

Sweat dripped into his eye and he wiped it away. There was a narrow band of steel left, with a wire beneath it. On either side of it, the saw had torn into the rubber in deep gouges. But Icarus didn't see any skin; he didn't see any blood.

"You okay?"

Helios's face was ashen, but he nodded.

Icarus pulled a large pair of bolt cutters from his backpack, hooked them around the remaining metal, and took a steadying breath.

"You're beautiful like this," Helios said. "So serious."

"We can talk about that later." Icarus was too scared to enjoy it.

He sent up another quick prayer, gripped the handles, and forced the bolt cutter shut with all his might. The last piece of steel gave way—and immediately the room filled with a terrible sound. The cuff was alarmed, as he'd known it would be. But that didn't matter. They didn't have the luxury of stealth. They were getting out of here *now*.

Icarus wrenched the closet door open and sprinted across the room. He skidded halfway, reared back and threw the bolt cutters toward the window. The glass exploded outward and the bolt cutters sailed into the night. Without hesitating, Icarus whipped the blaring restraint straight through the brand-new hole.

They both listened as the alarm got farther and farther away, until they heard the cuff bounce on the ground outside.

But the noise didn't stop. Far away, elsewhere in the house, there was another alarm. And with it, the sound of footsteps.

"We have to go. Laundry closet on the third floor with that platform we sat on when I came over before homecoming. We're rappelling off the roof," Icarus said. He grabbed the harness and pushed it into Helios's arms, thanking god that it was lightweight.

ORION

Icarus pulled out his baton, zipped his bag, and threw it over his shoulder, and then yanked open the door.

Mr. Black was charging up the stairs on one side of the mezzanine, but there was another set of stairs on the other side. Icarus looked back in the room and Helios had the harness half on. Helios was visibly terrified and still moving way too slow.

They weren't going to make it.

"We have to get to the roof," Icarus said urgently.

"I'll catch up," Helios promised. "I know where I'm going."

Icarus trusted him.

"*Angus! Get out of my house!*" Faster than Icarus had thought, Mr. Black was on the second floor. Icarus shook out his baton, then turned and ran.

He could feel Mr. Black catching up to him, before the noise of it really reached his ears. Mr. Black yanked Icarus back by one of his backpack straps and kicked him behind the knee.

Icarus fell forward hard and coughed the air out of his lungs in a wheeze.

Helios's father slammed his hand over Icarus's throat and lifted him up.

"You're going to fucking prison, you little rat."

Icarus scrunched his legs up and stomped Mr. Black in the chest. Mr. Black's nails scratched his neck, scrabbling for him, and Icarus shouted in pain. As Mr. Black fell backward, startled, his face darkened again.

Over his shoulder, Icarus saw Helios making his way to the other staircase. He was still too slow. Icarus had to buy him time.

"You can't keep him in here, you psychopath!" he shouted, hoping it was the right thing to say.

Mr. Black lunged at him, singularly focused on violence. Icarus blocked his hands with lashes of the baton, just barely managing to keep himself unscathed. Good fucking Christ, was this what Helios had been locked up with for the past few months?

Angus had said Mr. Black was athletic, but he hadn't said anything about this. Icarus had stupidly assumed that he'd meant back when they were in school, not as a permanent feature.

Icarus was a thief. He wasn't a fighter. He left an opening and Mr. Black got lucky.

He slammed his fist into Icarus's side and snatched the baton out of his hand, hurling it over the edge of the balcony.

Icarus sank to his knees and heaved as his mouth filled with acid.

Helios's father grabbed him and tore off his balaclava. He spared a single second to process the shock of seeing Icarus instead of Angus, but he adjusted swiftly. He yanked Icarus up by the hair and pulled his head back, sharp and merciless.

"What have we here? Not as valuable, but just as pretty. Sound familiar?" Mr. Black hissed. His face was a twisted mask, Helios's features in bas-relief, red with fury. The same color Helios turned from embarrassment and pleasure.

The hysteria of it all made Icarus want to laugh from fright.

"For months I've watched you and your rat of a father drain my fortune, scuttling around my home like vermin. The amount of investment property you've removed from this home? It was worth it. You'll never see the light of day again." Mr. Black's breath was hot on the front of Icarus's neck and it made him want to throw up all over again.

"And you in particular." He shook Icarus sharply, tearing out strands of his hair. "You think you can come in here and steal my art. Fine. Walk my hallways, eat my food? Fuck my son?"

Icarus hoped Helios was far away. He didn't need to hear this.

"I didn't want to take any of your shit. Did you think I fucking taught myself? I'm just a kid!" Icarus yelled. "I do what I'm told."

Mr. Black didn't need to let go to backhand Icarus so hard his teeth rattled. "Did your father tell you to destroy my wife's workshop?"

Icarus groped behind him so he could figure out just how far he was from the stairs.

"That was an accident. I'm sorry. I never intended for that to happen, and I couldn't stay to clean it up. If I could, I'd clean it now."

From this agonizing angle, he couldn't see Mr. Black's face. Couldn't read his expression to figure out how to say what Mr. Black wanted to hear. He was so good at that, *so good*. But with his head pulled back like this, Icarus was helpless.

"You have how many days left? Three, four, until you can be tried as an adult?" Mr. Black shook Icarus's head. "Ohhhh, this was worth the wait. I'm going to steal your whole life, Icarus Gallagher."

"You're just like him, then," Icarus said, and it cost him to admit it.

"You think you're so different, but you and Angus are the same." He panted. "You don't know how to love and you'll never be able to learn. All you do is take lives and live in selfishness. You deserve each other."

Icarus spat at Mr. Black's face and threw himself backward. He plunged down the staircase, reckless and unpredictable.

Mr. Black shouted in surprise as he jerked forward a few steps himself, before letting go of Icarus's hair to keep from toppling with him.

Icarus braced himself as his bones collided against carpeted floor. The pain jarred him, but he tucked and rolled and the years of gymnastics saved his life. The instant Icarus had a leg underneath himself, he sprang up and stumbled the rest of the way down the stairs.

He sprinted across the living room and up the flight of stairs on the other side. His head was pounding from the fall and he felt dizzy and nauseous, but he had to keep going.

"I'm not like him. I'm nothing like him!" Mr. Black roared, but Icarus wasn't listening and he didn't care.

He charged up the stairs to the third floor, breathing a sigh of relief when he didn't see Helios still struggling anywhere along the way. He must be in the laundry room already, waiting for him.

But Mr. Black was catching up quickly.

"Helios! I'm coming!" Icarus yelled.

He turned the corner and had made it halfway to the laundry room when Mr. Black grabbed him from behind again. Slammed him up against the wall.

"Can't you just let us go!"

"You are not stealing my son from me," Mr. Black shouted, spittle landing on Icarus's cheeks.

"I'm not *stealing* him," Icarus whimpered, pulling back. "We're running away. You don't even want him! Why do you care so much that I do?!"

Mr. Black shoved him again, harder, and spots swam before his eyes.

"Angus knows I'm on to him. He's gotten the threats, met with my attorney. Why did he send you in here again? What game is he trying to play?"

Pain hit Icarus like a typhoon as all the pieces of the past few months fell into place. The unexpected trips Angus took, the phone calls, the shouting in their storage room. His father was a coward and selfish to the end for not including him. For not trusting him to carry the weight of their undoing. He couldn't begin to process this betrayal right now.

Icarus shoved at Mr. Black's chest, but he was steady as iron. Frustration bubbled up in Icarus's throat and he could feel it rapidly turning into tears.

"I don't know! He just tells me what to take from here and he stopped doing that a month ago. I don't even get any of the money. He never said anything about any attorney. Didn't warn me about this," Icarus confessed desperately. "I even brought back your stupid disc when he didn't want me to. I'm just . . . I'm just . . . his delivery boy!" Icarus shrieked.

Mr. Black's eyes widened and the pressure let up enough for Icarus to get in a breath. Icarus used it to scream.

"Do you have any idea how that feels?"

Helios's dad reeled. He made the mistake of backing up.

Just enough for Icarus to jerk out of his grasp and again he ran.

DELOS AND PAROS

Icarus darted into the laundry room. Helios was waiting for him, open window at his back, ready. Icarus flung himself out the window and opened his backpack. He didn't know why Mr. Black had stopped following him and he didn't have time to find out. He pulled out the hinges that attached to the roof, nails, and his mallet and started pounding a hinge into the shingle.

This would be able to hold their weight as they swung down. It wasn't meant for two people, but the maximum weight limit was 350 pounds, and they had to be less than that together.

"Let go!"

Icarus looked up and found Mr. Black trying to tug Helios back inside. He left the hinge half hammered and leaped up to pull Helios away.

"Don't touch him, you broke his ribs!" Icarus ducked under Mr. Black's arms and pushed him back hard. "Leave us alone!"

"You can't handle him! He's mine to take care of!" Mr. Black hissed.

"You're really bad at it!" Helios yelled back and Icarus was too scared and angry to laugh.

"Helios, buckle yourself in," he commanded instead and turned back to Mr. Black. "We'll take care of each other. We're going to figure out how to be happy."

For as long as we can, Icarus thought in despair. While we are on the run from the FBI.

Mr. Black put his leg through the window and started to climb out. Icarus skidded down the incline and snapped his straps together with

Helios's. The hinge wasn't nearly as secure as it could be. He picked up another nail, but Mr. Black's feet landed on the roof.

Fuck.

Icarus turned around, closed his eyes, and with a groan of effort lifted Helios clean off the ground. He turned to face the diner across the street.

"Wait, don't—" Mr. Black screamed.

They jumped anyway.

LEBYNTHOS AND KALYMNOS

The ground reached up to catch them and for a moment, Icarus thought they were about to die.

But the cord did its job. They sailed down ten feet, then slammed against the resistance of it.

"Helios, pull the silver lock and let us down easy," Icarus commanded.

He was facing the ground and he could tell they were at least twenty feet up. They jerked down another three feet sharply and Helios screeched.

"Can you do it gentler? Slowly wind us to the ground," Icarus asked politely. His heart was in his throat and terror tasted like metal in his mouth.

"That wasn't me!" Helios shrieked.

There was a sound above them that sounded like hammering. "Oh god, oh god," Mr. Black was yelling.

"Icarus!"

Celestina and Luca were running out of the diner and across the street. A man was following behind them. But Icarus couldn't turn his head well enough to see. The blood was rushing to his eyes. He hoped to God it wasn't a cop.

"Icarus, I'm scared," Helios cried.

"It'll be fine; just pull the release and we'll be—"

There was a crack. The rope snapped like a whip in the air and his stomach lurched as they plummeted like a comet.

ICARIA

Icarus felt the grass on his face before anything else. Then he felt Celestina's hands touching him, moving him. He tried to reach out to her, to push himself up.

Then, agony. Bright and red.

"Oh fuck, I can see his bones."

Luca was talking. He could hear someone crying too. Celestina maybe. Or Helios.

"I'll go get my car. Try not to move 'im too much." He remembered that voice. The diner owner, not the police. Thank god.

At bare minimum, the weight of Helios had been taken off his back.

"His . . . ribs are cracked," Icarus murmured. "I got him out, but his ribs are cracked."

There was the sound of a car door and feet scrabbling. Icarus opened his eyes for a second, then slammed them closed again as the world swam and his stomach lurched.

"Okay, we've got to pick 'im up. You twos, grab his legs and I'll get his shoulders."

"I don't know if we're supposed to move him?"

"He can't just lie here! Did you hear that guy up there?!"

He could feel Celestina and Luca holding on to his feet, but the instant the diner owner touched his shoulders, he was awash in a pain so glorious the light drowned him, and far away he could hear the sound of screaming.

The agony ratcheted up to a level that made him feel less than human when they dropped him on the car seat. How he had been built to feel this kind of pain was beyond his comprehension. His entire body was lightning and he was burning alive.

"We have to drag him in farther," Luca said, "so Helios can sit under his legs."

"No, no—" Icarus moaned, but they pulled him anyway.

For one instant nothing hurt at all, and then the entire world went black.

HYPNOS

He was already crying when he woke up. The salt tracks itched his cheeks as they crystallized and Icarus turned his face to rub them into the sheets.

Nowhere but a hospital could ever be this white.

On the plus side, he hurt considerably less and was undoubtably on some kind of pain medication given to him by the same hospital staff that had put both his arms in casts. They'd even put him to sleep sitting up halfway.

His shoulders ached and he knew immediately that they'd popped out of the sockets and been reset. This wasn't the first time he'd fallen from a height.

He tested the rest of his body, gently flexing his muscles to see what else might have been damaged. His kneecaps and toes ached a bit, but otherwise the rest of him seemed to be fine. So, Icarus concluded he'd fallen face-first pretty much parallel to the ground. Reached out to catch them, shattered both his arms, and forced his shoulders out of their sockets, then his knees and toes had hit the ground and he'd immediately been crushed by Helios.

Could have been worse.

He sighed.

"Oh good, you're awake."

The curtain between him and the bed beside him snatched open.

Helios was lying on his side and looking vaguely green.

"So, it turns out my ribs were just lightly cracked and then when we fell they actually broke so I had to have surgery," he said, eyes bright. "I'm not sure what medication they gave me for it. But I'm so awake and I have so much energy, but I also feel like I'm going to throw up. How are you doing? How do your arms feel? I've never heard a scream like that in my entire life. Did you know you set off some car alarms?"

"Helios," Icarus whispered, exhausted.

"That diner guy was super nice. He brought us some food and coffee, which the nurses aren't letting me have, unfortunately. They won't let me get up and feed you either because of the rib situation. So you're going to have to let me know when you want to eat so I can press a button to call them. Since you can't press any buttons."

Helios took a second to breathe then soldiered on. "Anyway, your friends are really worried, but they had to go home because it's not visiting hours and they're not family. I think they called your dad and I told them not to call my dad. But I'm worried they didn't listen." Helios got quiet then.

"Hey, hey. It's okay, we'll figure this out," Icarus said. He could feel another wave of sleepiness washing over him. "Can you come a bit closer?"

Helios looked thoughtful. Then, he curled his ankle around the rung at the bottom of his gurney and reached over with one arm and pulled himself closer using the curtain. He paused, breathing fast through the pain. Then he managed to snag the edge of Icarus's bed and pulled himself even closer, until the tops of their gurneys were touching. He wrapped a wrist around his IV and slowly dragged his saline over until the line wasn't stretched tight.

"Okay," Helios gasped. "Hopefully they won't push us back when we go to sleep."

Icarus smiled softly. "Hopefully."

"Can I use your phone to call my mom?" Helios asked.

"It's in my clothes, wherever they are. Call a nurse and they'll get it for you." Icarus could feel himself fading fast.

"I'm glad you're all right," he mumbled before the dark took him. "I missed you."

FLY

When Icarus woke up again, Helios wasn't in his room anymore.

There was a Post-it note on his chest with the text facing him that said *"getting moved to a different room. They'll come for you too in a bit! laterrrrr"* He smiled. Helios's handwriting was terrible.

Unlike the first time he'd opened his eyes here, Icarus felt fully alert. He took a good look around the room. His clothes were in a neat stack on the chair by the window and they had left his bags and harnesses there for him too.

Icarus kicked the blanket off his feet to check if he was cuffed to the bed, and he wasn't, which was a relief. The food the diner owner had brought was on the nightstand next to him and probably stone-cold. The clock next to it said it was 4:03 a.m., but it was still dark out.

He closed his eyes again, even though he wasn't sleepy anymore.

"Son."

Icarus kept his eyes closed for a moment longer before facing his father. He looked at Angus and didn't say a word. Just studied him as he was: crouched in the hospital window, gloves, braces, harness, and socks. Dressed for stealing, silent as a predator.

Angus stepped down into the room and closed the window behind him.

"Did you know we have Ehlers-Danlos syndrome?" Icarus mentioned, looking at the extra gear his father wore when climbing. "It's why our joints hurt. Helios taught me that."

Angus didn't reply. As he got closer to the bed, Icarus desperately wished he could push him back hard again.

"Icarus, I'm sorry," Angus said.

There was no apology this man could give him that would suffice, so Icarus ignored it. He was so angry that it had tipped over into exhaustion. He didn't even have the energy left in him to yell.

"You should probably be fleeing the country right now," Icarus said. "What are you doing here?"

Angus swallowed. "This is the last time we'll see each other, I think. There are some important things I need to tell you before that happens."

Icarus closed his eyes again. "Important to me, or important to you?"

He was sure he was about to hear some kind of lecture about Orpheus's disc or about how reckless he'd been. Angus never spared an opportunity for that sort of thing.

Angus pulled a chair away from the window and settled into it. He leaned forward, elbows on his knees, hands steepled in front of his face.

"The house is in your name. The whole thing, all the units. You don't need to keep it, but if you sell it, please consider the people who live there. Don't raise their rents and take care of them when they need it."

"What?" Icarus had spent his entire life thinking they were renting. That was ridiculous! They didn't even have the biggest unit in the building.

Angus continued without elaboration. "They'll strip the entire unit while you're in the hospital. They're taking everything and they're freezing all my accounts. Yours should be fine. I had separate accounts for the money from our work at the Black house and the money I earned from restoration. That account is under review, but it should be available to you in a few months."

"They're gonna take my stuff too," Icarus insisted. "Mr. Black said he

377

was waiting for me to turn eighteen so he could prosecute me too."

Angus was shaking his head. "He . . . changed his mind. We had a call."

"What do you *mean* you had a call?" Icarus was starting to raise his voice. "You mean you could have just figured this out on the phone all this time?"

"Icarus, you know as well as I do that Mr. Black wasn't taking my c—"

Icarus wished he could stand up and he wished his arms weren't broken so he could punch Angus in the face.

"What, you chatted? Had a nice little talk and now everything is fine?" Icarus yelled.

Angus stood up and faced Icarus's anger without shrinking.

"Do you think that what happened tonight changed nothing?" he shouted. "You threw his son off a building. *You both could have died!*"

Icarus remembered the sound of hammering before the rope failed. The begging. He stayed quiet.

"The house will be empty, but it will be yours," Angus said, composing himself and looking at the floor. "When you get discharged, you can go home, but I won't be there. Stay for a few months, heal up, and then go where you need to."

"What's going to happen to you?" Icarus whispered.

Angus grimaced, and he'd never looked so much like one of Ramona's drawings to Icarus.

"Trials, fines, prison most likely. Depending on what charges are levied against me, I'll be there for child endangerment as well." He looked at the coffee on the nightstand. Then he cracked open the lid and took a sip. "Stuart didn't exactly forgive you as much as he agreed to levy your crimes directly on to me. Which is fine. As I'm sure whatever charges I'm getting for the art alone more than constitute a life sentence."

Icarus turned away from his dad and blinked hard.

"I wish none of this had ever happened," he whispered.

Angus stood up and put a hand on Icarus's forehead.

"I wish I'd done a better job," he confessed back, stroking through Icarus's hair just once. "You're a good kid, Icarus. And you'll be a better man than me."

Angus Gallagher opened the hospital window and crouched on the sill. Graceful, even now. Though Icarus knew it must hurt.

"Try not to fall again. You might not get so lucky," he said.

Then, he disappeared over the edge.

PASIPHAË

The sun on the wood floors was as golden as Icarus had always hoped it would be. It even smelled different in here, fresh and clean.

The Feds had indeed taken almost everything out of Angus's house. They'd stripped it down to the bones, taken out mattresses and dishes, even things that didn't have any connection to their crimes, until all that was left was a single spoon in the silverware drawer. They'd even taken Evangeline's ferns.

Luca, Celestina, Helios, and Icarus ate pizza on the floor in the middle of the living room.

Icarus lay on his back with his head in Helios's lap. His casts were itchy but he didn't mind. He couldn't when his heart was singing like this.

It wouldn't be so bad to start over in this place.

When it was warm and quiet like this.

They could make the workshop into a bedroom, fill it with things they thought were pretty. Turn the gutted-out storage room into a dance studio. It wouldn't be as big as the one Helios used to have, but it was better than nothing. They could do anything in this house.

The first place Celestina had gone when they came in with all the bags Icarus had packed was Icarus's old room. She'd opened the door, seen it was empty, and closed it sharply.

"You should put regular stuff in there, like a pantry," she announced.

"We will," Icarus said, as he stood in the living room, full of wonder.

Later, Luca and Celestina brought a mattress and some blankets from their houses for Icarus and Helios to sleep on. It was Thursday and they wouldn't have time to go shopping for basics until the weekend.

But that was fine.

Not being able to hold anything for six weeks was fine. Letting his plane tickets expire was fine. Having to sleep on his back was fine, with Helios curled around him, hot as the sun.

"Where did you decide we were going to go?" Helios asked.

"There's a job opening waiting for me in Paris," Icarus murmured as Helios dragged a hand through his hair. "Here's hoping it will still be there in three months."

Helios laughed. The thought was as ridiculous as the rest of it.

"You're going to paint again? Really?"

Icarus huffed, pleased at the question.

"As soon as I am able. I am second best you know. I am my father's son."

Helios leaned down, and Icarus grinned back. Tilted his face up to be kissed. They lay there awake deep into the night. It was too bright to sleep and the future was too exciting.

With no curtains, the room was filled with moonlight, blue as the sea.

He delivered him rules for flying, and fitted the untried wings to his shoulders. Amid his work and his admonitions, the cheeks of the old man were wet, and the hands of the father trembled.

He gives kisses to his son, never again to be repeated; and, raised upon his wings, he flies before, and is concerned for his companion, just as the bird which has led forth her tender young from the lofty nest into the air.

And he encourages him to follow, and instructs him in the fatal art, and both moves his own wings himself, and looks back on those of his son. A man angling for fish with his quivering rod, the shepherd leaning on his crook, and the ploughman on the plough tail, when they behold the pair, are astonished, and believe them to be divinities, who thus can cleave the air.

Soon the father began to be pleased with wicked accomplishment. Relishing his role as a guide, drawn by desire to show his son the heavens, he soared higher in bolder flight. The vicinity of the scorching sun softened the fragrant wax that fastened his wings. The wax was melted; he shook his naked arms, and, wanting his oar-like wings, he caught no more air. His face, too, as he called out the name of his son, was received in the azure water, lost.

The unhappy son, landing safely ashore, cried out, "Father, Father, where art thou? In what spot shall I seek thee, Father?"

Then he caught sight of the feathers on the waves.

AUTHOR'S NOTE

Aging is a strange thing—a wild thing—slow and strong and merciless.

I am much older now than I was when I left high school.

There is something peculiar about mining shades of my past to create something new for you. It feels like whalefall: a life well lived sinking to the bottom of the ocean to host a city built of bones.

Now, *Icarus* is a strange story about a strong child, with an inexplicable history and a night job that requires some suspension of belief. He is a chameleon, shambling across the narrative, serving everyone but himself.

There are so many books written about the weak learning to be strong and not many about the strong opening themselves up to weakness and vulnerability. Hardening yourself to survive has a cost, and it takes incredible bravery to begin removing that protection to allow yourself to grow.

Icarus is so good at everything. It's not a mistake or an oversight; real teenagers can be too. He's smart, he's athletic, he's cautious, he's guarded, he does his best and succeeds even when it breaks him.

A younger me knew a girl who got straight As, worked a night waitress job, parented a child, and got into Cornell at seventeen. A boy who worked construction with his dad from four a.m. until seven a.m., was on the honor roll, played football after school, and was so funny that everyone loved him, loved him, loved him. But he slept through his lunch break every day in his best friend's car.

Because other teenagers *always* notice. They're the first to see the bruises under their friends' eyes and catch them nodding off in class. To notice they seem absent-minded and figure out they aren't joking when they laugh about being tired. The first to open their arms for a hug when someone's eyes ask for it before their mouth manages to. They are the first to help.

Icarus and Helios are mirroring each other. Icarus notices what Helios refuses to say, like Luca and Celestina notice Icarus. Icarus tries to save Helios, without knowing a rescue mission was brewing for him too.

It is in our nature to do this for each other at that age, I believe. It's beaten out of us, or we are made to forget it. But the drive to help, even with very little resource, is something we have at our core.

There will always be things that you can't control. Icarus can't control Helios's abusive father or the crushing reality of Helios's addiction. Luca and Celestina can't defeat the brutality of Angus's grief or the criminal situation Icarus must participate in.

But Celestina can drag her fingertips through Icarus's hair, bathe him in cool water, and bed him down at the warm den in the back of her truck. Luca can turn to the people who can assure Icarus has a strong athletic future and call in favors from someone he knows might get the law on their side if Icarus needs it. Icarus can give his time, can give the gift of vision and companionship to a boy in a cage, and in the end he nearly gives his life. They do it without hesitation, bravely.

It doesn't feel like much being a witness, seeing something you can't handle happen to your friends. It feels awful.

But love and care and gentleness?

They are our *birthright*. They are not "too little"; they are what matters most.

When instinct tells you to pay attention, and choose tenderness, do it.

Community is humanity's greatest strength and community at its core, is just love. Work motivated by that love, comforts created out of love, bonds fed by love—or at least for the desire of it.

Being young is so frightening because it feels like you don't have the power to enact dynamic change. In cases like this, in stories like this, where what is happening is so inexplicable and out of control that all you can do is try to give the strong person in your life the pleasure of your time, or the snack from your lunch tray, or a hug in the morning, or the warmth and privacy of your car during their lunch hour.

If it is all you can give, it is enough. It has meaning. It *is* helping.

I love you for trying. And please, please, please don't let time steal this part of you.

Keep it, guard it, it is yours.

Love,
Kayla

ACKNOWLEDGMENTS

There is a moment in every author's life—after the great deed has finished, but before an editor has clapped eyes on it—where there is woe. Things are terribly fresh, the afterbirth still connected. These are my clever readers who saved your favorite girl from bleeding out. Thank you for the lifeline, Amber Khan, my sweet Anna Didenkow, Catherine Stewart, Celeste Moreno, my steadfast Colby Dockery, Colleen Curry, Dafne Perello, Heather Rose Walters, Janelle Findlator, Jessica Harris, Katelyn Wilson, Kudzanai Mutetwa, kind Katie Beasley, Liz Kelly, Marianne Delmo, Paola Mancera, my luminous Raviv, Sabina Bailey, Sarah Neilson, brilliant Anna Rodriguez, and the soft anonymous support of Pipabeths, Koopins1, and Saint Neptune's Girls. I love you all, dearly.

To Kyle, thank you for your ears and hours of sleeplessness.

To Eric, Stephanie, and Sophie . . . I'm holding my breath and my fingers are crossed.